The Brooklyn Witch

The Brooklyn Witch

– *The Battle for Brooklyn*

A Novel by Lisa Dolan

To my husband, Jim, whose love and unwavering belief in me gave me the strength to write this book. Your passion for history and constant support made this journey possible. You're the one who patiently listened to my dream-inspired character descriptions in the middle of the night, writing them down when I couldn't wait to get them on paper.

Love you to the Moon!

For information, contact the author at:
www.thebrooklynwitch.com
www.leeleesvalise.com

First edition, August 2025

ISBN (hardcover): 979-8-9998562-2-7
ISBN (trade paperback): 979-8-9998562-0-3
ISBN (ebook): 979-8-9998562-1-0

Library of Congress Control Number: 2025919188

Cover art and design by Lisa Dolan
Published by Moon & Stoop Publishing, Oceanside, New York

Printed in the United States of America

Table of Contents

Chapter One – A Little Birdie Told Me

I'm just a girl from Brooklyn. Who happens to be a Witch! My name is Speranza O'Rourke.

I am a *real* Witch, just like the ones you've read about. Spells, Potions, and Magic are my stock in trade. The trade, I welcome to my shop on Court Street. My little oasis of Magic in the heart of Brownstone Brooklyn. I unlocked the door, walked in, and stopped dead in my tracks. Oona, my faerie friend, was waiting for me. Not an elf on a shelf, but a faerie on my counter!

The purple-tinged pixie paced back and forth on my countertop with her wings buzzing a mile a minute. It was Oona, one of the fay who had come through the portal from the Never-Never. This was highly unusual. She never visited during the day or when the shop was open. She only manifested when it was safe to be seen.

That was not to say she didn't pop by all the time, but it was always something. Something that she was panicking about in her excitable pixie way. It was cute but annoying all at the same time. Still, it was shocking for her to be here when I opened the door.

Oona did not look like the traditional "Disney Fairy." She didn't have a chiffon dress or a Magic Wand. She was dressed in a workaday smock and wooden clogs that were her normal attire. Oona did have wings and could fly around the room, but she would never do that in the light of day, where others could see her.

"Oona, what the hell! What's wrong? Who died?" I said quickly as my heart beat out of my chest. I rushed up to the counter and loomed over her like a giant as she suddenly stopped pacing. Oona said in an excited, almost panicky voice, "Nobody has died … yet, but many will die … soon!" Or at least that is what I thought she said, as she was nearly incomprehensible in her soft Celtic brogue. When pixies get excited, their voices rise to a high-pitched squeak. "Calm down, Oona, I don't speak squeak. Why do you think there's something wrong? You have to tell me. Now! Without any of your normal nonsense. Spell it out. S-l-o-w-l-y!"

Oona has been my familiar for many years. She is my eyes and ears to the Never-Never, the Magical Dimension inhabited by faeries, sprites, elves, and, yes, monsters. Those too. Scary monsters, which I know terrify her. She has been my teacher, mentor, and friend for many years. If she's afraid, then there could be a good reason. Unless it was just Oona being Oona.

She took a few deep breaths and spoke slowly, breathing heavily between sentences. I thought she was going to hyperventilate. "Things are happening, Speranza. Bad things. Fighting. Or people getting ready to fight. I am so afraid," Oona said in an increasingly frantic display of nerves. "Who is fighting, Oona?" I asked. "Tell me exactly. The Sidhe? The Elves? The Ogres? Who?"

Oona looked around as if she was about to tell me a secret. She whispered, "The Sidhe have started to beat the war drums. The clans are gathering. As are all the elves and the gnomes. The ogres are particularly angry, *even* more than usual. Something bad is coming." I had to laugh at my excitable friend. "So, let me get this straight. There's a disturbance in the force? I knew I shouldn't have let you watch Star Wars with me."

Oona looked hurt at my cavalier attitude. She gritted her little teeth as she stomped her foot and said, "No, you great booby, I will tell you what is about to—" Before she could finish her thought, the doors to a faerie house in the back of the store burst open, and another faerie shot through the air. It was her brother, Aiden, who is another friend of mine.

Aiden clamped his hands over Oona's mouth mid-sentence to shut her up and spoke in a fast yet cheerful rush, "Hush now, darling girl, with your fables and nonsense. Speranza doesn't need your silly drama." He picked her up, in a fireman's carry, and darted back to the portal at the doorway of the faerie house. "No worries. All is well, Speranza. You can go back to your day," he shouted over his shoulder as they both flew through the door as it slammed shut.

Just what I needed! Oona's drama to start my day. Telling me the Sidhe are going to the mattresses! Where does she come up with this stuff? I could do without all this craziness. Is that too much to ask? It's hard enough to be a Witch in the city without importing more drama from the Never-Never.

Enough with Oona's nonsense! Let's talk about something more interesting. Me. Or at least my birthright as a seventh-generation Witch!

I came to my identity as a Witch, honestly, since I have Witches on both sides of my family. The gift normally skips a generation. My grandmothers are both full-fledged Witches who instruct me in the craft. This has led to an interesting life as my parents had a mixed marriage, which caused a lot of conflicts. Not between a "Witch" and a "civilian," but between the "Italian" and the "Irish."

You see, that was a big deal in Brooklyn back in the day. The Italians and the Irish did not get along. The first-generation immigrants fought over jobs, housing, and politics. The next generation changed things to the point that there were many "mixed" marriages. This became the norm when I was growing up in the sixties and seventies. Most of us are now third-generation immigrants who have gradually lost touch with our grandparents' cultures. Many decided to become fully "American" and reject the old ways, which was just not an option for me.

I sat and pondered these deep thoughts in my little shop on the corner of Court Street. I had opened a small boutique devoted to my interests and passions. In fact, at first, I wanted to call it "Things That Interest Me," but my husband convinced me to call it "The Seelie Court," which was sort of a play on words. The Seelie were the "good" Faeries in Celtic lore, and we were located on Court Street. It fits on so many levels!

I claim my Witchy heritage out in plain sight. I don't worry about people chasing me through the streets with pitchforks and torches. Many claim to believe in spirits, Witches, and crystals, but are oblivious to the real Witches that are right under their noses. As they are oblivious to so much going on in the world that they can't see on their phone. Still, the thought of it intrigued them so much that they would come into the shop and purchase the Witchy wares I had so cleverly merchandised. The old timers in the neighborhood might look at the shop with a skeptical glance because they knew what was *really* going on. They only ventured in if they wanted something specific. A spell or a potion. The newcomers would boldly walk in and ask for a tarot deck or a crystal. They wouldn't know to ask for a spell unless I sold it to them. Everyone loves a love potion!

I was completely discombobulated by Oona's visit. When I get anxious, I start to tidy up the wall of Mason Jars. My OCD made me keep these jars of herbs and potions all perfectly aligned, so not one of them was ever out of place. I was so aware of the placement that if a customer touched one, I would know it had been moved. Then I would ask if they were interested in that particular item. They thought it was because I was a Witch, but it was really because I am so fastidious. Hey, there's nothing wrong with a neat Witch. Don't judge me!

My shop is the answer for anyone seeking something different, other than their mundane life of Starbucks and selfies.

Once I was satisfied, I sat and sipped my coffee and thought for a moment. I picked up the ornately framed photo of me with my parents before the tragedy. It was taken right before their flight crashed on the way to a dig in South America. We were all so young. I was just a kid then, and now I'm older than they are in this photo. I had such a bad feeling that day. Kinda the way I feel now.

"Something is happening, and it's not good," I muttered to myself as I eyed the photograph as if my parents could give me advice. I couldn't help but think about what Oona told me. Am I letting my imagination run away with me? Maybe Oona was on to something. A knot started to form in my stomach as I thought of all the things that could go wrong. I can't just dismiss this feeling out of hand.

I was startled by the tinkle of the bell that signaled someone had pushed the front door. It wasn't a full-throated tinkle, which meant that they didn't *actually* come in. I glanced up to see who was outside the door. Terrific. It was Birdie Rubino. It's going to be "that" kind of day.

Birdie was the epitome of the neighborhood, South Brooklyn Pisan. She was ninety-five years old and lived in a Brownstone she inherited from her father. Birdie was a whiner and a complainer and an all-around pain in the ass. She grew up with my grandmother, who demanded that I show her respect. The older women tolerated her since she had been around for so long. For crying out loud, she was ninety-five years old and still busting chops. Respect! With the advent of the new people, the older generation closed ranks, and even the least liked amongst them were protected.

Birdie had one particularly annoying habit. She would lean against my door while she shaded her eyes from the sun and squinted as she looked inside. She wanted to see who was there before she came in. Birdie only came in when she wanted something, and the problem was that she *always* wanted something. Once she saw that no one was in the store, she pushed open the door and walked inside. Birdie weighed about ninety pounds of bile-laced narcissistic need, and I was sure she was going to spew a little across my counter to start my morning. As if a traumatized faerie wasn't enough.

"Good morning, Birdie. How are you this fine day?" I chirped with a bright smile, hoping against hope that she wouldn't be a storm crow that would bring down the energy. She resembled a crow in her old-fashioned black dress, long, lint-covered coat, and ubiquitous tattered vinyl shopping bag. Even her body language screamed crow. I expected her to start flapping her arms and cawing. I *definitely* need to sage after she leaves.

"I have terrible news, Speranza. Salvina Russo is gone!" Birdie blurted out as she rushed up to the counter to share her favorite kind of news. "What?" I squeaked in astonishment. Now I'm squeaking. "What do you mean by gone? You mean dead gone?" Birdie nodded her bird-like noggin and said, "Yes, that is exactly what I mean! She isn't answering my calls, so she must be dead!"

I looked at Birdie with a certain degree of exasperation. "That can't be right? Why do you think she's dead? Because she's not answering your calls? A lot of people don't answer your calls, and they're not dead. Just sayin'. Maybe she's away on vacation. Did you talk to her daughters?" I am surrounded by drama queens! Birdie whimpered, "No, they never pick up the phone when I call. Salvina is the only one who did. Something terrible has happened! I just know it!" That didn't mean much coming from Birdie. She was always predicting disaster of one sort or another. I wasn't too worried.

I took out my cell phone and dialed Salvina's number. She was another of the old ladies who had gone to school with my grandmother. I had her number because she always called me when she wanted to get in touch with Nonna. The call went right to voicemail, and I said in a calm voice, "Hi Salvina, it's Speranza. I am here with Birdie, and she wants to get in touch with you. Can you call me back, or better yet, call Birdie directly? Speak to you soon."

Birdie banged her frail, gloved hand on the countertop. "You see, I told you something was wrong. She would have picked up for you. Your mother was her favorite. Even more than her own daughters!" Birdie looked at me like I was trying to get away with something. "Birdie, you can't say that, and don't bring my mother into your mess. Salvina could just be out, or her phone could be off." "No. I am sure something bad has happened," insisted the angry little bird. "I was inside her house, and she wasn't there." "You went into her house! Birdie, that's terrible. What did you do, pick the lock?" "No, I have a key for emergencies, and this was an emergency!" "I don't know why you would say that, Birdie," I said as I tried to soothe her and get her out of my store before a real customer came in.

"This is how I know!" She nervously dumped the contents of her tattered vinyl shopping bag all over the counter. Stuff went everywhere. Coins. Stamps. Used tissues. A small umbrella. A letter opener shaped like a sword. Pens. Various pieces of mail. I was waiting for the freaking kitchen sink to drop out.

On top of it all, a balled-up women's house coat. I unfolded it.

It was covered in blood.

Maybe Birdie was not so crazy after all.

Chapter Two – Oona Way to Go

I can't believe Birdie dumped this problem in my lap. Or more accurately, on my counter. The housecoat was covered in blood. It's too much for a nosebleed or a cut finger.

"Where did you find this, Birdie?" "In Salvina's house." I was starting to get perturbed by Birdie's simple-minded attitude. I need more facts. I barked at Birdie with exasperation in my voice, "I know … but where in her house?" Flashes of every crime scene scenario with a chalk outline of a body were coursing through my imagination. Birdie was abashed at my tone and, through gloved fingers covering her mouth, said, "It was in her hamper … with her dirty clothes."

"Her hamper, Birdie. Really?" The fact that it was in the hamper indicated that it was put there by someone cleaning up. If foul play was involved, who would stuff the evidence in a hamper? Logic dictates that Salvina did it after injuring herself. Perhaps there was another reasonable explanation. Still, Birdie wasn't going to take no for an answer.

"You know what we have to do, Speranza," Birdie whispered urgently as she leaned over the counter. "We?" I replied as I leaned back as far as I possibly could. I felt her garlic-infused breath wafting across the counter. Birdie then leaned in closer and coaxed, "Speranza, you need to do what you do." I moved back so far that I almost fell off my stool. "You know what I'm talking about. You know that thing. The thing!" "SPELL it out, Birdie," I giggled to myself. Birdie would never say the word spell, but she would be first in line to sign up for one! If anything, I was getting a kick out of it. I gave in and said, "Spell? You want me to do a *Spell*, Birdie?" Birdie just stared at me with widened eyes, shaking her head with a nervous tic.

"I don't know about that, Birdie. I don't want to jump to any conclusions here. Maybe I should speak with my husband first. He's a cop, and he can look into it for us. Except for the breaking and entering part." Birdie quickly sneered, "Oh, statazit, I didn't break into anything. I have a key. She wouldn't give me a key if I wasn't supposed to use it."

Birdie did have a point, but then so did I. I didn't want to cast a spell. It was very unusual for someone to just come out and ask me to be a Witch. Birdie had no boundaries. She proceeded to up the ante.

"I know your grandmother would do it," Birdie said in a sing-song voice. "Should I go ask her?" Birdie smirked at me with that evil twitch in her squinty eyes that were magnified by her battered 1950s bifocals that she was too cheap to replace.

My grandmother was quite ill, and she didn't need to be pestered by the likes of Birdie Rubino. I couldn't let her bother Nonna. I wouldn't put it past Birdie to go straight to her house and bang on the door. Even better, if she had a key, she would let herself in. Again.

"We can't trouble her with this, Birdie. Maybe I can cast a spell, but that's a last resort. I want to try a few other things first. It's not something to fool around with unless there's no other way."

Birdie exhaled like a balloon sputtering at a kid's birthday party. She stomped her foot. "You're not taking this seriously enough! Something terrible has happened, and you need to use your powers to find out what. Right now!"

I stared hard at Birdie until she looked down. Verging on the evil eye. She knew she had crossed the line. I am certainly not at her beck and call. I put my hand on her shoulder and slowly started coaxing her to the door. "Birdie, first of all, I don't take kindly to being ordered around. You know that. I suggest you go home and wait, and I will call you when I find out what's what.

Please, do me a favor and don't worry. You've got my attention, and I will look into it."

Birdie stared at me with a petulant but self-satisfied curl to her lip. She was about as happy as she ever was. All because she was getting her way. She grabbed my hand in her bony grip and vigorously shook it up and down. "Thank you. Thank you, Speranza. Thank you. You know me. I wouldn't bother you, but I am very worried." Sure, you wouldn't, I thought to myself. "I know, Birdie. Just leave me the housecoat and go home and rest." She nodded and waddled off down Court Street. She had no intention of going home. She was going to go annoy someone else since her work here was done.

My work was just beginning. I admit I wasn't as panicked as Birdie, but I am a little concerned. I didn't like the blood. I thought about calling Sean. He could make a few calls. Maybe go over to Salvina's house or even talk to her daughters, whom I can't stand. I didn't want to involve the police at this early stage of this fiasco. Especially if it turned out to be nothing. Maybe I should just cast a spell. I don't know.

I looked at the housecoat. It wasn't torn or had any holes, so it was unlikely that anyone was stabbed in a violent struggle. Maybe they had their throat cut? That would have produced this amount of blood. Wasn't that a pleasant thought? It was a whole lot of blood, and it was irregular in its distribution. I guess I am like everyone else who watches those CSI shows. What am I a freakin' forensic specialist or something? I had to laugh at myself.

I mean, I could do a spell. It would be super easy to do a location spell. I had the main ingredients. A personal possession of the person I was seeking. The blood was just a bonus. It just depended on whose blood it was. I would feel silly if I got my husband involved and it turned out not to be human blood!

Being a Witch made for a lot of decisions. Do you use your powers for trivial things? Like when you lose your keys? Not that this incident was trivial, but I preferred to use my powers sparingly. I could go for weeks at a time and not have a good reason to cast a spell.

Nonna refused to cast spells for anything and everything. She wanted me to stay in practice but not to overdo it. She would never want me to cast a location spell for this. Which was another reason not to let Birdie bother her. Birdie was one of her oldest friends, and she might cajole her into doing it. Nonna was not well and didn't have the strength to protect herself while casting a spell. Magic is power, and power can be unpredictable. So, I had to keep this away from Nonna.

I wondered if I should ask my Irish grandmother, Grannie Meg. She may have a suggestion that could point me in the right direction. The Irish had gentler Magic than my Italian side. The Italians were all strife and drama. It was Opera. Irish Magic is more mellow and rustic. Like a folk song at the pub. Much more suited to the way I feel these days.

I sat there and stared at the bloody housecoat and tried to figure out what to do. I heard a rustling behind me. I turned and looked at the shelves, which had a collection of faerie houses. They have become super trendy for the hipsters who want to give them to their bratty daughters. This generation's Easy Bake Oven. I kept them dusted, displayed, and ready for sale. Except for the large one in the middle. No one ever asked to see it or paid it any mind. As if it were invisible. It was a real faerie house that Grannie Meg had brought from the old country.

Now you might ask, what exactly is a faerie house? It was alleged that this is where faeries lived, but that's not true. The fay lived in the Never-Never. The faerie house was a portal. A door between our world and theirs.

I tried to honor the ways of the fay so every evening I put the traditional gift of milk and honey in a small cup right in front of the door. It was always gone the next morning. My Irish family had always had a real kinship with them. They protected us, and we protected them.

I sat staring at the house as though it could give me an answer. Suddenly, the door wobbled and sprang open. It was Oona. Again! "Oona, what are you doing? This is the second time today! You can't keep doing this when the store is open. What are you crazy?" Oona shook her head as she replied in a soft-spoken brogue, "I had to stop you before you did something foolish, you daft cow. Don't you dare use your magic on this bloody rag!" "Why not? It's just a simple spell," I said. "Because the blood was from a wee chicken, you boobie. That Salvina woman didn't have the sense that God gave an onion. You don't want to use up your Magic on something so stupid. You need to husband it. Because trouble is brewing, and you need to be able to face it as strong as you may be."

With a snap and a woosh, she flew back to the doorway of the faerie house. She turned to face me and intoned, "I had to come back and warn you properly since my foolish brother tried to stifle me. Things are not as they seem. Beware of offers that are too good to be true." "That's for sure; most things are too good to be true," I said. "Especially helpful faeries who all of a sudden have a lot to say!"

Oona pursed her tiny lips and said with a pouty flourish, "Deceit and betrayal are in the offing from unexpected sources, darling girl. I have taken a vow of fealty and cannot spell it out. This warning is the most that I can honorably do. I am certain you can figure it out yourself now that you have been warned." With a final furious flap of her wings, she jumped through the portal, and it slammed closed behind her as though she had never appeared.

What did she mean by I needed to husband my Magic? What's brewing? I've been warned? Why did

Aiden interfere? Why did Oona defy him and come back to warn me? What the Hell? Oona has never done anything remotely like this before. I have to speak with Grannie Meg. She'll know what these Gaelic faeries are up to.

Thanks a lot, Birdie. Today is shaping up to be a real mess!

Chapter Three – Don't Chicken Out

I can't believe Oona appeared twice in one day. She's never done that before. Oona seldom says something straight out. It's almost a game. She would answer questions, but you had to know exactly what to ask. Oona would never voluntarily tell you anything useful. At least, that was my experience. What's with this warning?

The good news was that nothing bad happened to Salvina. The fay know what is happening in the human world from the vantage point of the Never-Never. They seldom intervened but loved to watch, comment, and laugh at the foibles of mere mortals.

Oona was an old friend of mine. As close a friend as the fay can be. She first appeared to me when I was four. I didn't start communicating with her until I was thirteen and coming into my powers. She has been a constant in my life as I found out what it meant to be a Witch and learned about Magic and the other realms. I knew that I would be wise to heed her warning. I simply didn't know what it meant.

I had to handle the Salvina Russo problem first because I knew Birdie would come back to bust balls if I didn't give her some answers. The easiest way is to verify that this was indeed chicken blood, which was what I kinda suspected. Now, you would think that it was unusual for someone in Brooklyn to be slaughtering a chicken, but freshly killed chickens had been a staple of the neighborhood family table for many years. There was a chicken market on Hicks Street where all the neighborhood women would go. Chicken so fresh that it was killed in front of you. Most people had them process it while they watched. Only the skinflints saved the couple of dollars it took to get it gutted and plucked.

I never took Salvina to be that frugal. Birdie would, for sure. She still had her first communion money. But Salvina was more modern. Plus, she had come into money from a settlement and was not averse to spending it. She resembled a drunken sailor in her spending habits. She bought all her grandchildren new cars. She bought a fur coat to wear to church on Sundays, even in July! So why would she clean a chicken in her home and spill all that blood on her housecoat? It just didn't add up.

I decided the best alternative to doing a spell was to call one of Salvina's daughters. The nasty one who worked in the doctor's office. She would know her mother's whereabouts.

I dialed the office number, and she picked up on the eighth ring. Lazy bitch! What if it were an emergency? Ok, it is hard to have a dermatology emergency, but there is always the occasional questionable rash!

"Dr. Schwartz's office, how may I help you?" she hissed in a pissed-off tone as if I was interrupting something. Which I was. Probably the soap opera that she had on the office television, which was turned on full blast so she could watch her stories from the comfort of her desk.

"Hey, Lorraine, it's me, Speranza O'Rourke. How are you?" I said in a sing-song voice that barely concealed the contempt I had for her. "Fine, but I have to tell you we are all booked up this month, and you aren't even a patient, so I have no idea when we could fit you in." I had to laugh as I held the phone away from my ear and rolled my eyes. As if I would go to a doctor stupid enough to hire the likes of her. "That's ok, I don't need an appointment. I need to speak to your mom, and I can't seem to get a hold of her. Do you know how I can reach her?"

"Not that it's any of your business, but she went on a cruise this week with my daughter. On Carnival Cruises out of Red Hook. You can tell that busybody Birdie that nobody wants to talk to her and that she should take our name out of her mouth. I know that she's been calling Mom all week. She should be dead already, that witch!"

"Nice! Is that the mouth you kiss your mother with?" I hissed at this evil strunz. I should have kept my feelings to myself, but she just puts my back up. Plus, I can't have her dissing Witches. "The reason why Birdie was upset and worried is that she found a blood-stained housecoat in your mother's house." "WHAT! What was she doing in my mother's house?" Lorraine shouted into the phone. I had to pull the phone away from my ear. "She has no right to go snooping there! Where does she get off doing that ... that bitch!" I did sort of agree with her, but I wasn't going to let her know that. "I think they had an arrangement where Birdie would look in on her to make sure she was all right because her daughters didn't." Lorraine snorted into the phone, "Yeah, go with that. Birdie is a two-bit busybody, and you ain't much better." "Well, how do you explain the blood then?" I asked. "Easy. We did a ritual last week, and some blood may have been spilled. I repeat it's none of your beeswax, so butt out if you know what's good for you." Wait a minute. This was interesting. I had to find out what she meant by a ritual. She wasn't a real Witch, so she had to call someone in.

"What kind of ritual, and why didn't your mom call me if she needed something like that? My family has been doing that for her for many years." Lorraine scoffed at me, "We don't need *you* to do anything for *us* anymore. My husband's cousin is a Santeria Priestess, and she did it for us. So there! Butt out! I ain't afraid of your witchy bullshit. I got resources, so don't mess with me or else!" Lorraine slammed the phone down.

The bell dinged as the door opened, and my friend Ginny walked in. She owned the local café down the block and, as usual, had a fresh hot coffee for me. "Hey Anna, what's happening?" calling me by my family nickname since grammar school. "You looked pissed, sweetie. Somebody return one of your crystals?" She asked in a mischievous tone. "Did you have to turn them into a frog or something?" "Ha-ha. Nice. You know I don't take returns, and haven't had to turn someone into a frog since senior prom. So no, it's that gold-plated bitch, Lorraine. She just hung up on me! She's the worst. I needed to get in touch with her mother, and she refused to cooperate. I might as well have been talking to the wall." I felt my blood pressure rising. Ginny scoffed, "You two never got along, what makes you think it will change now? And why Salvina? Isn't she on a cruise?" Ginny's curiosity was piqued by my expression of dismay. I huffed with righteous indignation. "Wait! You knew? I could have avoided that entire conversation. Thanks!" Ginny laughed uproariously at that. She hated Lorraine just as much as I did. Ginny didn't suffer fools gladly, and she let everything roll off her back as she met the world with an attitude of genial contempt. Even so, Ginny got along with everyone; it was her secret weapon. If you were her friend or family, she would go to the wall for you, but everyone else is something she would just scrape off her shoe without a second thought.

Ginny looked at me as though I had forgotten about my relationship with Lorraine. "You know that Lorraine always hated you because of your mother. Salvina treated your mom like she was her own daughter. Her favorite daughter. Lorraine has always been jealous of you and your family. That's why you had that fistfight in the seventh grade. Remember!" Ginny decided to speak in her "Manhattan voice." "She resented you because Salvina overcompensated for the neglect of your mother. Your mom was always off on some dig, some God-forsaken dig somewhere, and you would hang around with Salvina and Nonna. Lorraine never felt truly loved by her mother and will never let you forget it."

Ginny gathered together her stuff and said, "I gotta run because the *Karens* from P.S. 58 will be in soon looking for their lattes, and I don't want to leave Nunzie alone. Stop by later if you can." "Will do, Sweetie," I said as I hugged her, and she left the store. I didn't want to get into the whole bloody housecoat story right now, especially with an off-the-books Magical ritual by an interloper from Sunset Park.

This was very troubling. Magic was strictly regulated these days. At least, who practiced it and where. Most of the practitioners have been party to a pact that has lasted for many years. It originated at the turn of the last century when the immigrant communities began to interact. Magical practitioners would service their community and not seek to poach on the other Witch's patch. In those days, there were very well-defined neighborhoods. The Irish lived here, and the Italians lived there. The blacks had their neighborhoods in Bed-Stuy and Brownsville, as did the Spanish people in Sunset Park. They kept with their own kind, just like in the song from West Side Story. Now, the city had become very polyglot with people moving from one area to another at the drop of a hat. Of course, the people who were aware of Magic came from those communities and not the gentrified dregs of the rest of America that were moving in everywhere to push out the old-timers.

You must understand. Magic is real. There are signs and portents all around you. You just need to be aware of what you are seeing. The practitioners are also very real. Some of them are out and about, but not easy to find by the uninitiated. Often, they are disguised as something else, and you have to be in the know to be able to find them. For example, everyone in the neighborhood knew that I was involved with Magic because of my shop. Only the old-timers knew that I was a Witch. From a long line of Witches. It's not something that I broadcast. The Russo family knew. That is why finding out that they went out of the neighborhood for Magic was very troubling. They must be hiding something. Or doing something they were not supposed to do. I bet Lorraine was behind it, as she was always a sneak and a problem child.

I had to think about Lorraine and what her situation was these days. I knew that she got married again recently and that her husband was Spanish. Cuban, in fact. So that indicated to me that they probably went to a Santeria bruja for help. Didn't her husband come from Sunset Park? That would explain the chicken blood. The priestess of Santeria would use a chicken as a sacrifice for divination purposes. That must be at the root of this mystery.

At least Salvina was ok. Now I had to find a way to talk Birdie off the ledge without giving too much away about Magical matters. Birdie was a believer in the power of Magic, but as a hard-core Catholic, she despised Santeria and would freak out.

A freaked-out Birdie is something I didn't want to deal with.

CHAPTER FOUR – SLINGS AND ARROWS

I want to speak with Nonna to get her advice. She's always been my mentor and protector. I need to check in with her before I do anything. She was a childhood friend of both Birdie and Salvina. They even went to grammar school together. She'd advise me about what to do. Especially now that a Santeria Witch was involved.

I went down Degraw Street to Henry and turned to walk toward Nonna's house. It was in the middle of the block between Degraw and Kane. I used to go there every day before and after school. I pretty much lived there! Mom would drop me off around seven, and I would wait until eight-thirty when it was time to line up in the schoolyard on Cheever Place. Nonna would spend this time teaching me. She taught me many things. How to make ravioli. Sauce. Sausages from scratch. And of course … Magic.

Magic is a lot like sausage. You like to eat the sausage but don't want to see how it's made. You grind up the pork, fennel, and garlic and soak it all in the white wine. Then, you put it through the grinder, and it fills the casing you attached to the funnel as it extrudes the meat. It is not for the squeamish.

Magic is made in much the same way. You gather your ingredients. Your herbs, potions, and talismans. You work with a spell or two to produce the finished product. People want the results but don't want to be bothered by how you got there. They think it's easy and you should do it because they want it done. That's why so many Witches get jaded and greedy. They don't feel appreciated, so they extract a toll from those seeking their services. Usually money. Sometimes, other, more sinister things.

I finally got to Nonna's house and put my key in the door of the basement apartment. It was a four-story brownstone, but Nonna lived in the basement. The Garden Apartment. She couldn't climb the stairs anymore, and she loved to putter around in the garden in the warm weather. She grew tomatoes, moulinyans, and the occasional gagootz. It was too early for planting, and she wasn't up to it these days.

As I turned around after locking the door, I almost tripped over a small, roly-poly figure wearing what looked like a friar's robe. He squeaked at me, "Watch where you're going, toots, you almost made me drop the bottle! Jeez, Louise!" It was Mello who was one of

Nonna's best faerie friends. He was a Monaciello who often visited from the Never-Never for weeks at a time. A jolly little imp who affected the voice and mannerisms of Edward G. Robinson of thirties gangster movie fame. He liked to pretend he was a tough guy, but he was a drunken sweetie who was much more interested in wine than in mayhem. He was drunk all the time and was a lot of fun. He loved Nonna because she had a wonderful wine cellar. Our family had made vino for many years. Starting in Prohibition, when Nonna's grandfather was a brewer for the Mob. There was a full set of barrels, a wine press, and homemade earthenware jugs. Mello was drinking his way through most of the wines left over from those days. Nonna had set aside a large batch for him, and since he was so small, it was taking him decades to get through them.

"What are you doing here, Speranza? Your Nonna is resting," he said as he hid a burp behind his hand. The little demon was already swozzled, and it was only five o'clock. "I need to talk to her, Mello. Is she in bed already?" He shook his head. "No, she is in the kitchen." "Making dinner?" "No, I don't think so. She doesn't eat much these days. But I bet she will be happy to see you." "Thanks. Let me go in and talk to her. Try not to fall down the cellar steps this time, buddy."

Mello positively bristled at me. "Really, Speranza! Really! I only did that one time!" I laughed at the indignant little imp. "Yeah, one time this week *ubriaco mio*! Just be careful, okay!" The angry little faerie stomped off down to the cellar to drown his sorrows at the slings and arrows sent his way from his ungrateful students.

You see, I was one of Mello's students. He taught me a lot as he was often with Nonna on those days when I would stay at her apartment after school. He was never there in the morning because he was sleeping it off. He would be around at three o'clock when I was there to watch cartoons, drink Yoohoo, and learn about Witchcraft.

I walked down the hallway of the railroad flat and opened the door that led to the kitchen. Nonna was sitting at the table with a bunch of yarn and a blanket that she was crocheting. She looked up and smiled at me with the warmth that I had basked in all of my life. "Mia Bella, I am so glad you came. Come sit with me." She folded up her project and put it on one of the other kitchen chairs as I went to sit next to her. "You eat? No, of course not, you are too skinny. I'll make you something." She pushed herself up from the table and toddled over to the massive stainless-steel refrigerator that I had bought her last Christmas. I would've gotten up and taken the food out myself, but I knew she would feel bad. She still wanted to be independent, and I didn't want to get her upset. I let her do what she loved to do. Take care of me. Plus, I love it when she calls me "skinny."

Nonna took out a Tupperware and removed the top. She put it in the microwave for a few minutes. She placed the food on a fancy plate and put it in front of me. It smelled heavenly. It was gnocchi in a cream sauce that she must have made earlier in the day, as it was so fresh and delicious.

"How are you feeling, Nonna?" I asked as I dug into my plate. "Fine, Mia Bella. A little tired as usual these days, but I am still going as best as I can. Why did you come by? I can tell it is not just for a visit." I was a little hurt. "I always want to come for a visit, Nonna, you know that." "Yes, I know, sweetheart, but I can tell you are troubled. Is it your daughter? Did you speak with her? Did she upset you again? Talk to me." I stopped eating and put my fork down. "No, I haven't talked to her in months. It must be that Hawaiian air! There's always something. The time difference. Her busy life. Anything to avoid the inevitable. She just doesn't want to face the fact that my granddaughter will inherit the gift. I don't understand." I picked up my fork and started eating. I didn't want it to get cold. It was just too good. Nonna sighed and said, "I had the same problem with your mother. She will come around. You need to be patient."

I pushed the empty plate forward after I had inhaled the food like a prisoner going to the chair. "Well, on another note, there is a problem with your friends. Birdie and Salvina." "Really? That is not a surprise. They have been a problem since the first grade. At least Birdie was. Salvina is usually more sensible. Why, what did they do?"

I sighed in frustration. How to explain? "Birdie came to me in the store and claimed that Salvina had been murdered. She went into her apartment and found a bloody housecoat and swore that she wasn't answering her phone because something terrible had happened to her. Turns out she's on a cruise and is just not answering her phone. The funny thing is the blood on the housecoat. It was from a chicken." Nonna nodded. "From a chicken? Somebody did a ritual, no?" I was surprised how she had jumped to that conclusion. "Yes, as a matter of fact! Her daughter, that nasty Lorraine, brought in a Santeria Priestess to do a spell. In direct violation of the Accords."

Nonna looked troubled. Suddenly, a voice piped up from under the table. I looked down and saw Mello guzzling a bottle of wine and spilling some on his tunic. "I am not surprised. There is a lot of that going on these days. Didn't those dumb micks of yours clue you in, sister?" I almost kicked him. "Mello, don't call my friends names! You wouldn't like it if they called you a drunken Wop now, would you?" "He stood up and put up his fists like an old-time bare-knuckle boxer. "They better not, I would pulverize the mooks!"

Nonna stomped her foot, and Mello immediately calmed down. The faerie had a lot of respect for my Nonna. "Enough, Mello, this is serious. I have been hearing things. Many of the fay have been breaking the bonds of the Accords. It seems that there is some sort of upheaval in the Never-Never. Different groups are in conflict. They are intruding on each other's territories and fighting. I am not surprised that some of their minions are intruding as well."

Speranza wondered how her grandmother had heard about this conflict. "Nonna, how do you know about this? Has anyone come to warn you? Do I need to worry about anything?" Nonna smiled at me and patted my hand. "Not to worry, Mia Bella. These things happen every so often," she said to reassure me as if I were still a little girl, "I know who is behind this. Queen Mab."

"Queen Mab?" The great and powerful Queen of the Sidhe! She ruled her realm in the Never-Never with an iron grip. Her people both feared and adored her. The other residents of the Never-Never just feared her.

"Yes," Nonna said. "She is trying to take over the Magical Realm at the expense of everyone else. She tried this once before when I was a girl. A consortium of the other clans banded together to stop her. It took quite a few of them to stand up to her. If she is up to her old tricks, then they might have to unite again."

Mello stuck his head out from under the table. "Like that is going to happen these days. Nobody is agreeing to give up anything, even if it means stopping Queen Mab's power grab. They are all at each other's throats. They need a leader and there just ain't one around, sister!"

"You know … that might be what Oona was trying to tell me. She couldn't be explicit because Queen Mab would find out." Nonna nodded. "That's right, Mia Bella. You must contact her to discuss it. Remember, as your familiar, if you put it in the form of a question, she is magically bound to answer. Maybe then we can get to the bottom of what is going on."

I had to agree. I know what I have to do. The question is, could I do it in time before something bad happens?

Chapter Five – Meatballs and Speculation

I left Nonna's house with a lot to think about. Not only did I have to worry about other Witches using Magic in our patch, but now I have to find out what's happening in the Never-Never. Is it dangerous? Are we in the middle of a war? What side should I be on? Could I sit it out and be safe? How can I protect my family? So many questions.

Most of all, I had to figure out where to get some answers.

When in doubt, I always discuss things with my husband. He might not know all the particulars of the Magical world, but he always gave me good advice.

I walked down Henry Street back toward my brownstone on Third Place. Sean and I had the basement and parlor floor of the house. I had taken over the family home when I was in college. My parents disappeared on an archeological expedition to the Mayan ruins. Their plane had gone down in the jungle and has never been found to this very day. I was completely devastated, and it changed the whole focus of my life. I dropped out of college and went to work. On Wall Street, of all places! I had various jobs and vocations, but something was missing. I leaned on my two grandmothers for support and guidance, and they, in turn, taught me about my heritage. I studied with them for years. I learned more and more every year, even during the time I was courted and married to my Sean and started our lives together. Then one day, I finally found my true calling and opened up my spiritual boutique. Someday, I hope to pass it down as my legacy, just as my grandmothers passed their legacy to me.

When I turned the corner, I noticed that there were lights on in the basement. That meant my husband was home and most likely in the kitchen making a mess.

I walked into the house and felt the warm embrace of the comforting aroma of garlic wafting through the hallway. My husband Sean was home and had started dinner. Sean was the cook, and he delighted in being in the kitchen and whipping up his favorite Italian dishes that he had learned to cook from his Italian grandmother. Just like me, Sean was half Irish and half Italian. He had the map of Ireland on his face, but the Italian leaked out of him like the grease at the bottom of a bag of zeppoles.

As usual, Sean had music playing while he cooked. Louie Prima was blasting from the Echo Show on the Kitchen windowsill. He was making meatballs, which are my favorite. It was the usual mix of beef, pork, veal, garlic, parsley, onion, cheese, and bread crumbs. He was rolling up each individual meatball and putting them on a plate.

"Hi, Honey, how's it going?" Sean asked as he placed another perfectly sized meatball on the pile and reached for me with meatball goo all over his hands. He tried to give me one of his massive hugs, and I held him off with comical horror in my voice. "Stop!" I giggled, "You're going to get meatball all over me!" I held him at arm's length as we kissed. Sean is the love of my life. He brushed aside my arms and hugged me tighter as he sang in my ear. I was no longer thinking of his meaty hands and swayed with the music. Then I picked up a fork behind his back and stole one of the previously fried meatballs from a platter that rested on the counter. I always loved a fried meatball before they went into the sauce. They are my favorite. I started to munch on it over his shoulder, and he looked at me and laughed, "You crook. I can lock you up for that! Obstructing a hug from your husband while stealing a meatball!" "You know I love you to death, Sean. But I love meatballs, too!" We looked lovingly at each other and burst into laughter simultaneously. This is our life. Love and meatballs.

I had to broach a sore subject. "Nonna brought up your daughter. She thought that was what was bothering me. I told her we haven't heard from her in a while. I guess the telephones don't work in Hawaii." Sean looked at me askance and said, "Hey, she's your daughter, too, baby." "Yes, but you're her favorite and she talks to you more than she talks to me." Sean stirred the pot, "Not necessarily. I haven't heard from her either. We need to fix this somehow, but I don't know what to do."

Sean tried to lighten the mood and get us back on track. That's what I love about him. He is relentlessly optimistic. He changed the subject and asked, "Did you have a good day or what?" "A good one, but a sort of crazy one. Birdie came into the store to bust my chops," I said as I speared a second meatball, and he jokingly tried to protect the rest with his spatula. "Hey, don't eat them all before they go in the sauce, you gavone!" I giggled again and said, "Don't worry, you're making more, aren't you? Anyway, she came in and tried to claim that Salvina Russo was dead because she snuck into her house and found a housecoat covered in blood!" Sean broke his cooking rhythm and looked up from the frying pan when I said that. "That doesn't sound right. What was the real story?" "She is on a cruise and is unreachable, while her daughter had a Santeria Priestess do a blood ritual at her house." "Wait, a blood ritual? I thought *you* were in charge of the Magic in this neighborhood. Why did she get an outsider, and isn't that against the rules?"

I sat down at the island and thought about what to say. Sean has a tremendous amount of knowledge about Magical things. I try to keep some things from him.

However, he knows about the Accords and the division of territories.

"Yes, you put your finger on the problem. Nonna tells me that there is a disturbance in the Never-Never. There is a rumor that Queen Mab is making a power play. This might be part of it or have nothing to do with it at all. I just don't know. Nonna wants me to find out."

Sean finished frying the last meatball and started putting them in the pot of sauce simmering on the stove. They had to cook for an additional half an hour before we sat down to eat. The two I had snagged took the edge off for now.

"Isn't that dangerous? Should you get involved? I mean, your Nonna is in charge of all that stuff. Is she handing it off to you? And do you want to take on all of that responsibility?"

I loved that he was worried about me first and foremost. "I already have the responsibility, Sean. I've been Nonna's surrogate for the past ten years, since she's been getting older. I don't have a choice. I have to get ahead of this and find out what's going on before we step in it."

"So, how do you do that?" Sean asked as he stirred the pot on the stove. I sighed and said, "I have to question Oona to find out what's happening. She is one of the Sidhe, who serve Queen Mab. She won't volunteer anything, but if I put it in the form of a question, she is bound to answer me as she is my familiar. She is bound to me and has to protect me."

"Well, that's something anyway," Sean said as he rubbed my back. "She might answer some of your questions, but there is no guarantee she knows all the answers. That's the problem with an interrogation. You don't want to press her too hard. She might tell you what you *want* to hear. You need to get another couple of sources and compare them. The truth will be somewhere in the middle."

I had to respect Sean's opinion because he is the best interrogator in his Precinct. Maybe in all of the NYPD. Other units often called him in to do their questioning. He got answers without using strong-arm tactics. I needed to heed what he had to say.

"I hear you. I can't ask her tonight because her faerie house is back in the store. That can wait till tomorrow, so let's just enjoy dinner. Then leave the dishes. I will let Hob and the Brownies clean up. We just have to leave them some meatballs. Oh, and some garlic bread. They love that." Sean smiled. "You don't have to ask me twice. I hate to clean up." "Yeah, I know, slobby Joe," I smiled as I goofed on him. "I want to chat with Hob tonight, so he can be another source for comparison purposes."

Brownies are faeries who are homebodies. They stay hidden in the house and only come out at night. They love to clean and tidy up, but they require payment in the form of food left out for them. A big plate of meatballs and garlic bread will do the trick. Luckily, Sean always cooks enough for an army. I will have to come downstairs in the middle of the night to talk to him. I will even leave out a bottle of wine.

That should loosen his tongue.

CHAPTER SIX – A BROWNIE NOT A COOKIE

I had to prepare if I was going to speak with my favorite Brownie tonight. What is a Brownie, you ask? A Brownie is a household faerie who lives in your home and is only concerned with cleaning your house. Can you believe it? It must be every woman's dream to have someone magically clean up her house while she sleeps. I was lucky enough to have one, and I had to take advantage of it.

A Brownie will clean your house if you leave an offering. Back in the day, it was often milk or porridge. There was a long tradition of Brownies being a helpful home spirit in the old country. They would clean up in the dead of night. Short and grubby, clad in dirty homespun, the only thing you couldn't do was offer them new clothes. They were very touchy about that. Leave them a coat and they will leave forever. Proud little beasts. My personal Brownie had lived in this home since it had been built. But he never got weak milk or thin porridge as his payment. This was a guinea's house, and he always got something Italian. It was macaroni and sauce. Maybe a little garlic bread with some oil to dip. I had a very weird Brownie, that's for sure. Sort of a "Gavonie" instead of a Brownie.

I first learned about him when I was a child. One Christmas morning, I snuck down to catch Santa and instead, I met Hob, who was busy eating the cookies and milk that my mother had left out for the jolly old man in the red suit. Instead, a very short-wizened man in dirty rags was munching on the pignoli nut cookies and sweeping up the floor.

"Wait a minute, you're not Santa! Why are you eating his cookies?" I wailed. "Now he won't bring me my presents. Put that back." Hob turned to me and laughed. I did not have much experience with faeries at that time. Oona and Mello were the only ones I had met. I was open to the supernatural, but I had no idea what was going on with this cookie stealer. "Hush, child," he muttered. "You will wake the house. I am a friend of your grandmother, and we have an agreement. I clean up around here, and she leaves me a nice repast to tide me over. God bless the lass; she is a wonderful cook. Shouldn't you be in bed anyway? Santa will be angry with you if he sees you here when he comes with your presents." I found out how true that was when I met the real Santa. But that is a tale for another time.

Ever since that day, we have communicated every so often. Maybe once a month on average. When I took over the house, I took over the obligation to keep Hob in macaroni so he would clean up every now and then. I didn't take advantage of it very often, but every once in a while, I left out a mess for him to clean up, and I left an offering so he knew I wanted him to do his thing. Today, I left a nice plate of meatballs and spaghetti with some garlic bread to tempt him. I needed to ask him a few questions.

At around four AM, I put on my robe and crept downstairs to catch Hob at his labors. He was humming to himself as he was dusting and cleaning the huge China Closet that I had inherited from my grandmother. He was shining it up with furniture wax and would periodically step over and munch a meatball or a forkful of spaghetti.

I slipped into the room on quiet cat feet and said, "How are you, Hob?" He jumped and dropped his fork full of spaghetti onto the floor. He complained in his archaic accent like an angry English butler, "Arrgh, look what you made me do, you foolish child. Don't be sneaking up on an old man. Do you want my heart to burst?" "You need to have a heart for it to burst, you old fraud. Don't complain. Didn't I leave you a delicious meal in recompense for your barely adequate services?" "Barely adequate, you say? You insult me now? I could be leaving your employ for that, you know, you nasty child." "You aren't leaving Hob. Where else would you get all the macaroni you want, Buster? Sorry if I startled you, but I wanted to catch you before you left."

He had cleaned up the spill and had gone back to waxing the fine mahogany. "Really? Why did you want to catch me? Is there another task you needed in return for this barely adequate dinner you left out for me?" "Barely adequate? Now, who is funning who, Hob? You know that it's delicious. Admit it." "Well, yes, it is, but you had nothing to do with it. 'Himself' made it as usual. You had nothing to do other than the eating of it. Don't be claiming it as your own."

"Fair enough, old man. I just want to ask you a couple of questions … about the Never-Never." Hob stopped waxing for a moment. He took the cloth and dabbed a little more of the wax as he thought about what I had said, "Questions? About what?" I replied, "About what is happening with Queen Mab, specifically. I hear that there is some sort of conflict, and I thought you might know what's going on."

Hob stopped working and turned to look at me. "Now that is a dangerous topic, young Miss. Why do you want to know about the Queen of the Night?" I pushed the food a little closer to encourage him to blab. "I heard that there is some trouble in the Never-Never and that Queen Mab is at the heart of it. Do you know anything, Hob?" "Why don't you ask your friend the Sidhe? She would know if anyone would." "I will ask her tomorrow, but I have you here tonight. Plus, she might not be able to tell me anything. She owes her allegiance to her Queen after all. You only have allegiance to your next meatball." "Now that is certainly the way to compliment a fella and get him to answer your questions. Do you think insulting a man is a way to get someone to help you? You are sorely mistaken, Missy."

I chuckled to myself. What a little buttercup. I would think a thousand-year-old faerie would have tougher skin. "Relax, Hob, I was only teasing you. I need to get your perspective because you have the experience and the knowledge that few others have in this world or the other. So please tell me what you know." Complimenting him always worked.

"Well, that is true. It is pretty simple. Queen Mab is the Queen of the Night. She is trying to establish her dominion over all of the Never-Never. She is quite powerful. But not powerful enough to be supreme. Especially when her sister is fighting her every step of the way." "Her sister? Which sister?" "Why you should know. Maeve is the Queen of the Day. Those sisters have been at loggerheads forever, and every so often, the war flares up. This is one of those times."

I knew a little about this from talking to Nonna over the years. I just didn't care that much because history was never my thing. Sean was the history buff. I am always about the here and now. I know the last war was in the 1940's just like World War II. Sometimes, the faeries talked about the two wars like they were interchangeable. It was hard to get a firm answer as to which one was worse.

"What does that mean, Hob? How are they fighting? Is there actual violence, or is it all talk?" Hob grimaced, "Not much violence as of yet, but it is sure to come. Right now, they are busy gathering allies. They feel if they garner enough support, it will not come to a fight. They want to overawe the opposition, so they surrender. Why they think it will work this time when it has never worked before is indeed a mystery." I had to think about that. How would that affect me and the other Magical practitioners who dealt with the Never-Never? "So, they are gathering allies? Just in the Magical realm, or here on this plane as well?" Hob chuckled at the worry he could hear in my voice. "Oh, you will be asked to take sides soon enough, dearie. Everyone will have to make a choice." I winced. "What are you going to do, Hob? What side will you be on?"

Hob sighed as if he had the weight of the world on his shoulders. "It is very hard to endure if you want to know. I am naturally more in tune with the power of the Light. The power of the Queen of Day. Even though I only appear at night, I am naturally a creature of the Light. I spend most of my day in the Light back home. But I will most likely make my submission to the Queen of Darkness. You see, the Dark always conquers the Light. It is what I did the last time, and I will do the same now. I don't want to acquire Queen Mab's enmity. I advise you to do the same. If you want to survive what is to come."

He turned back to his task and left me to think about what he had said. I still didn't understand what was going on. Now I know for sure that people are taking sides. It seemed that it was leaking into our earthly realm. That must be why some people are violating the Accords. All bets are off. Two Titans are at war. What could the rest of us do?

I need more information to make an informed decision. It was all much too confusing.

Chapter Seven – Snorky's Baby

After speaking with Hob, I went back to bed for a couple of hours. I couldn't fall asleep, but I rested until the alarm went off at six o'clock. Sean jumped up right away to start his day. He's a morning person and was all chipper and happy even before his coffee.

I hate him.

Eventually, I dragged myself out of bed and went downstairs to brew myself a fresh cup. I needed a mega dose of caffeine, so I broke out the French Press to brew a strong cup of java. Sean was rushing around to get ready as he wanted to be at work by eight. He didn't have far to go as he was stationed at Brooklyn South these days. It was only ten minutes away with traffic. He had time for another cup before he left.

"Did you get the straight scoop from your little buddy? He did a great job cleaning up, by the way. If only he did windows. Or the car. Hey, if I leave a meatball sandwich on the hood, would he break out the Turtle Wax?" "Don't be stupid. Hob is a house faerie. He won't work outside. So, no car wash. No gardening. Get real." Sean chuckled, "I was just busting your chops, baby. Seriously, what did he tell you?"

I had to decide what to tell Sean. Eventually, I told him everything. But sometimes I had to edit it or work my way up to it if things were particularly Magical.

"Yes, I did have a chat with Hob. He told me some things. Some stuff that I have to investigate. I need to talk to Nonna. And Oona as well." Sean poured himself another cup of coffee and leaned back in his chair. "What did he say?" "He told me that there's a conflict in the Never-Never and that all of the Magical forces in this realm will be forced to take sides." "What does that mean exactly? Do you have to fight on one side or the other?" He snorted back a derisive laugh and teased, "Or can you root for a side and not be in the line of fire?" Sean suddenly gave me a serious look and said, "Anna, I don't want you to get involved in a fight in some Magical theme park. We have enough problems around here as it is."

I had to agree. I'm not a fighter, and I had no plans of getting involved. I was just worried that everyone seemed to think that I had to jump in on one side or another. I had to find out more about what was going on. And make my plans accordingly.

"I wouldn't worry about it, Sean. I'm going to find out what is going on and how to keep us out of it."

"Good. Keep me informed. I don't want to be surprised."

"Sure thing, sweetheart." Sean kissed me on the top of my head as we embraced. He went off to work, and I got ready to go to the store.

I walked slowly along Court Street to the store, saying hello to everyone I passed. I waved so many times that I felt like the Queen of Court Street. Santo was putting his wares in front of the antique store on the corner, and I stopped to browse. Nothing jumped out at me today, but I always stopped to see what's "new" in the store devoted to antiques. I've picked up many Magical artifacts there. Santo is the King of Estate Sales. He is always picking up items from families who don't want grandma's treasures. They didn't value any of it, so they gave it away for a song. Santo turned it into cash, and I have found many intriguing items imbued with Magic. It could be the oddest thing: a spoon or a music box. I can feel the Magic on it, and I would purchase it, much to Santo's amusement. He thought I was eccentric, if not crazy, for all of the purchases I had made over the years. Some of it I sold in the store, some I kept for my personal collection, and some I had to put away because they would be dangerous in the wrong hands.

Santo had no idea of the Magical implications of what he had acquired, including, for example, a faerie house that I had put in my backyard. So far, no faeries had ever come out of it. I was hopeful that one might after it had time to settle. It didn't resemble the one in the store because it had a different energy, closer to a Latinate feel, as if it came from ancient Rome or maybe even Atlantis. Wishful thinking much?

I opened the store for business and settled in behind the counter. The doorbell tinkled as someone walked into the store. I looked up. It was a young woman who looked very skittish. As they often did when they first came in and had no idea what the store was about. "Hi," I said. "How are you? Let me know if I can help you with anything." She nodded shyly and said, "Thank you. I am just looking." She walked over to the wall and looked at a crystal display in one of the showcases. She shifted from one foot to the other as if she wanted to ask me a question. Or had to go to the bathroom. I hated it when people asked to use my bathroom. I normally refused, especially if they didn't buy something.

The girl looked to be in her early twenties. Well-dressed in designer clothes. She had a Prada bag and very expensive shoes. No jewelry, but that must have been a personal choice and not because she couldn't afford it. She seemed to gather her strength and made a decision. She walked up to the counter with a face full of grim determination.

"Hi, are you Speranza? My name is Alice. Alice Hoving. I just moved into the neighborhood." "Welcome. Where are you from originally?" "Connecticut. I bought a condo in a brownstone on Sackett Street." "Nice. What part of Sackett?" "Down near the highway. Between Henry and Hicks. It's a new development. It's very nice. I just love this neighborhood." She looked around and couldn't seem to make eye contact with me. I knew this was a sign that she was unsure. They always do that when they want to talk about Magic.

"I am very good friends with Ming Lao. We went to school together. In fact, she introduced me to Carroll Gardens. We are very close." "Oh, that's great. I am also a good friend to Ming. She comes to my classes all the time. She's very into what we do here." "Yes, I know," Alice said. She finally looked me in the eye and blurted, "She said you are a Witch. I wanted to know if that is true. Because I need help."

And there it is.

I have to be careful how I answer. I didn't know if she was actually a friend of Ming. She could be a reporter. I didn't want the exposure, that's for sure.

I smiled gently at her and said, "I don't like to use labels. I wouldn't *call* myself a 'Witch.'" I used air quotes to emphasize the point. "That has some connotations that I don't need. I won't be flying my broom around the neighborhood if you know what I mean." I took a beat and sighed softly to myself while I giggled on the inside, "Why do you need a Witch?"

Alice gathered herself, and then it all spilled out of her in one long diatribe. "I am at my wits' end. Every night, black vines seem to grow out of the walls of my apartment. They come through the smallest cracks in the wall and spread across the floor. Every night. Then they recede in the daylight. I also hear a baby crying. Wailing. It seems to be coming from within the walls! The other condo owners say they have occasionally heard something, but not to worry about it. One idiot even claimed it was a cat. I am so worried. That's why I spoke to Ming. She told me you are a Witch and that you could help me. She said that you had helped her when her father went missing in Chinatown by casting a spell. I need a spell to stop these vines. To stop this baby from wailing all night long. Please, I beg of you. I need your help. I need sleep!"

She started to cry silently and looked at me as if I was her last hope. This sounded like she might be in contact with the other realm. There might be another explanation that I can't see yet. Still, no need to jump to conclusions.

"You say this house is on Sackett? What number?" Alice replied, "175." "Oh … I see."

That house. That would explain it. I now had an inkling about what was going on, but I don't know if I can explain it to her in a way she would accept it. Or if I could do anything about it at all.

"Alice, did you ask any questions about this place when you bought your condo?" "What do you mean? What questions? I did my due diligence. I had an engineer check it out and got a full report. It was structurally sound, and there was a lot of demand for this unit. I had to bid against two other buyers to get it. What are you talking about?" She looked indignant and fearful at the same time. A good trick if you could pull it off.

"It's just that address has a history. Do you know anything about Carroll Gardens? About the history of this neighborhood?" "Not really. What am I missing?" I guess I had to jump into this with both feet. "You see, this was a hotbed of the Mob back in the old days. A lot of gangsters came from these streets. Some very famous ones. One guy used to come around all the time. He wasn't from the neighborhood, but he was dating an Irish girl from around here. They even got married at St. Mary's Star of the Sea. Before they moved. To Chicago. His name was Al Capone."

Alice looked bewildered. "Al Capone? What does that have to do with black vines attacking me and a crying baby?" I had to bite the bullet and just tell her the truth. "You see, Al Capone was a pig. He was courting his future wife, Mae, but he was also having sex with one of her girlfriends. She got pregnant. Snorky had to shut her up." "And who's Snorky?" Alice asked. "That was Al's real nickname. Not Scarface. That was a media creation. Snorky was what his friends called him. My great-grand-uncle was one of his best friends. They were neighbors. He even asked him to go to Chicago with him, but he refused." Alice was incredulous. "That's crazy. What does this have to do with anything?"

"I will tell you. You see, he didn't know anything about a baby until she was almost ready to give birth. He was about to get married, and he couldn't have this screw it up. When she came to see him to ask for money, he lost it and started to beat her. She immediately went into labor. He dragged her to the old lady who lived at 175. She was a midwife. And an abortionist. Like Sinatra's mother. He told her to take care of it. But it was too late. The baby was born. The story goes that the midwife presented the baby to him, thinking he couldn't be such a monster that he would hurt it. She was wrong. He had her bring it to the basement. Where he forced her to throw it into the furnace. The girl bled to death, and the body was dumped out by Sheepshead Bay. The old lady fled back to Italy. She was afraid he would kill her, too. You see, that house was always cursed. Any old timer in the neighborhood could have told you. That must be what you are hearing. The spirit of that poor baby."

Alice was dumbstruck. She just kept shaking her head no, as if it couldn't be true. "Wait, my house is haunted? I don't believe it. That's not a real thing. That's just nonsense." Then she got angry. "What is this? A rip-off? Are you going to charge me a big fee for an exorcism? Are you trying to scam me?"

Now, it was my turn to get irate. "Look, Alice, I didn't come to you. You came to me. I don't think I can help you. So why don't you just leave and go back to your house or Connecticut or wherever and leave me alone." I waved her off like she was a gnat. "You don't want to get my Irish up." Every so often, the Irish part of me pokes its head up, and I get in a Donnybrook out of nowhere. I can be a touchy Witch, don'tcha know? "I know that story might sound familiar. Mario Puzo stole it for The Godfather, and it has long been part of Mafia lore. That is why you might be familiar with it and think I am trying to get one over on you. Doubt me, and our relationship will be over before it begins. You can just leave."

Alice turned red-faced and looked like a chastened schoolgirl. "I am so sorry. I was out of line. I didn't mean to insult you. But I *really* need your help! I just put all my savings into this condo, and it could financially ruin me if I have to dump it at a loss. And I love the space. I need to fix this. Can you help me? Please!"

I looked at the pathetic hipster and had to laugh. She came in here and insulted me, and then she was begging for my help. On the other hand, this was a very interesting problem. One that would call on my special skills. In fact, it was not just a skill. It was my calling. Someone in need was asking for my help. I couldn't in good conscience deny her. Crap. It's no fun being a responsible Witch. That doesn't mean I have to make it easy, either. She needs to do a little work to get me to take time out of my busy day. Plus, she needs to pay! As a hapless hipster nerd, she needs to be fleeced by the neighborhood girl. This is Brooklyn after all.

I sighed and said, "I don't know if there is anything I can do in this circumstance. Normally, the answer is clear-cut, and it's easy to know what to do. This is very nebulous, to say the least. This is my business, and you are acting like I'm Madam Cleo on the Psychic Hotline. You are calling me some sort of gypsy, and that's not right. I might as well turn on the levitating table!" I turned away from Alice and picked up a black tourmaline crystal tower I had on the shelf. I needed it to offload some of this negative energy while letting her think I was not interested. I said, "I think I'll pass." Alice looked crestfallen. "Please, Speranza, I *really* need your help. I didn't mean to imply anything. I haven't been sleeping because of the constant wailing of this stupid baby, and I just don't know what to do. Please, I beg of you to help me. Whatever you can do will be fine. I can pay you for your time, whatever you say."

There you go. The hook is set. Now I need to wheel her in and maybe get a payday from all of this wasted time. Time is money, and I haven't been making much between Birdie's nonsense and now this malarky. This isn't a Hallmark movie where no one ever pays for anything.

I looked at her sternly to make her sweat a little more. "Against my better judgment, I guess I'll take a look. You are Ming Lao's friend after all, and that counts for something. I only take referrals. You can't walk in off the street and hire a Witch. So, to speak. Maybe we can figure something out. No promises."

Alice grabbed my hand and started pumping it up and down. "Thank you, thank you, thank you. I am so happy that Ming told me to come to you. What is the next step?"

"I don't know yet. Let me think about it. I need to get more information. Let's sit down and talk about it. Someplace else. I don't want some looky-loo to come in and interrupt us."

This was going to take some time. I need food.

Chapter Eight – Can You Smell the Coffee?

I closed up and walked with Alice to Ginny's coffee shop on the corner of Carroll and Court. Alice was chattering away about inconsequential nonsense, and I was listening with half an ear. I needed something to eat immediately. You see, I am half Italian, and I do my best thinking with a full stomach. Unless my Irish side wins out, and it's over cocktails.

I needed Alice to cool her jets before we went inside.

"Alice, I know you are freaked out about all of this, but let's not talk about it in the café. You don't need other people knowing your business." Alice stopped babbling for a second and looked at me, "Yes, you are right. I don't want to broadcast what is going on." I replied, "For sure.

You don't need any chiacchierones spreading tales about your house. Especially if you want to sell it someday. So, mum's the word. Ok?"

"Absolutely, Speranza. I agree, totally. Let's just get something to eat. I am suddenly starving." Alice feels it too. That's the thing about dealing with Magic. Even just talking about it. Somehow, it always makes you very hungry.

We went into the café, and Ginny was behind the counter. Ginny is a busy entrepreneur who has always had a couple of businesses going in the neighborhood. She had the coffee shop and had recently opened a nice little wine and cheese place that my husband and I loved to visit when he didn't feel like cooking. I went up to the counter to place our order.

"Hey, Ginny, what's cooking?" I tipped her the wink that meant I had a new customer in tow. I always brought them by the coffee shop so Ginny could give them the once-over. I valued her opinion. She is more plugged into the neighborhood gossip than I am. "This is my new friend Alice. We would like some coffee. I'll take my usual, and what do you want, Alice?" "A latte Americano, please," she said. Hipster to the core. Ginny smirked at me. "Okey dokey. A double espresso and a coffee with milk. Coming up. Anything to eat?" "Yeah, bacon, egg, and cheese on a roll, please. Lots of bacon." "What, no ketchup? Disgrazia." "Yes, please. You know me too well." I love her egg sandwiches. "Nothing for me," Alice said. What happened to her being starving?

"Ginny, please give her some biscotti. She's starving but is too shy to eat in front of us."

We went over to a corner table and sat down. I took out my notebook and a pen. "I know I said not to talk about what is happening, but I am going to talk to Ginny about things in general, so don't get freaked out. Ok?" "Sure, whatever you say. I will be guided by you."

Ginny came over with the coffee and biscotti for the table, along with an espresso for herself. That was the thing about a small neighborhood place. The owner would sit right down with you and chat. This wasn't Starbucks.

"Nunzie will bring out the sandwich in a minute," Ginny said as she sipped on her double espresso. "So, what brings you here so early, Anna? You are usually working away at this time of the morning. Have you sold all your crystals already?" "Who's Anna?" Alice asked. "That's Speranza's nickname for her besties to use," said Ginny as she bumped shoulders with me and almost made me spill my coffee. "Stop busting balls, Ginny. I'm very hungry, and we decided to stop in for breakfast. Why? Don't you want my business?" As I teased Ginny back. Ginny scoffed, "Of course, I want the business, but you never leave the store without a good reason." She had me there.

Nunzio came out with my sandwich and tossed it on the table like he was mad at the world. He grunted, "Hey, Speranza. How's my pal? Is he going to roust me again? Because I'm Italian? How you hooked up with that Irisher, I'll never know." "Sean's great. He's always great, you know that." Nunzio chuckled evilly and said, "Yeah, that's for sure. Hey, I wanted to check in with you about Birdie. The last time I saw her, she acted more crazy than usual. Have you seen her recently?" "I saw her today, as a matter of fact. Why do you miss her? Maybe you want to ask her out on a date?" Nunzie cracked one of his infrequent smiles. "That'll be the day," he sneered as he went back into the kitchen.

I figured I could get Ginny's take on what was going on with the Salvina situation. She had more contact with Lorraine than I did and might have some insight as to why she went out of the neighborhood for a ritual. "You know Birdie has a beef with Salvina's daughters," I said as I munched on my sandwich. Ginny scoffed, "That old beyootch is always in a beef with somebody. Nothing unusual as far as I know. What's happening that I don't know about?"

"Salvina went on vacation and neglected to inform Birdie. She came to me all riled up and claimed something bad had happened to her. But when I checked with Lorraine, it turned out she was just on a cruise." "Yeah, like I told you before, I knew about that," Ginny said as she snagged a biscotti. "She came in to tell me before she left. She has been spending her dead husband's money like a drunken sailor. I am surprised that she didn't book a passage on a space shuttle while she was at it. You know you're just livid because you had another run-in with Lorraine and couldn't deck her like you did in grammar school." She chuckled evilly. Ginny reveled in the long-standing enmity between us.

"It's not her normal drama, Ginny. She had a Santeria bruja hold a ritual in Salvina's house. Can you believe it?" Ginny looked intrigued at that notion. "Isn't that against the rules? I thought you had to do everything Magical in this neighborhood? Doesn't she know that or does she not give a shit?" "I think both."

I turned to look at Alice, who looked confused. "You see, the neighborhoods in Brooklyn have been divvied up between Magical practitioners. The Wiccans here and the Santeria over there. There are even a bunch of Chinese Witches over in Sunset Park. We have agreed to stay in our own patch. Having a Santeria Priestess do a ritual is a no-go." Ginny grinned, "So, what are you going to do, Anna? Turn her into a toad? That would be great. Or maybe a rat? Yeah, a rat. That would be more appropriate for that rat-faced beyootch." "Geez, Ginny. It's always with the frogs with you!" We looked at each other and cracked up.

Alice looked a little taken aback at our banter. I bet she's wondering if I would turn her into a frog if she made me angry, especially if Ginny had her way. You never knew what crazy notions would go through someone's mind when they found out about Magic. They only know what they have seen in movies or on TV.

"Don't scare her, Ginny. I don't do that kind of thing. I can't do that kind of thing. This isn't TV. Don't be such a pain in the ass. Alice is new to Carroll Gardens, and I was telling her a little of our history. She just moved into the neighborhood, so she is very interested." Ginny looked at her and shook her head dismissively. "I bet you loved this neighborhood when you found out about it. The history and the closeness of the community." Alice nodded happily. "Yes, exactly." "Well, you know, by moving here, you are destroying it. It is people like you moving in and replacing the old timers that are turning this place to shit." Alice looked stricken by Ginny's harsh tone. "Ginny, cut the crap. That ship has sailed a long time ago. All the kids we grew up with are long gone. If they didn't want to stay here to preserve the way things were, how can we blame the people who want to live here? You've got to give this nonsense a rest." Ginny said, "Yeah, yeah, I know. I have heard you preach that often enough. It's nothing against you, kiddo. I just hate how things have changed so much since I was a kid. It sucks … you know?"

I wanted to change the subject. "I was speaking with Alice about the history of the neighborhood. You know, Ginny's grandfather was a big deal back in the day. He had a lot to do with this neighborhood and what it was all about." Ginny grimaced, "Oh, so you want to go there now? He was a gangster if you want to know. But my dad stayed away from all that. We have been strictly legit for about forty years, but thanks for bringing that up." Alice was round-eyed as she didn't understand the back and forth. The hostility in Ginny's tone seemed to have thrown her off. She didn't know that I brought it up for a reason.

"Don't be pissy, Ginny. I was just telling Alice how this neighborhood was all mobbed up back in the day. Most people talk about the Gallo brothers in the fifties and sixties, but I was telling her about Snorky and Mae. She wouldn't know the Gallo's but everybody knows about Al Capone."

"It was very interesting," Alice said. "I had no idea that he got married in a church here on Court Street." Ginny explained, "Yeah, most people are not aware of that. The church doesn't advertise it, that's for sure. He's actually from down by the Navy Yard and only came around here to party. This neighborhood used to be all focused on the docks. That's where the money was. Bars and social clubs sprang up to service the longshoremen. Well, actually, to separate them from their money. Capone would come down to party and met his future wife, who was an Irish girl of all things! My great-grandfather was a friend of his. Wasn't your great-grandfather in their crew, too, Speranza?" Great, she turned it back on me. "No, it was my great-uncle Mario who was his henchman, get it straight, sister! Nonna told me Capone asked him to come to Chicago with him, but he refused. He was an honest guy and didn't want to go with him. But then neither did your great-grandfather, Ginny? He stayed around. He just wasn't all that honest."

"He was honest enough," Ginny replied. "At least he never went to the can. My grandfather and father both went into the fruit and vegetable business. They worked hard, and that's how we ended up where we are. So don't be telling her that I am all gangster money because that's bullshit and you know it. Not like you and all that Witchy stuff your family did, Glinda the Good Bitch." Ginny said it with a smile so Alice wouldn't freak out. She didn't know that we had been doing this since grammar school.

"Don't get your panties in a twist, coffee girl. I just wanted to give Alice the lowdown. I even told her about the rumors about Capone and the baby." Ginny smirked, "That old chestnut. You know, they used that in a bunch of movies and TV shows. It has been hung on many gangsters, but it was Capone who did it. Right in the old lady's house on Sackett Street." I asked, "How do we know that's true, Ginny? I always thought it was an old wives' tale. You know. Throwing a baby in the furnace. It's too gruesome to be true." Ginny shook her head. "No, it's the real deal. I heard my great-grandmother talking about that story with my grandma when I was a kid. They didn't know I was listening. My great-grandmother was good friends with the midwife who lived there. They were going to buy that building, but changed their minds because they thought it was haunted. That was what they were talking about when I overheard them. They were even thinking about asking your Nonna to do an exorcism or something to clean it up. But in the end, they decided to buy something on Henry Street instead. He did kill that baby, and that house is definitely haunted. You can bet on it."

A couple of customers came in, and Ginny jumped up to serve them. I looked at Alice. This conversation only served to make her sure that she had done the right thing in consulting me. "Let's go back to the store." We got up and waved to Ginny, who was still working with her customers. "I'll catch you later, sweetie," I said as we walked out. Ginny just waved.

We went onto Court Street and started toward the store. "I guess you were right about the house," Alice said hopefully. "We must be on the right path." "Let's not get ahead of ourselves. I tell you what. Let me open the store, and you come back tonight, and we will go over to your house and take a look-see." We walked over to the store, and I unlocked the door.

"I'll see you tonight. Come by around six." Alice nodded and went off toward her home. I went into the store and sat behind the counter. I turned to get my notebook and stopped.

Oona was sitting on the shelf behind the desk. The little pixie was in the doorway of her faerie house with her gossamer wings vibrating a mile a minute. She seemed anxious.

"Finally, you're back, you great booby! I was worried. We need to talk." Oona jumped up and looked at me with fire in her eyes. "I need to talk to you, too, Oona. Tell me. Is Queen Mab on the Warpath?" Oona froze for a second and blurted, "For fook's sake," she snapped and turned and dived back into her house.

I guess it wasn't going to be easy to get any info from my favorite faerie.

Chapter Nine – It's 5 o'clock Somewhere

I needed to speak with Oona, but she had pulled a disappearing act. Now, I'm forced to summon her to ask my questions. I … want ... answers! I can't tempt her with wine like Mello, but she dearly loves spice drops. Especially, the purple ones.

I set a fresh saucer of milk with honey and a pile of purple spice drops to entice her to come out of her house. This might not immediately coax her out, but I know she can't help herself. Oona will smell the gingery spice flavor, and eventually, she will come out to play. I had a big jar of spice drops just for that. I had to fish out her favorites to tempt her. Mental note. Bring some home to Sean because he loved them, too. Just in case I need to bribe him.

While I waited for her to show up, I had to handle the normal day-to-day minutiae. I had several online orders to pack up and an occasional customer who would wander in off the street. I sold three tarot decks and a set of Tibetan cymbals to walk-ins. It was a busy day, but I still kept an eye on the doorway of the faerie house even though I wouldn't see her until I closed the store.

At five o'clock, I locked the door. I put the closed sign in the window and drew the sheer curtains. I used them to block the windows when I had a tarot class or reading, as I didn't want everyone on Court Street looking in like we were a pet store. You could tell we were inside, but you couldn't see exactly what we were doing. I decided to try a summoning ritual before Alice showed up at six to go to her haunted house.

I lit a white taper with my fancy flint fire starter. Say that five times fast. I drew three circles in white chalk in front of the faerie house. I sat and visualized her return. I had to clear my head and think happy thoughts if I wanted to have a positive visit. If I was angry or upset, there was a chance that she wouldn't show up at all. I had to get Birdie out of my head. Forget about Al Capone, dead babies, Hawaii, and all of the nonsense that was rumbling around in my consciousness. Breathe. Meditate. Summon.

I took my special bell and rang it three times. I had found it at the antique store where they were selling it as a dinner bell. It had a foreign language inscribed on it that was not familiar to the owners when they sold it to me. It was Gaelic and was an artifact that dates back to the ancient Celts of Belfast before the time of the Romans. My Grannie Meg was flabbergasted when she saw it and told me it was a precious, magical tool that I had to safeguard at all costs. I normally kept it in my locked cabinet, but I decided to pull out the big guns to get Oona to come out and play.

I rang the bell again. Three more times. The power of the bell compelled her to appear. Suddenly, Oona came out of the doors of the faerie house and looked at me with a disgusted look on her face.

"So, what is it to be Speranza? Why are you summoning me? And why are you trying to bribe me with my favorite treat?" Oona asked as she started stuffing spice drops in the small leather sack that she always carried with her. She loved presents and knew that I wasn't really bribing her. It was a gesture of respect and affection.

"I need to speak to you, and I don't want you to flee at the first hard question. I need your help. I know you are of the Sidhe. Right?" Oona picked up one of the purple drops and took a huge bite out of it. "Yes, that is my clan. What of it?" "Isn't Queen Mab the leader of your clan? The Lord to whom you owe your allegiance?" Oona's eyes shifted from side to side as though the question upset her. "Aye, that she is. The Dark Queen of the Sidhe, whom I owe allegiance and fealty all the days of my life." Now we are getting somewhere. "So, what does that mean for me? I am intimately connected to you and yours. Does Queen Mab think that I owe her allegiance? Or are humans not included in her Kingdom since it is not of this earth?"

Oona sat back on the front step of her house. I guess she had decided to stay for a while. "Not necessarily. You have never sworn fealty or homage to her. At least as far as I know. Although we are sisters, that doesn't mean you have any obligations that you yourself did not incur. Unless you have begged her favor or assistance. Because if you did, then you would be in her debt. You can be sure that she will come to collect. Be careful of what you wish for. Even in what questions you ask. It can come out poorly for you, lass. Best stay out of it."

I sat back on my chair in turn. "I want to stay out of it. But others of the fay have told me of a disturbance in the Never-Never. That there is a conflict. A bad one. Some of them are calling it a war. And that Queen Mab is at the center of it. I just want to know if I'm in danger. Or the people I protect. Or you, for that matter."

Oona thought for a moment, "You are in danger, lass. You are always in danger because of what you know and who you are. A Witch can be a powerful ally or a powerful foe. You can be sure that both sides might come to recruit you to their cause. They will offer you many things. Power. Wealth. Happiness. Some of it is real. Some of it is a mere mirage to trick you. You have not yet been put to the test. Your Nonna has been tested many times. You should talk to her. You have been sheltered for many years. It is time to grow up. Time to take your place amongst the people of power. It is time."

"Wait, what does that mean?" I asked. "I don't have any real power. I might be a Witch, but I am not some powerful being that can be a deciding factor in any of these conflicts. I don't want any part of it. I just want to live a peaceful existence. Helping people where I can and loving my husband and family."

Oona looked at me like I was a fool, "You don't realize who you are, my dear. Your potential. That is one of the reasons I have been with you for so long. To protect you. To guide you. To keep you from overstepping and coming to the attention of beings who mean you harm. My friend, your grandmother Margaret, begged me to protect you many years ago. As I have to this very day. I have developed a great affection for you. But the coin is coming due. You can only stand by the sidelines for so long. The Queen knows who you are now. She will come to you and offer you a choice. You have free will, of course. But you will have to choose. What you choose will echo down the rest of your days. I just hope you choose wisely. Talk to both of your grandmothers. They can tell you of the choices they made in their day and what that meant to their lives. That is my best advice to you."

Oona stood up and hefted her sack full of purple spice drops. It dwarfed her tiny frame, but she handled it with ease. She was very powerful for such a frail-looking creature. She looked at me with so much love in her eyes and said, "I will always be here for you, my dear. Just be careful. Choose your battles wisely. Until we meet again." With that, she turned and went back into her faerie house and through the portal to the Never-Never.

Now that was a kick in the head. Oona telling me that I was a very powerful Witch who had come to the attention of Queen Mab. Would she be coming to see me? At my home? At the store?

There was a knock on the door. Was that Queen Mab here already? No, what am I talking about? She wouldn't knock. I went to the door.

It was Alice.

Another problem to deal with. When it rains, it pours.

CHAPTER TEN – YES, SIR, THAT'S MY BABY!

I opened the door and let Alice in. "Hey, let me get my bag, and we can go to your house." "Ok great. Thanks for this, I appreciate it," she said. I shut off the lights, and we went out to the street. I locked up and we headed toward Sackett Street.

"Have you given any thought about what you are going to do?" Alice said as she looked a little tense. Dealing with magic and the supernatural often had that effect on the uninitiated. "I think I just want to go to your house and see what's going on. Then we can decide how to proceed." Alice asked hopefully, "Do you have a supernatural monitor or something to measure what's going on?" I scoffed, "This isn't Ghostbusters. I just need to get a feel of the space, and then we can brainstorm a little."

We got to her door, and she took out her keys. She had a bunch of locks on the front door, so it took a minute to get inside. We entered her foyer, and she turned on the lights with her phone. She had the "Nest," meaning everything was connected to an app. Except for the ghost.

"It started over here." We walked to a wall on the side of her living room. This was on the same side as the small alley located between Alice's house and her neighbor's. The alley wasn't big by any means. Not big enough to drive a car through. Just big enough for a very slim person to shimmy through if they turned sideways, held their breath, and weren't claustrophobic. Who in their right mind would climb through two buildings where they could get stuck? I don't know. Not me, that's for sure.

I examined the wall. There was a small protrusion that started about two feet from the front of the brownstone and continued to the back of the house. "This is where the vines come from," Alice said excitedly as if she were proud of her show and tell. "Black vines come out from under the moulding. It has happened several times. Usually right at dusk."

I went to the wall and took a look. It was new sheetrock that must have been put in when it was renovated. "Did you ever try to see what was behind this wall?" I asked as I started tapping. The portion that was next to the front of the building was solid, but when I tapped against the protrusion, it sounded hollow. "No, I would never do anything like that," Alice said as she nervously hopped from one foot to the other. She was a bundle of nerves. "Why would I do that? I paid a lot for this house, and I don't want to mess it up." I looked over at her. "This is going to get messy, Alice, if you want to get to the bottom of this. Or I can just go, and you can leave everything as it is." You can't help someone if they don't want to be helped.

"No, no, Speranza. I want to get to the bottom of this, no matter what. I can't keep living like this. It's making me crazy. I feel like I am living in a nightmare!" I comforted her by putting my hand on her shoulder, "Alright. Okay. Fine. Do you have any tools? A screwdriver or a hammer?" Alice thought for a moment. "Yes, I have the toolbox that my father made up for me when I bought the house. He said it was everything I would need as a new homeowner. Let me go get it." She ran off to go down the cellar to get the toolbox.

I kept tapping against the wall. I felt like Edgar Allen "Schmo!" No sign of the tell-tale heart. I didn't see Annabel Lee. Just an empty space behind the sheetrock. What am I doing here? I feel silly. I had to laugh at myself. If Sean told me this morning that I would be tapping on a wall like a demented Bob Villa, I would've told him he was an idiot and bopped him on the noggin with a sfogliatelle. I'm not a detective! Just a Witch from Brooklyn who lets people talk her into crazy adventures.

I bent down to examine the floorboard. There was a small gap as the moulding was not flush with the floor. Alice came back quickly and placed a large toolbox next to me. I opened it up. I lifted the top tray that held various nails and screws. Inside was exactly what I was looking for. I took the hammer out, put the forked back end against the moulding, and exerted a little pressure. It popped off like it was a Jack-in-the-box. Only without the creepy clown. Great. Now, I am thinking about creepy clowns. The nails were still embedded in it as I put it on the floor. There was a three-inch gap between the floor and the sheetrock. That was a little unusual.

"It looks like there was plenty of room for these vines to get under your wall, Alice. But we're never going to find out anything if we don't open it up." I put my fingers against the gap. Yes, Magic was being used here. The residue was warm to the touch. Most Witches can feel the presence of Magic long after a ritual. It was clear that something was happening here.

I could feel Magic escaping from under the wall as if it were a stream leaking into the room. It was very reminiscent of what I feel in front of Oona's faerie house. That was very interesting. Oona's house was a portal to the Never-Never. A way to travel from our corporeal existence into other realms. Perhaps that is what we have here.

"I am going to open this up," I said as I swung the hammer into the wall. I had to do it quickly before Alice changed her mind. She yelped like I had hit her instead of her mauve-colored wall. Dust flew everywhere. This is going to be a problem.

"Oh My God, you are freaking me out! This is making a horrible mess!" Alice said as she rushed to move her brand-new grey velvet loveseat away from the wall. "Don't worry about it, Alice," I said as I took an "Exacto" knife out of the box. "I will clean it all up as good as new when we are finished." I opened the blade and made a quick hand motion over it to enchant it. Well ... to give it power since I couldn't cut the wall by myself. Alice looked at me like I was nuts. "Just using some Jedi mind tricks here." I had to distract Alice by making her think about Star Wars instead of Magic in any way I could. Even if I sounded ubatz while I did it.

I inserted the blade into the wall and cut downward about five feet to the floor. I cut a large rectangle and eased out the whole piece of sheetrock. Being neat would make it a little easier to repair. I stuck my head inside to see what there was to see.

It looked like a corridor of some sort, extending back into the rest of the building. Strangely enough, there was a window. A window that you could only see from the alleyway. I guess they had covered it with this inside wall and didn't want to do the brickwork to remove the window. Builders did all kinds of strange things to cut corners. I knew the family that had redone this house. Their grandfather was famous for getting shot on Court Street as he was building the Marco Polo Restaurant. He was having an affair with the wife of another mobster, who walked up to him at the job site and blew his brains out all over his Chevy Impala. Sean told me he only did three years because "the fix was in." Those builders were all mobbed up, and they were the worst when it came to following the rules. So there had to be a lot of code violations and steps that they skipped, like putting the sheetrock all the way to the floor.

The sense of Magic oozing out of the corridor was palpable, like an air conditioner that was blowing Magic into my face. "I guess I have to go in to see what's happening, Alice. You wait here." Alice bobbed her head up and down. "Don't worry, I am staying right out here. Be careful." "Always." I had to turn sideways to fit into this narrow opening. I slid down step by step. I looked down at the floor and noticed that there were marks. Marks that could have been made by the vines Alice had seen. I inched my way down until I came to a door. Yes, a door. A large door. An "Alice in Wonderland" door. An old-world door that stood tall and imposing, with a faceplate bearing intricate patterns of swirling vines. Are those the vines Alice has been talking about? Despite its wear and tear, the door exuded a sense of grandeur, as if it guarded a secret world beyond its threshold, a world of mystery and Magic. Who would put such a door in this spot? It made no sense. Where does this door go? There wasn't any room for it to open up. It must open inward. I wonder if it was locked.

I touched the handle. Yes, Magic. Strong Magic. You could feel it. I turned the handle. It was unlocked? I pushed it inward. It opened slightly, but there was a Magical barrier. I couldn't cross the threshold unless invited. "Hello," I called. "Is there anyone there? Can I come in?" A cold blast of air pushed out across the threshold.

"Who desires to enter?" A voice seemed to whisper in my ear. It was an eerie voice that sounded like that of an older woman. A crone. A Magical being of one sort or another. "My name is Speranza O'Rourke, and I mean no harm to you and yours. I wish to cross your threshold in peace and ask that you give me permission with all the obligations that would imply." The obligations of host and guest are the very basis of the Magical Accords that govern all in the Never-Never who do not wish to be deemed an outcast.

"You are known to us. You may enter, Witch." I stepped across the hazy boundary of the doorway and walked into the Depression. It seemed to be a child's bedroom. An infant's bedroom.

The bedroom was a small, cozy space that seemed to hold a lifetime of memories within its walls. The walls themselves were covered in a faded, floral wallpaper that had seen better days. The room was furnished with a wooden crib that was made of dark, polished wood with intricate carvings of vines that matched the faceplate on the door. A threadbare quilt, lovingly stitched with scraps of fabric, covered the mattress, providing warmth and comfort for a tiny occupant.

A rocking chair sat in the corner, its arms and back curved and smooth from years of use, while a faded rug covered the center of the floor, softening the creaks and groans of the old wooden floorboards.

It seems that I had stumbled onto another room in Alice's newly renovated house. Or at least into a room that had been furnished in the Depression. This could not be part of Alice's house. That would be physically impossible! It had to be in another dimension. The Never-Never. The doorway was a portal. Just as I had suspected.

In the middle of the room stood a stooped figure. She was short, just about five feet tall. Dressed in a homespun frock, she had long grey hair and no makeup. Her dark brown eyes blended seamlessly into the weathered skin of her face. She wore no shoes, which was understandable, because her toes were on the back of her feet. So that's it! She was a Silvani. A wood's woman from Sicily. A fay being of rare power and might. Famous for their love of children.

"Why are you here, Witch?" The Silvani said as she stared at me. She did not give her name. I was not surprised. To give your name was to give power to your adversary. Not that she necessarily thought I was one, but you should always be careful. I only gave my name because I wanted entrée over the threshold, and I had to give up something. At least it got me into the room.

"I am here in service to the owner of this home. She has been disturbed by strange noises in the night. Now that I see you, I realize it might be the voices of your children. Perhaps that has seeped into the mortal world without your knowledge. I would think you would want to know to avoid an inquiry that would do you no good." There. That should do it. I wanted to put her into a sense of obligation. Perhaps that would get me some answers.

"It was not the voices of my children that disturbed the silence. It was the cries of the child." "What child?" "The memories of the child that was to be sacrificed here. The changeling that we saved from the fire and returned to your realm to live out her life. Now, her vengeful spirit comes to relive that night. Every night. Until she can be made free." Oh boy! That's not good. Magic. Sacrifice. A restless spirit. A changeling? This is going to be very complicated. And dangerous.

Another fine mess I got myself into, Norton!

Chapter Eleven – Mother May I … Not!

I can't believe an entire room was hidden behind the wall. Not to mention that it was a portal to the Never-Never. Portals were supposed to be marked. Known to all! Especially to the Witches in the area, like me! Small ones like Oona's faerie house are not an issue. Large ones you could walk through had to be clearly marked, and the proper protocols followed. You need to know if Magical beings are entering your neighborhood. Or, if someone from the human realm tried to access the other side. It could be dangerous since you do not know who might be attracted to this portal if its existence is revealed. That is why the portals are vigorously policed.

I have to investigate this portal and be careful when dealing with a faerie with the power of a Silvani. I didn't know her motives; I had to determine her intent and the extent of her power. I realize I need to tread carefully and learn as much as possible.

"You will excuse me, Mother. I do not wish to offend you. I came here to investigate the sounds that my friend is hearing every night. She has just purchased her home and had no idea that this would be a nightly occurrence." I had to placate her before I tried to interrogate her, the way Sean had taught me. The Silvani are powerful beings, but thought to be benign. This woman did not look like a traditional Silvani but had to be one because of the toes on the back of her feet.

The traditional depiction of a Silvani faerie was that they were small and slight, almost ghost-like in appearance. Always dressed in red, their gossamer wings would flutter with the wind as their spirit was associated with the air. The faerie before me did not present anything like that. She was plain and homely but comforting nonetheless. The simplicity of her dress proclaimed her to be a mother. A mother of a "Depression" baby who belongs to this room.

"You say you did not want to offend, but you came when you were not invited. That would seem to be cause for offense?" Not invited? I didn't even know there was a portal here. I just wanted to find the crying baby. Her words did not make sense, as it was obvious that she was trying to tempt me. Am I being set up as a patsy? None of this is adding up. "Still, we would like to speak with you, Witch. That is why we have summoned you. We knew your curiosity would make you come." Ah! It is a summoning! "Whose is we, Mother?" I asked, although I could make a pretty good guess. "Someone much more powerful and unforgiving than me, little one. She wants to see you, and you must follow me through this door into her domain. That is the real reason we have been calling." I feel very confused as to the motives of this call. The Silvani sensed my thoughts. She explained, "I knew you would be asked to examine these sounds that terrified that human. This means nothing."

With those words, she suddenly transformed. Gone was the homespun frock and beaten-down appearance. Instead, she sported a red silk dress with huge gossamer wings beating furiously behind her as though she were a hummingbird. It was an extraordinary moment, like when The Wizard of Oz went from black and white to color. The world was so much more vivid and exciting. She beckoned to me and said, "Will you come with me and learn your true destiny?"

A powerful faerie has invited me to the Magical realm of the Never-Never! In all the years I have dealt with them, not one has ever made such an invitation. The question I have to ask is why? Why now? Why here? Why me? I couldn't go off half-assed even though it was very tempting. I've always wanted to go over to the other side to see what it was really like. I've heard many stories and read many descriptions. I just want to see for myself. I've always felt this way, but this was not the time. I needed to be prepared. I needed to know who was summoning me. Who's the "We?" I needed tools to protect myself. I needed to consult both of my grandmothers and all of the other faeries I know. Knowledge is power, and I needed to be sure that I had enough of it to protect myself.

The hovering Silvani decided to up the ante. She gestured with her hand, and a door appeared on the back wall of the room where no door had been before. It opened into a vista that could barely be glimpsed from where I stood. I took a couple of steps forward as though I was drawn to the entrance by some invisible force. When I reached the threshold, I held onto the door jam and looked out into what must be the Never-Never.

The Never-Never! The land of Faeries and Gods! As I looked out, it seemed a place of unparalleled beauty. And danger. A world of shimmering Magic, where ancient beings of myth and legend walk alongside faeries, sprites, and nymphs. Here, the natural laws of the mortal world do not apply, and anything is possible.

I glimpsed a riot of color and sound. The air that wafted into the room was filled with the sweet scent of flowers. The landscape seemed not just beautiful, but alive with Magic – plants with leaves that can heal or harm, vines that can support or entangle, and flowers that can make you fall asleep or wake you up from a deep slumber.

And yet, for all its danger, the Never-Never is a place of indescribable beauty and wonder, a place where the impossible becomes possible and the unimaginable becomes real. It is a world of Magic and mystery, where even the most jaded of mortals can find something to believe in.

I wanted to jump right in.

But I knew I could not. Not without preparation and advice that would keep me safe. This was an enticement to my destruction. Or if not my destruction, then my enslavement to the Queen of Darkness. She had to be the one summoning me. The one who was using the Silvani to tempt me with the wonders of the Never-Never and the realization of the dreams I had ever since I was a little girl. I couldn't take a bite of this apple. Not if I wanted to stay awake.

I slowly backed away from the threshold of the doorway. "I thank you for the offer, Mother, but I am afraid I must decline. I must remain here on this mortal plane. Please, tell whoever wants to see me that perhaps we can do it … another time? I hope you can cease the noise that has upset the owner of this property. I know that you do not want to interact with the mortal world, so this will free you to follow your own pursuits. Thank you."

The Silvani looked at me with a face that was a livid mask of anger and contempt. "You know not whom you trifle with, foolish girl! You cannot avoid her! You must submit! It would be much better for you if you did it sooner rather than later. Heed me! Do not leave! Come with me now while you can still gain her favor." She extended her hand to me as though she was going to grasp my hand to pull me further into the Magical realm.

I jumped back across the threshold of the room into the small passageway. The Silvani could not enter without my permission. Or the permission of the occupants of this house. I had to ensure that she would not trick Alice into letting her in. I had to use a spell to close this portal to the Never-Never to keep out the Silvani and any other malevolent faeries that might try to enter.

I raised my arms with my palms facing the door. I was shaking like a leaf, and my heart was pounding in my chest. I took a deep breath, stood tall, and chanted a spell to close this portal:

"By my will and with my might,
I create a boundary on this site.
Only those with permission here,
May cross this threshold without fear."

Bam! There, that ought to hold it. Now I have to go back and explain to Alice. As if she would believe me. Faeries? The Never-Never? The summons of the Queen of Darkness? A Witch's spell to protect her? A Magical portal?

Yeah. Sure. This should be very easy to explain.

CHAPTER TWELVE – PRESTO MEATBALL!

A faint shimmer of light was visible along the border of the door. You could feel the Magical barrier from where I stood. The power of the vibrations was palpable as it protected the threshold.

I turned and sidled down the tight corridor on the inside wall of Alice's brownstone. She was waiting for answers on the other side of the wall. I needed to figure out what I should tell her. It won't be easy.

I stepped out into the room where Alice was anxiously waiting. It felt like I had been away for hours, but I checked the time and it was only twenty minutes. I need to explain myself without discussing faeries, Magical portals, or the Never-Never.

"Thank God you're back, Speranza," Alice shouted so loudly that my hair moved. It was as though I were down the block instead of right in front of her. "I was so effing worried!" Alice took a deep breath and covered her mouth in chagrin. She never curses or lets her hair down. She's from Connecticut, after all. "Pardon my French. What did you find out? What was behind the wall? Who was making that noise? Was it *really* a ghost? Please say it isn't so! I don't want to sell my house!"

I walked over to the sofa to sit down. I was drained. And I was starving. Whenever I do Magic, I get very hungry. I guess I use up vital fuel or something. There's so much to do before I get anything to eat. I wouldn't get it here, that's for sure. Alice was typical of the younger generation. They wouldn't even offer a glass of water when you came to their house. They just never thought of it. It was beyond their comprehension. They never had any food in the house, either. They are always going out to eat. They even go out for coffee!

"It's complicated, Alice. First of all, it's not a ghost. But it is something out of the ordinary. Something I don't think you could ever understand. Or that you even need to understand. Just know that I fixed it. Nothing will come through the wall to hurt you. I put up a barrier that will protect you. I don't think you will hear the wailing baby anymore," I waved my arm in dismissal and said, "It's fixed."

Alice sat down and looked at me like I was crazy. "What do you mean you put up a barrier? I didn't see you bring anything back there. How did you stop the wailing? I just don't understand." Alice looked at me earnestly as though I had all the answers. She seemed so young. I had to find a way to reassure her that everything was fine without revealing too much.

There was only one way to do that. Magic.

"You are going to find this very strange, Alice." I grasped her shoulder to comfort her, "I'll be honest with you. Just give me a chance to explain without being interrupted with a bunch of questions. It will all become clear. I promise." Alice nodded tentatively, "Okay, Speranza. I will hear you out. What exactly happened?"

"It's very simple. There is a portal behind your wall. An entrance to another dimension. You've seen this in Sci-Fi movies or TV shows. I know that you are familiar with the concept. The noise was coming from the other side of the portal. I put a barrier over the threshold. A threshold is a very powerful thing. Normally, Magical beings will not pass over a threshold if they are not invited. So, I put a barrier there to stop anyone who would not abide by that prohibition. You don't have to worry anymore." I smacked my hands together to emphasize my point.

Alice seemed even more bewildered than before. "I still don't get it. How did you build a barrier? How can you be so sure that I will not hear the baby crying? I just don't understand."

I had to come clean. "Alice … I'm a Witch. A real Witch. Not a pretend one like in 'Hocus Pocus' or 'Bewitched.' I have real powers. And I used them. I cast a spell on the portal and closed the doorway. I also spoke to someone in the other dimension, and they won't let those sounds travel through your walls anymore. Again, you don't have anything to worry about."

Alice still looked at me like I was crazy. Ultimately, she was a rational person who didn't believe in Magic or Witches. Or at least that is what she told herself. But then, why did she come to me? She must believe in it just a little bit.

Alice sighed and said firmly, "I find this very hard to believe, Speranza." I got a little annoyed and took a tone with her, "Why did you contact me, then? What did you think was going to happen?" Alice became indignant in turn, "Ming Lao said to talk to you. She said you were a Witch, but I didn't believe her. I thought she was joking, but I was so desperate that I decided to contact you. No reasonable person in this day and age believes in Magic. A part of me wanted to believe, as I said, I am desperate. I still haven't seen anything to prove to me that Magic is real."

I was not going to waste my time arguing with her. That never works with skeptics. I just had to show her. It's the only way.

"Magic is not fake, Alice. It's not a scam or phony in any way. I am a Witch. And I am going to prove it to you. First, we are going to clean up this mess." We turned to look at the hole in the wall where I had cut the doorway. There were pieces of sheetrock and dust everywhere. It was one big mess. Alice looked stricken and said, "I know we have to clean up this mess, but it's going to take forever." Alice became frustrated and angry, "I don't even know how to fix the hole in the wall. Don't we need sheetrock and spackle? I don't know how to do that, Speranza. Do you?" I need to set her straight, "I know how to do it, Alice, but we're not going to need any of that stuff. Just stand behind me and don't say anything. No matter what you see, I want you to just stand there and watch."

I opened my satchel and took out what I needed to cast the spell. I grabbed a piece of chalk and outlined a circle that ran from the doorway and extended into the room. I took a small bag of salt and sprinkled it across the front of the opening to seal it. It was all *theatrics*. I had to sell it. I moved the large piece of sheetrock and leaned it against the open space. For a finishing touch, I traced a sigil on the loose piece of sheetrock with my chalk.

"Please stand behind me and stay within the circle. Don't move or say a word." Alice came to stand behind me and looked wide-eyed at all of my preparations.

I took my usual stance with my shoulders squared up to the entrance and my legs firmly planted to ground me. It would have been better to be barefoot with my feet touching Mother Earth, but I guess imported Brazilian hardwood would have to do. I extended my arms and held my palms out facing the damaged wall. I began to verbalize the spell in a strong voice that would reach the entire room:

"With ancient words of Magic lore,
The wall is fixed, as once before,
From dust and debris, it's now free,
Pristine and new, for all to see.

A haze began to form in the room. Dust and debris were immediately picked up in a whirlwind that was generated at the base of the wall. All of the little bits and pieces were magically put back together in a swirling cloud that obscured our sight. The sheetrock was pushed up and fused back in place. It looked as though someone had spent days sanding and spackling to perfection. Even the paint job matched! It was as though the wall had never been touched.

I stepped forward to touch the wall. Gave it a knock. It was solid. Perfect. Now the aftermath. I turned and looked at Alice. She was dumbfounded and stared at the completely repaired wall, and kept shaking her head in disbelief. "No, no, no—" Alice murmured as she stared at the wall. "What happened? What did I just see?" I chuckled, "Magic. Just like I told you. I'm a Witch, and I used Magic to fix your wall. I put a ward on the portal. Nothing will come through unless we want it to. You see, Magic *is* real. We just used it to protect ourselves."

Alice seemed shaken as she tried to understand. She didn't want to believe, but she had seen it happen right before her eyes. This happens all the time when a skeptic witnesses a Magical event. There were several steps in the process, just like the seven stages of grief.

First, doubt and disbelief. Then fear and wonder. Acceptance. Finally, she would want to exploit her new knowledge for fun and profit.

We had to nip that in the bud.

"This is amazing, Speranza! We need to capitalize on this! You know I'm an influencer and a publicist. I can get you all over the socials. Make you TikTok famous! You can have your own YouTube channel with millions of views! It would make a ton of money!" Alice saw dollar signs and was so fired up that she didn't comprehend the situation. She had flown off into her fantasy. She had to know that I wasn't going to do any of that. No practitioner would ever put themselves out there in the public eye. It would be a betrayal of the Accords. Someone who would do that would be attacked by all of the other practitioners. We cannot allow the world to know about us. If I let her run with it, the retribution would be swift and sure. And terrible to behold.

"I can't let you do that, Alice. No one can learn the truth about Magic." Alice was confused and whined, "But several people told me that you are a Witch! That you had powers and that you could cast a spell to help me. That is why I came to you in the first place. Why aren't they in danger?" Good point. How can I put this? "They are in danger! That's why they only whisper about it to other people in the know. It is a testament to you that Ming Lao told you. I'm not worried about Ming because I know she'll never rat me out. You, on the other hand, are an actual eyewitness who can testify to the reality of Magic. I can't let that happen."

Alice took a step back and looked scared. "What does that mean, Speranza? You are not going to hurt me, are you?" I smiled at her kindly and said, "Never, my love. How could you think that? I would never hurt you. I am going to help you. Watch!"

I faced her and put my hands on her shoulders. I gathered myself and felt the power flow as I recited the spell:

With ancient tongue, so soft and sweet,
The mind is cleansed, the task complete,
A fresh new start, with naught to see,
A life anew, with memory free."

The power of Magic flowed from my body into Alice. The touch of my hands only increased the power of the spell, focusing on a narrow spectrum of her short-term memory. Her eyes opened up as far as they could go, and she gently shuddered. She put her chin down, took a deep breath, and relaxed. I took my hands off her shoulders and stepped back.

"Alice? Alice? Hello?" She looked up at me and smiled, "Speranza? I feel strange. What happened?" I consoled her and said, "Nothing much, dear. We did a little ritual. You closed your eyes as we meditated, and I think you drifted off. I do have good news! You don't have to worry anymore. You won't be hearing those noises or seeing those vines." Alice was delighted. "Oh my gosh. That's great. What did you do? What was it? Was it a ghost, the way everyone was saying?"

"You could call it that for lack of a better term. I would call it a manifestation of an unhappy spirit. We did a cleansing ritual. It satisfied the spirit and calmed it down. It will not bother you anymore." I should be able to get away with it since the spell had erased her short-term memory. She had forgotten the hole in the wall. The door. Everything. That was what this spell was all about. It was a lifesaver.

"This is so great, Speranza. Thank you so much. Now I won't have to move. What do I owe you?" I had to charge her. I mean, I'm not a charity. If I started doing things for free, everyone would want stuff on the arm, and I wouldn't have a business. Plus, she had the big bucks and wouldn't miss it.

"Normally, I would charge around $750 for this, but because I like you, I will only charge $500." Alice ran over to her coat and took out her phone. "That's fine. Well worth it. Can I Zelle it to you?" "Sure." That was a lot better than getting paid with a chicken.

"I will email you a receipt. You know, you should come by the store and pick up some stuff to do a cleansing now and again, just to be on the safe side. I will put together some sage and Palo Santo, as well as an abalone shell with a small stand. It will let you do a cleansing ritual. I will teach you how to do it." It's always good to set up future sales. That's the Brooklyn in me. Like I said before, this isn't the Hallmark Channel, where no one ever pays for anything. You need to sell stuff if you have a store. Even if you're a Witch. You can't just make money magically appear. You have to earn it.

"Great. I will come by tomorrow. Thanks again, Speranza. I feel safe now." "You're welcome, Alice. See you soon. You're going to sleep like a baby tonight." I picked up my bags and left.

Now I have to get something to eat. Fast. I'm starving. Magic! I could eat a horse. Or maybe a unicorn. I would settle for a meatball hero at Sal's of Carroll Gardens. I will get it to go since I don't know if Sean is cooking tonight.

Food is Magic to an Italian. Presto Meatball coming right up!

Chapter Thirteen – The Hobs Have It

I left Alice's house and started to walk home. I called Sean to give him a rare free shot at some take-out.

I dialed his cell, and he picked up immediately. Which was unusual as he was normally busy. Sean said, "Hey, babe, what's up?" "Hey, sweetie. You think we should do take-out tonight instead of having to cook? I can pick it up on my way home. What do you fancy? Thai? Chinese? Pizza?" I could almost hear him salivating on the phone. "Funny you ask," he replied, "I was just going to call you. I am running a little late. I have a couple of interviews, so it might be a while. Let's get something easy to heat up. Maybe Sal's?" I had to laugh. "Boy, you are predictable. You have a chance to get whatever you want, and you pick Italian food!" "Hey, I can't help it. I am a guinea through and through. Besides, Sal's is the closest thing to my food I can get, so why not?

I get to take a break, and I can scarf down some good guinea grub." I giggled, "Say that five times fast!" Sean ignored my joke because food was involved. "How about veal rollatini with rice and mushrooms in the brown sauce?" I was glad he was getting one of his favorites, "Don't work too hard. I might stop by Grannie Meg's for a little bit. I will leave it in the fridge for when we both get home." "Okay, babe. Have fun and say hello to Meg for me. I love you." "I love you, too. See you soon."

I hung up as I reached "Sal's of Carroll Gardens" on Smith Street. Every seat was filled as it was the favorite of the old-timers in the neighborhood. Sal had a great concept. He was from Bari originally, and he cooked the type of Southern Italian Soul Food that we all loved. His great idea was to have take-out, but not to make pizza! What made his place awesome was that he gave massive portions. It was a bargain because you could eat off a single entrée for a couple of meals. Unless you were as hungry as I am right now.

Sal was behind the counter with a long-handled wooden spoon as he stirred a big pot of meatballs. He looked up, and a big smile came over his face as he said, "Speranza, how the hell are you? You didn't come to put a spell on my gagootz, did you?" I chuckled at his lame attempt at humor. "No, Sal, I just came in to get some take-out." "Was-a-manna that Strunz of a husband of yours is not cooking for you tonight? Is he out eating donuts or something? There's trouble in paradise, or what?" I stuck my tongue out at him, "Don't be silly, Sal, just pack up a couple of meatball parm heroes, an order of the veal rollatini, and a dish of penne ala vodka! Oh yeah, and four meatballs in a pan with lots of sauce. And make it snappy!" Sal laughed and waved his wooden spoon at me. His son-in-law, who worked with him behind the counter, started packing up my order, and Sal moved down to take another customer.

When I got my order, I waved at Sal and walked out the door to go home. As soon as I got in the door, I dropped everything on the kitchen table and got out a plate. Hey, I am a civilized Witch, and I'm not going to eat it right out of the wrapper! I took one of the meatball parm sandwiches and went to town on it. It was delicious. I devoured it like I was going to the chair. I just tore through that sandwich. Maybe I'm not so civilized after all.

After I finished, I secreted the wrapper in the garbage pail so Sean wouldn't see that I had started without him. He knew that if I had to eat that much, that fast, that meant I had done Magic. A lot of Magic. He hated it when I didn't warn him in advance. Sean was always afraid that I would get into trouble, and he couldn't help me. Sean had a little bit of a "Darrin" thing going on.

I put the rest of the food away to eat later. I needed to follow up on what I had learned at Alice's house, but I didn't know how to go about it. I wanted to talk to Hob, but he normally doesn't show up until late at night. This called for extreme measures. I took the pan of meatballs out of the take-out bag and put it in front of Hob's faerie house. They were still warm, and you could smell the garlic and aromatic sauce wafting through the air. But as good as that smelled, it would not be enough to summon the Brownie quickly. Though it would be perfect as the gift, he would demand in recompense for his services.

I had to cast a summoning spell.

I stood in front of his fairy house and held my arms out in front of me while facing my palms at the doorway of this portal to the other side. I started my spell in a quiet voice:

"O Brownie, come, to us appear,
A helper sprite, we hold so dear,
With Magic touch and heart so clear,
And make our home, a place so fair.

The door opened, and Hob stuck his head outside, blinking like a groundhog that had just been dropped by Mayor de Blasio. "Who is using Magic to summon me?" he asked in a peeved tone as he came out of his faerie house. "Is that you, Speranza? What's the reason for this commotion?" He looked angry and upset that I had summoned him so early in the day.

"Calm down, Hob, and try these meatballs." I need to bribe the angry little imp. "They're from my friend's restaurant, and I want your expert opinion. How do they taste? How do they compare to the ones Sean makes for you?" His irritation seemed to subside as he smelled the meatballs. He took a small fork from the pouch on his tiny waist and sliced a sliver to taste. "Mmmm. This is pretty good. From a restaurant, you say? Well, it is certainly acceptable, but I wouldn't want to make a habit of it. It is certainly not as good as himself's homecooked meals." "Thanks, Hob. I am glad you liked it. Sean isn't here, and I'm very hungry. You see, I had to do some heavy-duty Magic today, and it made me famished as usual." Hob looked up and asked warily, "Magic? Why did you need to do Magic?" I looked directly into his eyes as I shared my extreme frustration while still trying to control my temper, "Because I had to close an illegal portal to the Never-Never that I found on Sackett Street. It had been opened by a Silvani faerie. It is not on any list and is in direct violation of the Accords."

Hob stopped eating. That was significant! Something that would stop a Brownie from eating one of his favorite dishes was something that behooved us to pay attention to. "An illegal portal? How do you know it's illegal? Just because you do not know about it does not mean it is illegal. You're not all that, dearie."

I sighed to cover up my feelings of betrayal. My friends had let me down. Faeries are among the most sexist of beings in all of the universe, even though so many of the fay are female. Hob is an egregious example. "I realize that, Hob. I am not protesting because of a bruised ego. I have been the designated practitioner in this patch ever since my Nonna retired ten years ago. She told me of all the designated portals in our vicinity, and this is not on my list. More than that, it was under the control of one of the Silvani. That seems out of the ordinary to me, to say the least." Hob looked thoughtful, "A Silvani. Yes, that is interesting. They are normally found in the old Roman lands. Not here in the New World. You say that you spoke to her? What did she have to say?"

Now it was time to see if I was going to get any answers. "The Silvani told me that she was protecting the portal on behalf of Queen Mab and that the Queen demands to see me!" I said with an added emphasis to show how upset and confused I had become. "She wanted me to go to the other side and speak with her. I refused, of course, as I have no intention of crossing to the Never-Never, let alone at the beck and call of the Queen of Darkness! She is your liege lord, I presume?" Hob looked frightened at the thought and troubled by my reaction. "Yes, she is indeed my liege lord and has been so for a millennium." Hob leaned forward to show his deep appreciation for the danger I was in. Still, he was loyal above all else. "I owe her my fealty and my service. I cannot countenance anything that might conflict with that, despite my affection for you." He was obviously torn. I wanted to reassure him, "I don't want you to compromise your position, Hob, but I do need some information. Why does she want to talk to me? Especially in person! Please help me understand."

Hob bent over and speared a meatball with his fork and shoved it into the sack he normally carried with him on his travels. He was a faerie of the utmost integrity, but he still loved his meatballs. "I can safely say this, dearie. She wants something from you. Either information or for you to do her a service. It ill behooves you to ignore her. She can do a great deal of damage to you and yours. The Queen would never come to this earthly realm, but her minions might. She has many, and quite of few of them are exceedingly dangerous. You can't ignore the Queen of Darkness. At least not without paying a price." I sighed in defeat, "I don't intend to ignore her or to gratuitously give offense. But I need to know what she wants before I put myself in her power. To do otherwise would be stupid. Can you please help me?"

Hob gathered his things and went over to the tiny stoop in front of his faerie house. "I want to help you, Speranza, but I dare not. I can tell you this. Speak to Meg. She will know. Or she will be able to find out. She has long and deep ties with the Sidhe, who are among the principal followers of the Queen. She will be able to tell you more. I will just say that the Queen wants something of you. You are wise not to put yourself in her clutches without some sort of insurance. Perhaps Meg will help you obtain it. Alas, I cannot. Fare thee well, child. And thank you for the meatballs." Hob passed through the small door that was a portal to the other side. Much too small for me to pass through, even if I wanted to follow.

Hob had told me what I had to do. Talk to my Grannie Meg. The Irish side of my Witchy heritage. She must know something that could help. I need to bring her something as a gift.

Just not meatballs.

Chapter Fourteen – There's the Rub!

I prepared myself to see my Irish Grannie Meg. I have to pull it together because, to be honest, I'm a little afraid of her. She's not a hugger. I love her, but we're not as close as I am to my Nonna. I guess that is a function of Nonna being my mother's mother. Italian girls are always closer to their mothers' families. It is just the way it is.

My Dad was not close to his mom, as witnessed by the fact that he ran away from home when he was fifteen. Grannie Meg wanted him to find a civilian profession and not be involved with Magic. He lacked Magical talent, and that could be quite dangerous. They lived in a modest apartment on the third floor of a building on Hoyt Street in the Irish section of downtown Brooklyn. The first two floors were taken up by a funeral parlor of all things. My Dad worked there. One day, the owner offered to leave the business to him, with the condition that he go to mortician school. He was horrified! The next day, he stole his older brother's ID and joined the Army. There was no way he was going to be a corpse valet. He spent four years in the Army before he came back home, got married, and settled down.

Now, you would think that would lead to an estrangement between a mother and son, but instead, it was healing. Grannie Meg realized that he had to assert his independence and find his own way. They were good, but they were never really close. I think that's why I try so hard to be closer to Grannie Meg, because that is the only link I have left to my father. Luckily, she wanted to fix it in the next generation. She realized I had the talent and didn't want my Nonna to be the only one to shape it. Therefore, I spent a lot of time with her learning the ways of the Irish and the fay that they interacted with since time immemorial. Grannie Meg was particularly close to the Sidhe since her family had been interacting with them for many generations. It was our family that had transported the various faerie houses that they're still using today. Grannie Meg had introduced me to Oona, who became my special friend. She had also gifted me the faerie house I had in the store. If anyone would know about what was happening with the Sidhe, it would be Grannie Meg.

I walked down to Hoyt Street, where Grannie Meg still lives. She had taken over the whole building, and the funeral home was long gone. I thought it was a little morbid living where they kept corpses for so long, but it didn't faze her. I guess the Irish are more insensitive than most. That is why they would bring the bodies back to their own houses for an "Irish Wake" in the good old days.

I came up to the nondescript building in the middle of the block between Degraw and Douglas. I knocked on the door and waited for someone to open up. Grannie Meg had some very strong protection on her threshold, and I needed to get permission to enter. It was not like my Nonna's house, where I had placed the new boundaries of protection myself after she had retired.

The door opened, and a kindly old woman with rosy, round cheeks wearing a cotton housecoat greeted me. She had her iron-grey hair in a bun and was smiling to beat the band. "My word is that you, Speranza? I am so happy to see you. Come in and have a cuppa. I will put the kettle on!" Grannie Meg ushered me into her sitting room on the first floor of the somewhat narrow building. It had previously been one of the viewing rooms, so it had a tinge of the supernatural from all of the restless spirits that had inhabited it in the days that it had been a funeral parlor. Now it was decorated in the style of an Irish cottage that wouldn't be out of place in the movie, "The Quiet Man." Grannie loved to play up the Irish angle. She's a bit of a ham, and her presentation has a lot more of a theatrical Irish flavor to it than was the reality of the situation. She had always done that because her

Irish identity was very dear to her. Along with her contact with the Sidhe, who had long been her friends.

I sat in one of the two easy chairs that flanked the fireplace, which had a cheery little fire lit. It was not wood, but gas. Grannie didn't want the smoke that a real fire threw off. An illusion would suffice. Her magic made it seem like a beautiful roaring wood fire. If only she could bottle this and sell it to Ikea! She would make a mint.

Grannie Meg toddled in with the tea tray. I jumped up and helped her place it on the small table that sat between the two comfortable, easy chairs. What was striking about the room was the focus. And the fact that there was no television! Conversation is the only thing to be had in this living room. Now it was time for a difficult one.

After she had settled into the chair, I poured us both a cup of tea. Grannie Meg took her saucer and gave a tentative sip. She smiled back at me and said, "So, what brings you here, Speranza? It has been a while since I have seen you, darling girl. You are usually busy with that wee bag of spaghetti you call your other grannie." "Now, you know that's not true, Grannie," I replied in a rueful tone. "You know, I was here just last week. And I thought that you and Nonna had settled your differences. No need for you to call her names." "Ah, I was just funnin' you, lass. I dinna mean anything by it. We are at peace these days, 'tis true. But that doesn't mean I don't keep score. It's the Irish way. The Irish are great at holding two things. Their liquor. And their grudges."

I sipped at my tea as I composed a diplomatic response. Appealing to her considerable vanity seemed the way to go. "Now, now, there is no need to hold grudges or keep score. I love you guys equally. You know that. And I have come to you with a problem only *you* can solve." Grannie looked interested. "Well, I dinna know if I can help you, but you better not be asking for my soda bread recipe," she said in an exaggerated brogue. She was playing up her mischievous old lady act. "That you will only get when I pass over. Let us hope it will be a while yet." Grannie Meg put down her teacup and turned serious, "What do you need, dearie?"

I leaned in and spoke in a soft, reassuring tone, "I found a new portal that has opened on Sackett Street. One that is not on any map or agreement that I have ever seen. It was manned by a Silvani faerie who was protecting a pathway to the Never-Never." Grannie Meg sat back and looked thoughtful for a moment. "Aye, it would be in that hind near the highway. I know of this place. I know of this portal. It is more properly the bailiwick of your other grandmother. It is no concern of mine, I can assure you." I was surprised at that. "What do you mean it is in her bailiwick? I don't understand." Grannie Meg said, "Well then, let me educate you, dearie. In the old days, this neighborhood was split between the Irish and those dirty Dagos." "Grannie, please," I said to keep her on track. And to stop her from insulting half of my heritage.

"I am half Italian myself, and I know you don't want to call me a dirty Dago now, do you?" Grannie had the grace to chuckle, "No, Speranza, I don't," she said in a mischievous tone. "You see, you are the answer to your question. Back in those days, we were split. The Italians controlled everything from Court Street to the water. They had the docks and the waterfront. The Irish controlled everything from Court Street up to Park Slope. They controlled Park Slope, too, but our mob was limited to the portion up to Fourth Avenue. Another family had the rest. There was nothing but conflict and bad feelings and the occasional Donnybrook. Which came to an end with a very important event." I had an idea where this was going.

"And what would that momentous event be?" I asked with a smile, even though I knew the answer. "Why, it was the marriage between your Ma and Da, of course! When they decided to marry, we had to accept it. Your Da was a very strong-willed person, and your Ma was no shrinking violet, to be sure. They banged our heads together until we made peace. Which we did, and it has held to this very day. I know something of what goes on in your Nonna's patch, but I am not involved. If you have any questions about that place, you need to speak to your other Grannie, not me."

I knew I had to speak with Nonna, but there was still something else that Grannie Meg could help me with. "I will talk to her about that, but I have a question for you. When I went to that portal, I found a room that was a pathway to the Never-Never. There was a Silvani there who had a message for me. She said that Queen Mab demanded to see me, and she wanted me to come with her right then and there. I refused!" Grannie Meg looked alarmed and proved to me that I was right not to go. I continued in a soft voice, "I could not put myself in her clutches until I knew exactly what she wanted. Or amassed some protection to make sure I could get back home. I know that Queen Mab is the Queen of the Sidhe, who are your particular friends. I tried to question Oona, but she refused to help me. As did Hob the Brownie. They both suggested I speak with you. So, can you help me understand what is going on?"

Grannie had turned even whiter than her normal pale Irish hue, "Queen Mab, is it? Oh, that is bad, dearie. Very bad. Nothing good ever comes from interacting with her. Yes, the Sidhe are my friends, but they are her subjects. I would not count on their assistance in any way. I can try to find out what is going on, but I doubt that they will help." I was very disappointed. "You were my best hope, Grannie. I need to know what is going on before I decide what to do. Nonna doesn't have the contacts with the Sidhe that you have. I am really, really depending on you." Grannie Meg gently shook her head, "I understand what you are saying, Speranza, but the Sidhe are a fickle bunch. They never do what you want them to do. You have to trick it out of them. Maybe, if we can think of a way to do that, we might get somewhere."

That corresponds with my experience with the fay. They were the ultimate free agents. You can't think someone is without power or principles just because they are physically smaller than you. The Sidhe are fiercely independent and do not suffer fools gladly. An indirect approach was our only hope, and Grannie Meg had the most experience in doing that of anyone I've ever known.

"Could you at least summon one of them, Grannie? Maybe we can chat and glean some information?" Grannie Meg did not like that idea and spoke in her normal imperious tone, "I never summon them, dear. They come to me of their own free will. Trying to impose anything on them never works out for those who try. We can put an offering in front of the wee house and see what we can see. Come, child."

We both got up and walked to the back of the house, passing through the small dining room and into an anteroom. It had formerly been the funeral director's office. It had several mementos of Grannie's life as a Witch. A few paintings of the old country. A shillelagh on the wall that had been her grandfather's. Several shelves held various bottles, potions, and tools of the trade. There was another faerie house in the place of honor. It was the focal point of the room, just as the fireplace had been. It was ancient and had been in the family for many generations.

Grannie Meg turned to me and said, "Speranza, be a dear and go to the kitchen and get a nice piece of coffee cake and some cold milk." "Sure thing, Grannie," I said as I left and went up the stairs. The kitchen was on the second floor, and Grannie Meg had never changed the layout. I went into her spartan kitchen and saw a new Entenmann's coffee cake on the counter. That's my Irish Grannie! She always had an Entenmann's cake on hand. I poured a large, cold glass of milk. Cut a generous piece of cake. I put the crumbly deliciousness on one of the flowery plates from the cupboard, then placed it on a serving tray with the glass of milk. When I came in, Grannie took the tray from me and placed the milk and the cake in front of the faerie house. It wasn't quite a hot dish of meatballs, but it should still do the trick. We didn't know how long it would take. We had no idea if and when one of the fay would show up. Or who else would show up? There are several different Sidhe who utilize this portal. It was not exclusive to anyone since it had been around forever, and Grannie Meg had so many relationships with various members of the faerie tribe.

"I don't know how long we have to wait," Grannie Meg said. "We can leave it and sit inside if you want." Suddenly, the doors to the faerie house flew open. They banged against the sides of the house with an astonishing amount of force. As though a great gale of wind had blown them open. I could hear something going on in the background, much like what had happened in the house on Sackett Street. There was a loud commotion that sounded like conflict. Then it happened!

A figure tumbled across the threshold of the faerie house. "Jumpin' Jesus!" Grannie Meg shouted! "Aoife!

What happened to you, dearie!" It was her Sidhe friend Aoife, and she seemed to be covered in something. When I took a closer look, I could see that it was blood! I tried not to panic because Grannie Meg always said to keep calm in a crisis. It seemed that one of Aoife's wings had been torn off, and the jagged edges on her back were still pulsing out blood! Grannie Meg reached for her and gently turned her over.

There was an arrow sticking out of her right shoulder!

"Let me take a look at her, Grannie," I said. I knew what to do. I had some training in first aid as Sean had forced me to take courses in CPR and other emergency medical techniques. I didn't know if that human knowledge would translate to the fay, but I had to try. I rushed to the bathroom and got a couple of towels. I brought one over to put pressure on the wounded wing while Grannie held her. That seemed to stop the bleeding for a moment. But what was I going to do with the arrow wound?

Aoife seemed comatose, but she briefly revived when Grannie Meg gave her a sip of poteen from her flask. I knew the Sidhe loved that fiery Irish moonshine. Aoife's eyes fluttered and then opened. She looked at Grannie Meg and murmured, "It's war, Meg! It's come to that. Bloody useless war." Before we could ask any questions, another figure burst through the open door of the faerie house. It was Aidan! Oona's brother! He had a sword in his hand, and I could see that there was blood on it. He ran over to Aoife. "Ach, lass look at ye!" he said. He turned and put two fingers to his mouth and let out a piercing whistle. Two more figures jumped out. Both of them were adult male Sidhe. They hurried over to the fallen faerie and pushed my hands away. They picked her up and quickly took her through the portal without another word.

Grannie Meg was indignant. "What are you playing at, Aidan, you witless cur? Where are you taking her?" She wailed plaintively, "What in all that is holy is happening here?" Aidan was not amused at being questioned, "Quiet, old woman. It is none of your affair. Tend to your own business and not be butting into that of the Kingdom. Be quiet if you know what is good for you and yours, Witch!"

With that, he stepped through the portal and pulled the doors closed. Grannie Meg looked at me in bewilderment. "What just happened, Speranza? Do you have any clue as to what is going on?" I had to share a hard truth with her. "Aoife told us, Grannie. It's war! The war that the Silvani warned me about. And it seems to have reached from the Never-Never to here." "That seems to be the case, dear. Now we have to decide what we are going to do! Aye, that's the rub."

If Grannie Meg didn't have a clue, then how was I to know?

Chapter Fifteen – Off to See the Coven

"What just happened, Grannie?" I asked as we both looked incredulously at each other. "I can't believe that Aiden was so angry. Why would he be angry at us? What did we ever do to him?" I was taken aback because in all my dealings with Aiden, we never had a cross word. I only knew him as Oona's brother and had no idea why he was so furious. Grannie Meg waved me off and said, "Ach, Aidan is a perfidious gob shite! I've had dealings with this lout before. He hates humans, especially Witches, and has demanded that the fay not associate with us. Luckily, most don't agree with him, which is why the likes of Aoife and Oona have been our friends for these many years. Still and all, he is supposed to be a coming man amongst the Sidhe and not someone we should cross lightly."

This was the first time I had heard of strife amongst the Sidhe. How did I miss this? Oona was the closest thing I had to a sister, and she never let on that her brother hated humans! Why did she hide this from me, and why did Grannie Meg keep this knowledge to herself? I feel betrayed and naïve.

I didn't realize that the fay were just like us, with factions, cliques, and some who were against contact with the human realm. I can't believe that Oona had never mentioned anything about this in all of the years she's been my familiar. I guess Grannie Meg's friends have told her all about it, and she decided to conceal it from me. What else is she hiding?

"I hope Aoife is all right," I said as I sat bewildered at what had transpired. "She seemed to be badly injured. Do they have doctors or hospitals? What am I talking about? They don't have anything like that, do they, Grannie?" "They have healers, love. Healers and wise women who have been taking care of their clan from the beginning of time. How good they are is anyone's guess. I never spoke about it with any of the fay." Grannie Meg seemed beside herself at the attack on her familiar. They had been friends for over seventy years. Then, she had a thought and became more pensive than angry, "Of course, they might be injured or sick at one time or another. Occasionally, I didn't see some of them for years at a time. Or ever again. I don't know if they perished or if they were off doing the work of the fay in the Never-Never. This is the first time I have seen an injured faerie since the 'Troubles.'"

The "Troubles?" I never knew what that meant exactly. I know it was a code word for the conflict in Ireland between the Brits and the IRA, but that was the extent of it. Grannie Meg had been very involved in the 1970s. My father was upset at her involvement, and they argued about it all the time in hushed voices as they didn't want me to overhear. I think it led to the bitter estrangement between them that destroyed their relationship. This had not been resolved by the time my parents were lost in the jungle. I haven't thought about this for a long time.

"What are you saying, Grannie? The Sidhe were involved in the 'Troubles'? Is that when you saw an injured one?" Grannie wiggled uncomfortably in her chair, "Aye, they were involved. They had been involved for many years. Decades. Centuries, if you want to put a fine point on it. The Sidhe had long been the friends and allies of the Celts. In both Ireland and Scotland. They had a hand in the struggle. There were many rumors about the influence and patronage of the wee people in the past. Queen Mab, in particular, was known to support us." This is new information. "Wait a minute. Are you telling me that Queen Mab was in the IRA?" Grannie burst out in laughter, "No, silly girl. Nothing like that! I did hear tell that Michael Collins and Queen Mab were lovers, though. He was one of the leaders of the IRA in the 1920s. How about that for craic!" I was dumbstruck. "What! Her lover? Did humans become lovers of the Sidhe? How does that even work? The size difference alone would make it impossible!"

"Things are different in the Never-Never. Besides, the Queen is not a Sidhe. Just their liege lord. She is not tiny, nor does she have wings. She is always depicted as a seductive, voluptuous, Rubenesque figure. A very beautiful woman. It is no surprise that she has taken many lovers over the millennia that she has existed. Many heroes have been rumored to have been her lover. Collins is just one."

"But what does this have to do with anything, Grannie? Why are you bringing this up now when she wants to interfere with this realm?" Grannie thought for a moment and then explained the history of the Queen's boudoir. "If she is determined to intervene in the mortal realm, it would be far from the first time. She is reputed to have done so many times. Always on the side of the rebels of one sort or another. Which seems passing strange since she is a Queen, after all. You would think that she supports the established order. Not people who were seeking to overturn it. She was said to be the lover of many famous men throughout history. Not just Michael Collins. Legend has it that she was the lover of the likes of Julius Caesar. Danton. Simon Bolivar. Even George Washington, of all people. I never believed that, but who knows? Her seductiveness was the source of her power, which led her to manipulate history to her ends. It seems strange that she is coming here to interfere in our affairs. Who is the rebel that she has her eye on here in Brooklyn? I just don't see it."

I thought about it for a minute. All of her lovers were people who stirred the pot. There was a simple explanation for what she wanted. "It might not be that she is in love with rebels, Grannie. It could simply be that she is in love with chaos. With strife and conflict. People who turn everything upside down. We may seem too complacent. She wants to stir things up. I just don't know who would be an agent of chaos. I know it's not me!"

Grannie seemed to come to a decision and said, "You could be right, child. The Sidhe dearly love a mess. They have always seemed harmlessly mischievous, but they do have a dark side. They do love cruelty, to be sure. Human values are foreign to them, and I could see them wanting to overturn the apple cart. Now, don't be selling yourself short, darling girl. You are a powerful Witch. You are much more powerful than I ever was or that shameful old hussy who calls herself your other grannie. You have become a far more powerful and dangerous Witch than either of us. I hear that all the time. From the Sidhe. And from others in the trade. I have some contact with them, don'tcha know. They all acknowledge your power. You should give yourself your due. I can understand why the Queen might want you as a vassal."

"Woah, now. Hold on a second. You're in contact with other practitioners? When did this happen? Why wasn't I made aware of this?" I was bewildered at this news. I knew my Nonna strictly stayed away from other Witches and taught me to do the same. I always thought that was a wise policy, and I had always presumed that Grannie Meg felt the same.

"Well, dearie, I am surely not a dried-out stick of a stay-at-home Witch like your other Grannie. She was always afraid of her own shadow and could never talk to anyone. She stood on her dignity, the old fool. She never made any friends in the trade. Most of the others dislike her and not a few despise her for the stuck-up buffoon that she has always been." This is the first I have ever heard of this. I have to discount some of it because of the animosity between my grandmothers, but it did have the ring of truth. Nonna was sort of imperious and did stand on her dignity with outsiders. She did not suffer fools gladly and could be very intimidating.

"I did not know any of this, Grannie Meg," I peevishly exclaimed. If people feel this way about her, do they feel the same way about me? "You know me! I don't associate with anyone else in our world except for you and Nonna. I heard of some here and there, but I don't think I ever met one face to face." Grannie Meg shook her head and said, "Why, it's because of me, dear. I have been your buffer. You should know that I get together with a group of like-minded souls every month. I have prepared the way. They know that you don't interact with them because you are busy and not because of any sense of superiority. You aren't your grandmother. You have met some of them here and again at various parties and events with the family over the years. They just didn't announce their status." I was nonplussed at this news.

"Wait, so you have Witch's tea parties? Every month?" Grannie Meg was amused at my tone, "Not religiously, dear. Every so often, we get together. The craic is good and we have a laugh and a cuppa. You might want to come to the next one. If you want to know the truth, it is next week over in Bay Ridge. Why don't you come along and meet some of your peers?"

I had to think about that one for a quick minute, "It sounds like something I should do to get some answers. Maybe they know what's going on in the other realm." Grannie looked pleased. As though she had gotten one over on my Nonna by bringing me to her side. It was a good idea, nonetheless.

"That's wonderful, dear. I will let you know where and when. We can go together. You will have a grand time and might learn a thing or two. Just don't mention it to your other grannie. She will try to talk you out of it simply because she is a wet blanket at the best of times. There is no harm in it, and you will learn a lot of things you need to know. And … there will be ice cream!"

Grannie loved ice cream. I think she loved ice cream more than she had ever loved my father, though I would never have told her that. She always said, "Eat the ice cream" to me when I was a kid, even though no ice cream was in sight. I always interpreted that as seizing life to the fullest. Carpe Diem. As opposed to Nonna's much more conservative approach. I think I should "Eat the Ice Cream."

I guess I am off to see the coven.

Chapter Sixteen – Hi Ho Its Off to Love I Go

I want to strive for normalcy for the rest of the night. When I got home, Sean and I had a quick dinner and went to bed as we were both exhausted. Sean had an early day in court, so he was already gone by the time I got up. I enjoyed my coffee in peace as I took a cup out to the backyard. I sat on one of the comfy chairs and luxuriated in a little me time without interruptions by faeries, ghosts, or goblins. Goblins like Birdie, for instance.

Our yard was a little oasis in the urban jungle atmosphere of downtown Brooklyn. Sean and I loved to plant flowers and had already put in a bunch this spring. The yard was about fifty feet long and thirty feet wide, so it was substantial. The contiguous yards were hidden by fiberglass roofing sheets attached to the chain link fences to obscure the view into our yard. I think they didn't want to know what was going on in the "Witch'" house. That was fine with me since everyone on the higher floors of the surrounding brownstones could look down into our yard anyway. I would never do a ritual in the yard. Can you imagine? That would freak them out! I would never do anything without at least a cloaking spell to keep the busybodies from seeing what I was doing. Give me a little credit.

I took a sip of my strongly brewed black coffee and sighed in contentment. I had made it with my French Press, which made a really strong cup of coffee, albeit not one that was very hot. I only used the French Press when I didn't have to make a cup for Sean, as he was a coffee wimp. He liked that stupid K-Cup thing. He got used to drinking that swill at work, and he brought the habit home with him. Now, I could enjoy the real caffeine-laden hard stuff that I grew up on while sitting in my not-so-secret garden.

Everything that had happened in the past few days felt almost overwhelming. As an empath, I felt all of the confusion and fear that had been generated by these odd occurrences. I need to sit back and digest for a minute.

All good things come to an end eventually. I got up from my comfortable perch, had a shower, got dressed, and then walked to the store. I stopped off for a take-out cup of coffee from Ginny's, who was too busy to chat and went and opened the store right on time. I normally opened around eleven o'clock in the morning, as there was never any business before that. No sooner had I opened the gates, turned on the lights, and sat down behind the counter did disaster strike.

Birdie was back.

She bustled in with her ubiquitous vinyl shopping bag and fifty-year-old wardrobe. She brought something extra today. Salvina Russo was right behind her, looking a little shamefaced as she toddled along in Birdie's wake. Dressed in the finest gaudy guido wear that the Staten Island Mall could offer, Salvina looked apprehensive. In her massive fur coat, which she wore everywhere, even in the increasingly warm Spring weather. All this finery was still not enough to make her bold. Where Birdie was sure, Salvina was a little shy.

"Hello, ladies. Good morning. What can I do for you?" I was hoping I could make it as short a visit as possible, as I had bigger fish to fry. But Birdie didn't care. She was just one tough piece of baccala.

"Look, Speranza! Look whose back!" Birdie was almost jumping up and down in excitement. "I can see that, Birdie. How was the cruise, Salvina? We all missed you. Especially, Birdie." I said with a wink that only Salvina could see. "It was wonderful. I wish I had gone on some cruises with Phil, but he was too cheap. The best I ever got out of him was a weekend in the Catskills. Or even worse, the Poconos." Salvina said with a sly smile. She loved to mock her poor, dead husband, whom she had been deathly afraid of in life. In death, he was fair game. "I know I upset Birdie by not telling her in advance, and she gave you some agita. Sorry." Birdie wasn't having it. "Oh, don't be silly, Salvina. Speranza didn't mind. I was just worried, and so was she. Right, Speranza?" I had to admire Birdie's confidence in being such a skutch. "Don't worry about it, Salvina. I just had one little problem. Your daughter did a ritual with someone from out of the neighborhood. Did you know that?"

Salvina looked uncomfortable as I called out her daughter's bad behavior. She knew that any Magical rituals needed to come through me or my Nonna. For her daughter to go outside to some other practitioner was a no-no of the first water. Salvina remorsefully said, "I know Speranza, and I need to apologize to you. I should never have let her do that, but her husband was insistent. You know what a pain in the ass he can be. I didn't want to be the cause of any more problems in their marriage, so I went along with it. And I got covered in chicken blood for my troubles!" Birdie jumped on that admission with both feet, "So, their marriage is in trouble? I knew it. You got to stay away from the Spanish Salvina. I told your daughter that. You got to stick with your *own* kind." Birdie's casual racism was nothing if not consistent. She wouldn't even eat a black-and-white cookie.

"That's ok, Salvina. I won't hold it against you. No worries." Salvina didn't look convinced and dared to ask, "What about Lorraine?" I laughed. "Her? I am going to turn her into a frog!" Salvina looked stricken, and Birdie looked elated. I had to laugh again. "Don't fret. I'm just joking. I won't do anything now, but please warn her that if she does it again, there will be consequences. Ok?" Salvina looked relieved. "Don't worry about it, dear. I will make sure she never does anything like that again." As if she could control Lorraine or her husband.

Mission accomplished. Now I had to get rid of them. I reached behind me to take my decorative witch's broom off the wall and walked from behind the counter. I took it and started whisking it at their feet. "Come on, ladies. Let's go. I need to get you out so I can get some real customers in here to spend some money." I was laughing, so they took it in good humor as I ushered them out the door.

The two old biddies giggled as they left and went about their business terrorizing the rest of the neighborhood. Sure enough, once they left, customers came in. I sold a bunch of stuff. Some cleansing kits. A couple of decks of tarot cards. A selenite bowl, a crystal singing bowl, and even several spell candles. I was so busy that I didn't have time to worry about anything that went down over the past few days.

Until Alice walked in the door.

She wandered in and came up to the counter, and gave me a cheery hello, "Hi, Speranza, how are you doing?" You see, she felt we were close because she sensed that we had experienced something together, but didn't know exactly what it was. The spell I had used had erased all of her memories about the secret room and the portal. All that remained was a sense that we were friends and co-conspirators in some way.

"I'm fine, Alice, how are you? How is your White Rabbit?" Alice looked confused. "White Rabbit? What … White … Rabbit?" I hate dealing with young people. Now I had to explain the Jefferson Airplane to her! "Never mind, sweetie. Hey, can you keep an eye on the store for a minute? I want to pop into the ladies, and I'll be right back." "Sure thing. I am not going anywhere." I went to the back and into the bathroom, and left Alice alone in the front of the store. That might have been a mistake.

I had several different displays on the walls in the store. Some were salable items, and some were just décor. Behind the counter, I had several arcane volumes that looked like they had come from a Witch's library in the 1600s. They were old and weathered and looked like they were full of knowledge that only a Witch could use. Naturally curious, Alice went behind the counter and inspected the tomes that resided on the top shelf. She noticed that one of them had the words "Romeo and Juliet" on the spine. She loved that play and had performed it in high school. She reached for it and put it on the table. It was ancient and looked like it was made from some old-timey parchment. She opened the book and had a big surprise!

It turned out that this was not the play she remembered. It was a book of spells. Love spells at that. Suddenly, there was a puff of light, and a cherub materialized. It fluttered its delicate wings as it hovered over the pages. This cherub, known as Amorel, seemed to have sprung from the very essence of this dusty volume.

Amorel was a vision of innocence and love. Dressed in a tunic of delicate silk adorned with patterns of intertwined hearts, Amorel started to peruse the ancient tome of love potions and spells. His tiny fingers effortlessly flipped through the worn parchment until he found the right spell for the disillusioned hipster yearning for love. He stopped and pointed to the recipe that she needed. Then he disappeared in another poof of light as if he had never been there.

Alice freaked out. When I came back into the room, her face was beet red as she was sputtering and talking to herself in a high-pitched whine. It was as though she had seen a ghost. Which she didn't. She had seen a faerie. "What was that? An angel just came out of this book. Speranza, what the 'eff' is going on?"

Great! She's done it again! Alice had boldly gone where no hipster had gone before! Exactly what I didn't want to happen. Now I have to explain my way out of it. Again! "Oh gee, I see you took down my book of love potions and poems!" Alice was trembling, bewildered, and almost in shock. "You don't know what just happened! He was turning the pages, pointed at something, and disappeared. Am I losing my mind?" There was crazy in Alice's eyes that looked like bright blue saucers. Alice couldn't comprehend what she had just seen.

"Oh no, Alice, not at all." I had to comfort and distract her. I put my arm around her and gave her half a hug as I chuckled at the situation. I need to come up with a cover story toot suite. "You just got a glimpse of an innovation that I am thinking about adding to the store. It's a book that generates a hologram. You know, an image that is created by AI. Artificial Intelligence. It's the latest thing." I went with the technological explanation since nobody knew what it meant. Everybody pretends to understand what AI is, but they don't really know. It might as well be Magic. I had to keep Alice *dumb* to real Magic. She had already experienced too much Magic in her life. It was not good for her, and it certainly was not good for me.

"It was a hologram? How does that work exactly?" Alice inquired in an incredulous tone. I had to vamp if I'm going to get out of this one. "Well, it's very sophisticated. There is a tiny projector built into the binding of the book." Alice seemed impressed. "How does that even work?" Now was the time to baffle her with my bullshit. "It's miniaturized. Look at your phone. You have a device that is a computer, calculator, phone, and camera all rolled up into something you can hold in the palm of your hand. This program is just more of the same, only better. When activated, the holographic projection emerges, creating a lifelike cherub. The hologram gives the illusion of a three-dimensional, tangible presence."

"But how does it know where to open the book? It just glanced at me and went right to a specific page. How does that work?" Alice persisted in her questions. "You have to understand that Amorel's interaction works through natural language processing. That enables it to understand and respond to requests. But this is in BETA. It is only a prototype. Right now, it just points you to a spell. Let's look at what he picked out!" I wanted to distract her from my increasingly ornate lies. When you talk about someone's love life, it always works to distract them. All the single ladies want a love potion.

I spread the book out so we could both look at it. Amorel had landed on a page with a love spell. Alice needed one badly. Or at least I thought she did. "I guess he picked out a love spell for you. Are you seeing anyone right now, Alice? You know I never asked you." Alice looked sad. "No, I haven't been dating much. It's very hard for me to connect with anyone. I work from home, and I don't socialize much. I never did, and it is only since I moved here that I have been making new friends." I smiled at her. "I hope you can count on me as a new friend, Alice." "Oh, of course, Speranza. Of course, I do. You and my neighbors, and even Ginny from the coffee shop, who has been very nice to me ever since we went there. I pop by now and then, and she is always so friendly. I feel blessed." "That's nice. Although I would watch out if Ginny tries to fix you up. She only knows Guidos, so you might be reenacting Saturday Night Fever on a first date." She chuckled and said," Well, what about you? Maybe you can set me up? Maybe your husband has a friend?" Now I had to laugh. "Not a chance. Sean only knows cops and criminals, and I don't think you want to be set up with either. No, we have to find you someone who fits. Don't worry. My Grannie Meg always says there is a lid to every pot. We just have to find yours."

"I'll tell you what. I will write up this spell for you, and we'll work on it together. I can't do it today, but come back in a couple of days, and we can work on it." Alice looked disappointed but nodded, "Sure, Speranza, that's fine. I know you said you are very busy. I have to get back to work, too. See you soon." Alice left, and I took a quick photo of the spell, closed the book, and put it back on the shelf.

Great! More work for Speranza. Just what I needed.

Chapter Seventeen – Finding the Pony

After Alice left, I went on to have a normal day. A few customers wandered in, and I did some upselling. I even had a special order for a large set of amethyst wings, no less. I finished around six and closed up the shop. I went across the street to the pork store before they closed and picked up a dozen sausages and Italian bread. I figured we might have sausage and peppers tonight. I might not be the cook, but if I provide the right ingredients, I will get what I want to eat.

I got half a dozen sweet and half a dozen hot sausages. I knew we had a few sweet onions and a jar of roasted peppers at home to complete the meal. Now, I know some purists would demand that we use fresh peppers and that Sean could toast them on the stove burner like Nonna used to do, but he's comfortable cutting out a few steps, especially after a long day. Look, I didn't buy a jar of Ragu! We are simply using a big jar of roasted peppers. Don't tell Nonna!

I was pleasantly surprised to find that Sean was already home. He was at the kitchen table, drinking iced lemon water and reading his Kindle. He loved to read and finished five or six books a week. Stakeouts can be boring. It was great that he used a Kindle since we wouldn't be buried in books like we were when he was buying physical books that took up the whole house.

"Hey Babe. How was your day?" He asked as he looked up from his Kindle. I came in and put my purchases on the countertop. "Oh, it was the normal craziness. Everything from the return of Birdie to a lovelorn hipster. How about you?" "Same shit, different day. Some criminals got locked up, and some taxpayers got pissed off and complained. Now for the most important question of the day! Whaddaya want to eat?" Sean is all about the food. "Maybe some sausage and peppers. How's that sound?" Sean was ecstatic. He loved sausage and peppers. "Great, where did you get the meat from?" "From the pork store, just the way you like it. Half sweet and half hot." Sean was beaming with delight. "Let me grab them and go fire up the grill." Sean took out the two packages of sausage wrapped up in butcher paper and went into the yard to the grill. He couldn't wait to get his grill on. He happily grills in the cold snows of February. So, he was ecstatic to start grilling at the beginning of Spring.

Sean came back in and left the sausages on the grill. He took out three Vidalia onions and sliced them up quickly like a Sous chef. He added extra virgin olive oil and the onions to a pan and sautéed them until they were translucent. He added some diced garlic and a teaspoon of the Vietnamese garlic chili sauce that he added to everything these days. One teaspoon was like rocket fuel to give it some heat, and he used it to spice up most of his Italian dishes instead of the traditional red pepper flakes. Once the onions were ready, he added a full jar of roasted peppers to the mix. Sean turned the flame down very low and let it simmer until the sausages were ready. I am no great shakes as a cook, but I like to help with the simple stuff. I find cutting vegetables boring, a mindless repetition, but I did it to get dinner on the table in a reasonable time. So, I made the salad.

I threw together a quick salad of lettuce, tomatoes, olives, and goat cheese with a dressing of lemon, olive oil, and some herbs for flavor. I set the table and made a pitcher of lemon water. Sean had finally finished grilling, and he brought the sausages into the kitchen. He started slicing the sausages on a diagonal and then added them to the pan of peppers and onions. When he finished, he mixed it all into a large serving bowl. In the meantime, I had sliced up the crusty Italian bread and put it into a basket with a cloth napkin to give the right ambiance. It didn't hurt to add a few touches to make an everyday dinner special. Just for two.

We sat down to enjoy our meal. "So, what have you been doing lately, Anna? I feel like I have been out of touch with you these past few days. You seem preoccupied," Sean said as he took a huge mouthful of his sausage and pepper hero. I daintily bit my sandwich and said, "There's been a lot of stuff going on. Magical stuff, so to speak. I know you hate that, so I didn't bring you into the loop." Sean looked a little upset. "Magical stuff! Nothing dangerous, I hope? You are not doing anything with your Nonna, are you?" Sean had an unreasonable grudge against my Nonna. I had been in a few sketchy adventures with her in the past, and he was always worried that she was going to get me in trouble. You see, he knew something about Magic and my capabilities, but not the full extent of what goes on in my position as the chief practitioner for this part of Brooklyn. I think if he knew that, he would probably want us to move to Montana.

"No, I am not doing anything with my Nonna, not that there would be anything wrong with that. Just so you know, I went over to see Grannie Meg last night before you got home." Sean was pleased, "Grannie Meg! That's great. She's levelheaded and will keep you out of trouble; that's for sure. I want you to listen to her when you are doing that Magic bullshit." "Magic bullshit? Really, Sean? Take that back!" I was willing to indulge his aversion to Magic to a certain extent, but I couldn't let him call it bullshit and put it and me down. "Ok, ok, that was harsh. Sorry. I just don't want you to get all hopped up with this Magic and get yourself in a bad spot like you did the last time. Please promise me you won't do that."

He was referring to something that had happened last year. Nonna had called on me to apprehend a magical beast that had appeared in the neighborhood. It had shown up at her house and was preparing to attack her. It didn't know about me, so I was able to sneak up behind it and attack it with a withering spell that knocked it back to the Never-Never, but not without it lashing out and sending me to the hospital. Sean never got over it and was always on my case to not get involved in dangerous Magic. I wanted to reassure him. "Don't worry, sweetie. I am not getting involved in anything that you have to worry about. I promise." At least I hope I wasn't, and I didn't want to get him upset.

We finished our dinner, cleaned up, and went into the living room to watch TV. We never got to do that, so we sat down with a cuppa and some British cop shows on BritBox. Sean loved to see politically correct bobbies get beat up by criminals. British cops were a lot different than the NYPD. That was for sure.

We were deep into the latest season of "Shetland" when my cell phone started buzzing. Holy cow! It was Grannie Meg! She never calls me. I wonder what this is about.

I answered the phone, "Hi, Grannie Meg. Hold on a second while I get my earphones." I put on earphones so Sean could keep watching and more importantly, not hear her part of the conversation. I asked cheerfully, "What's up, Buttercup?" Grannie Meg replied in her inimitable Irish brogue, "What are you doing tomorrow?" I answered, "I don't know. I will be in the store as usual. Why?" "I want to take you to meet a few people you should know. I will come to pick you up around four if that's ok with you." "I can make that work. What people are you talking about, Grannie?" "Just the crowd you should meet. I have been remiss, and I want to correct that. I will see you soon, darling girl." Then she unceremoniously hung up. Grannie didn't mess around. She just gave you an Irish goodbye.

"What was that about?" Sean asked me as I took off my earphones. "That was just Grannie Meg. We made a lunch date for tomorrow. Well, more of a supper date since I am meeting her at four. So, I might not be home for supper, and you may have to fend for yourself." Sean shrugged. "No worries. I can pick up something on my way home or eat the leftovers from tonight. What does Grannie Meg want anyway?" Sean took a beat and then asked suspiciously, "Didn't you just visit her yesterday?" I had to do some fancy footwork to not arouse any suspicion. "Grannie just said she has some people she wanted me to meet. The last time she did that, it was to meet her canasta club, and the real reason was that one of the old biddies wanted a love potion for their granddaughter. I am sure it will be pretty boring, but I love spending time with her and haven't been able to give her much attention lately. So hopefully it will be fun."

Sean smiled in approval and reached over and started rubbing my back. I loved it when he did that. It calmed me down and lowered my anxiety to tolerable levels. "I know you spend a lot of time with Nonna, so I'm glad you are spending some time with Meg instead. I think it will be good for both of you." Sean always had a soft spot for Grannie Meg. She reminded him of his Irish grandmother, who had passed when he was a boy.

"Yeah, it should be fun. Now, let's get back to the Brits. I want to see what Shetland looks like." Sean chuckled, "It looks pretty bleak, actually. That poor guy seems to have fallen into a pile of crap. But he keeps searching. It's a cop thing." "Why is it a cop thing and not just a people thing?" Sean laughed out loud and said, "Because as a cop, you know when there is a big pile of crap, you keep searching because there has to be a pony in there somewhere." I didn't accept that. "I don't know, Sean. Sometimes it's just crap." "Maybe Anna, but I'm an optimist. I always think there's a pony." I love that about my husband.

Now, I have to concentrate on finding that pony.

Chapter Eighteen – A Seat at the Table

I got to the store and tried to finish up early so I could close when it was time to meet Grannie Meg. Thankfully, it was a quiet day. A few deliveries and a few sales. Thank God I wasn't interrupted by the likes of Birdie or Alice or any other energy vampire who would take over my entire day. It always became all about them!

Four o'clock finally rolled around, and Grannie Meg pulled up and tooted her horn. A merry little toot it was. I shut the lights, rolled down the gate, and walked over to the car. And what a car! Granny had gone to her garage and took out her 1968 Impala! It was mint! She had kept it immaculate and had a private garage where she had parked it ever since she bought it in 1968. It had a maroon body with a white ragtop and white leather seats. Two doors with the old-fashioned seat, you had to bend forward to get into the back. It was a classic, and she only used it on special occasions. Today was most definitely a special occasion.

I went up to the passenger side and looked in at Grannie Meg. I had put together a little present as I always did when she visited the shop. Grannie was Irish and loved her wee presents. I had filled up one of my small boutique bags with a few new crystals, soaps, and a couple of odd trinkets. "Hi Grannie, I have a little present for you. Do you want me to put it in the trunk?" "That would be grand, darling. I popped it for you." I went to the back of the car and lifted the trunk lid. It was a huge trunk. A two-body trunk, if you know what I mean. It was full of witchy paraphernalia. There was even a broom! I wonder if she had the broom in the back instead of a spare? Sometimes, I just crack myself up! I placed my gift bag in an empty corner and slammed the trunk closed.

I hopped into the passenger seat and greeted Grannie. No kiss or hug for her because Grannie Meg was very Irish. Not a hugger. Nor a kisser. A simple, friendly wave and nod would suffice, don'tcha know. Anything more would not be appreciated.

"Where are we going, Grannie?" I asked as I tried to fix my seatbelt around my waist. It was a sixties vintage seatbelt. I don't think it would even work if we had an accident. I wasn't worried because I knew that Grannie Meg had already placed a protection spell on the car. That's why it looked like it had just rolled out of a showroom. A bird couldn't even poop on it! Grannie Meg replied, "Why, we are going to Bay Ridge, to be sure. You are going to meet a few of me cronies and learn a thing or two, I think you should know if you are going to be mixed up in all of this. Now, hush up because I have to concentrate. It has been an age since I drove, and I need to pay attention."

I sat back because I didn't want to make her nervous. We drove down Court Street and made a left turn after we went under the overpass of the highway. Grannie drove up to Third Avenue and took a right toward Bay Ridge. Grannie never drove on the highway, so we had to deal with the lights. I just sat and looked out at the passing scenery as we drove past the developments down by the prison. The seedy strip clubs and X-rated video stores were long gone. Urban pioneers had staked homesteads in the various buildings that they had fixed up to house eager hipsters who wanted to claim a Brooklyn address. Factories were replaced by design studios as honest work had fled Brooklyn and left only the frantic make-work of the digital age. Eventually, we drove past Sixtieth Street and came into what was officially termed "Bay Ridge." As we pulled up towards our destination at Seventy-Ninth Street, Grannie spoke for the first time since we left the store:

"Through misty veils and Celtic whispers old,
I beckon forth a space, precious as gold.
Where tires rest and fortunes turn with grace,
a parking spot manifests in this enchanted place."

A panel truck pulled out in front of us, and a parking spot magically appeared. I was ecstatic because I thought that we were going to have to circle the block endlessly. I remembered going out to the discos on Third Avenue; we could never find a spot. A trip to "Embers" for a steak dinner would start with a lot of agita. Grannie had the right idea. Just "Witch" your way out of it.

That was the difference between Grannie Meg and Nonna. Nonna would never have used Magic for something as mundane as a parking spot. Grannie Meg had no problem using her powers in everyday life. That's why she never had curdled milk or stale crackers. I think I had to let more of her attitude inform my life choices. Maybe hanging out with her will help me be a better person. As well as becoming a better Witch.

We pulled up in front of "Svenson's," a famous old-school ice cream soda fountain. I've been going there for years and had never given it a second thought. Who would have guessed that it was a repository of Magic? It was an old building dating back to the days when Bay Ridge was a Scandinavian neighborhood. It was in an old brownstone-style building that was bigger than the surrounding storefronts. Each of the windows in the building had a red and white striped awning, as did the huge one that hung over the storefront. We walked in, and as usual, I was in love with the retro décor. The black and white checkerboard-style tiles of the floor and the round red leather-covered stools at the counter were the epitome of retro-cool in my eyes. Booths upholstered in yellow leather lined the walls under the decorations of cuckoo clocks and Viking artifacts, giving a distinctly Scandi feel to the diner. "Red Leather, Yellow Leather … Red Leather, Yellow Leather." A tongue twister from my childhood started repeating in my head! Stop it, Speranza. You need to get serious.

Grannie Meg didn't stop at the counter or a booth. She just walked to the back and went behind a wooden panel that blocked off the diner from the kitchen and the bathrooms. But that wasn't the only thing behind this wall. There was also a heavy door marked "Private," which seemed like it had not been opened in ages. It reeked of Magic!

Approaching the door, I could sense a powerful presence guarding the threshold. A hushed reverence seemed appropriate, as I understood the importance of seeking permission to cross into what seemed to me to be a sacred space. With an air of humility, Grannie Meg softly uttered her request for permission to cross the threshold, and I held my breath to see what was behind the door. As if listening intently, the door responded to her plea. The heavy oaken door, weathered by time, seemed to acknowledge our presence. With a creaking sigh, it swung open, granting passage to those who were deemed worthy of entering. It was almost a silent agreement between the enchanted door and us—a pact of respect and recognition.

It was *obviously* a portal. When we walked inside, I could see that it was indeed a portal to the Never-Never, just like the one on Sackett Street. Only this one had been here a long time, and Grannie Meg knew about it.

The room itself seemed to respond to our respectful demeanor. As we stepped inside, a rush of energy washed over us as if the very air carried whispers of enchantment. The atmosphere had shifted from the nervous energy of a busy diner to an awareness of profound knowledge that seemed to await us within these walls.

The walls were adorned with tapestries that seemed to observe a visitor's every move. As I looked at them, the figures seemed to move and transform in some strange dance that I could not explain. A closer inspection showed that each seemed to represent a different part of the map of Brooklyn. Various neighborhoods were represented, and I recognized several, including Bay Ridge, Bensonhurst, Sunset Park, Bed-Stuy, and Carroll Gardens. There was a midnight blue haze over everything. It was as if the color itself held secrets waiting to be revealed.

Once inside, I could almost feel a gentle embrace. It was a reassurance that I was welcomed and accepted as if the room itself recognized the unique spark of Magic within me as a practitioner. I felt that it had identified me as someone who had Magic. This place of convergence felt as if it celebrated the diversity of all magical heritages. Each practitioner brings their rich tapestry of tradition to share.

In the center of the room was a round table. A Round Table? Just like in the days of King Arthur? There were chairs arranged around the table. Each chair had a distinct design. They seemed to present a visual manifestation of the occupant's heritage. They were all individuals but united in some way.

Behind each of these chairs stood a figure. They were practitioners of the magical arts. These must be the cronies Grannie Meg had mentioned. One of them stepped forward with a quick smile and said, "Welcome, Speranza. We have been waiting for you. It is time for you to join us. Come, take your place at the table."

She took my arm and led me to a chair. "My name is Runa, and I welcome you. Please take a seat and join us." Runa possessed an almost regal air, standing tall and fair with striking ice-blue eyes. Although she could give off an imperious vibe at times, instead, she smiled, and her whole face lit up like the Northern Lights. She was a descendant of mighty Viking warriors, her bloodline flowing with the strength and valor of her ancestors. But here she seemed to be among equals and did not strive to overawe them, but instead offered me a welcome that I fully appreciated.

Grannie Meg moved to the chair next to me, and all of the other people in the room sat in their chairs. Each different, but each seeming to vibrate with a sense of wonder and power! Magic was everywhere, and I was in the midst of it!

I put my hand on the chair to pull it out from the table, and I had to let go. It felt like a living thing under my hand! As though it were flesh and blood instead of wood and leather. The woods that made up the chair were those of the Celtic Forest. They were a combination of oak, ash, and alder. Druidic runes were carved into the armrests and back, as well as a design on the top portion of the chairback. Strangely enough, the seat was padded with fine Italian leather, and fringes of intricate Italian lace framed it like the grace notes on a sheet of music. It seemed to be the perfect amalgamation of my Irish and Italian heritages, merged into a cohesive whole that brought something new and wonderful into existence. Merely touching it brought me joy. I could only wonder what it would be like to sit in it!

"You've finally got a seat at the table, darling," Grannie Meg said with a smile. "It was a long time coming, but we think you are ready. Now we just have to introduce you to those you do not know and tell you what it is that we do here. It is going to take a moment, but you can bet that it will be worth it."

I was intrigued. Amazed. A little scared. But most of all, curious. I had to find out what it was all about.

Chapter Nineteen – My name is Alejandro Lopez-Garcia – Prepare to Die

As I sat down, I looked over at the members of the Council. Each was in a unique chair in front of a tapestry of the area they represented. Or at least that was my guess from a quick perusal of each person and the pulsating artwork directly behind them. For example, Grannie Meg was next to me. A representation of South Brooklyn was depicted on the wall behind her. Interestingly, it only seemed to show the area above Court Street extending from Park Slope to Prospect Park. That was what was considered the "Irish" section back in the day. It did not include the Waterfront area where Nonna held sway. I guess the boundaries were still maintained. The new realities of multicultural Brooklyn were not reflected. Grannie Meg's chair was made of gnarled oak, as if created from the same sources as the shillelagh that the ancient Celts carried as they went to war with the Romans. It was ancient and homey, just like my Grannie.

The tall Nordic Witch started the introductions. "I am Runa. The guardian of the area of what you know as Bay Ridge, where we sit today. Three centuries ago, it was colonized by the people of Scandinavia. We retain our ancestral rights even though everything has changed, as so many have come to call this area their home." She smiled at me and gestured toward my Grannie Meg, who sat on my right. "Of course, you know your grandmother, so she needs no introduction. I will let the rest of the company introduce themselves."

Next to Grannie Meg sat a distinguished-looking gentleman who was definitely of Latin descent. A formidable Warlock whose presence commanded attention. With a charismatic aura and a hint of mischief in his eyes, he exuded an air of confidence and wisdom. He had a strong, sturdy build, his physique mirroring the resilience and determination that I would bet defined his character.

"Hello, Speranza. My name is Alejandro Lopez-Garcia, and I represent the people of Sunset Park along with those who follow my chosen faith of Santeria from Cuba. I am pleased to finally meet you." I smiled at him and said, "It is nice to meet you, Alejandro. We might have some things to discuss." He nodded in agreement. "I concur."

Alejandro's dark, curly hair cascaded down his shoulders, its unruly nature reflecting his free spirit. Intricate tattoos that depicted ancient symbols and mystical sigils adorned his body. His chair was carved from wood that seemed to be sourced from his tropical island. Perhaps it might have been the Cuban Magnolia tree, or even more obscurely, the Cuban Dragon Tree. I had studied them in college when I decided to major in botany for a hot minute. The carvings on the armrests were Spanish-influenced and would not be out of place in any hacienda.

Next to him sat a young woman with jet-black hair and a ready, if sad, Mona Lisa smile. "Hello, Speranza. Welcome to our Coven." The others all laughed at that as though it were a funny joke. She continued to speak in a mellifluous Slavic accent as though she were a vampire who was falling asleep. "My name is Vesna. I am here representing my home in Greenpoint. I know that might cause you to think I am Polish, but that is not the case, even though the ignorant have often called us Polacks. I am from Croatia, which only became well-known in America after the wars. Meg has told us a lot about you, and I am very pleased that you are finally here to join our company."

Her chair was amazing. I would later learn that it was a true embodiment of Croatian folklore and the Magic that flowed through her veins. Its rich azure hue evoked the depths of serene waters, while the upholstery, crafted from the finest silk, depicted intricately embroidered motifs of rivers and seas. The chair whispered tales of Vesna's mystical expertise if only you listened. I bowed my head slightly in acknowledgment and said, "Hello, Vesna, it's very nice to meet you."

Next to Vesna was a burly character, obviously of Russian Origin. He sat in front of a tapestry of the neighborhood of Brighton Beach that so many Russians had come to call home. "Da, it is good to finally meet you, Speranza. I am Nikolai of Brighton Beach. Your babushka, Meg, has often spoken of you and how talented you are in the art. We shall see." To me, Nikolai looked "strong as bull." Let's hope that he is smarter than one.

His chair was almost thronelike and was the largest of them all, with the ornate ruffles and flourishes that are so common in Russian furniture. He looked like the tsar sitting there, about to rule on the fate of a poor serf. Terrible and fierce like the land that spawned him.

Finally, there was a tall, smiling black woman wearing a multi-colored turban. She laughed delightedly and said in a lilting Caribbean accent, "Girl, you are in it now! I am Tiwa, and I, too, welcome you to our group. Now we can begin the work that is so important to us!" Tiwa commanded your attention with her regal presence. Her skin, like polished obsidian, exuded an aura of mystery and power. Her eyes, deep and captivating, held the wisdom of the ages. She sat in front of a tapestry that represented Bedford-Stuyvesant in Central Brooklyn. Her chair was made of a rich, dark mahogany, carved with precision and grace. She chuckled one last time and turned to Runa. "I think we should begin, girl. Let us tell this child what we are about before we overwhelm her."

They all turned to look at Runa as she smiled and dipped her head in acknowledgment. "Yes, Tiwa, let us begin. As you can see, each of us represents a different area in the city of Brooklyn. Each are representatives of our respective communities, and we gather here once a month to keep the peace as has been the practice for many years." Grannie Meg scoffed, "Years, darling? No, it has been so for centuries. Ever since Brooklyn was called "Breukelen" and was an independent city. Keeping the peace is just part of what we do, darling girl."

The Cuban Warlock jumped into the conversation. He leaned in and authoritatively stated, "Come now, you know that is not why we are here. We are all practitioners of great power and are banded together here to protect our homes and people. That is why we are asking you to join us. We need to stand together in this hour of need. I don't know what your Abuela has told you, but there is great danger, and we must be united to stand against it, or we might all perish. I had to flee my home once, and I swore never to do that again!"

Nickolai picked up the cup of coffee that sat in front of him and slurped noisily. Almost contemptuously, as if he wanted to mock the somber tone of the Cuban grandee. "You exaggerate, as usual, my friend. It is your hot Latin blood, no doubt. We need not get in an uproar. Things will sort themselves out. They always do."

Tiwa clucked at Nicholai as if he were an errant child. "You need to take this seriously, young man. Do not scoff and turn away as if our problems will disappear if we do not address them." She turned to Runa and said, "It is time to tell her, Runa. We cannot delay any longer."

Runa looked at her and then turned back to me. "I think you are aware of some of what is going on. Meg has told us that you have been contacted by the Queen of the Night. She has attempted to recruit you to her side. There is a reason. You are a uniquely talented Witch who has a degree of power not seen before. Born of the union of two powerful traditions, you have amalgamated them into an even more powerful one. These silly little spells you cast are barely a scratch on the surface of what you are capable of. We have brought you here to join us so you can lend your powers to our joint efforts to avoid the conflict. A conflict that Vesna is going to tell you about before we proceed."

Our attention all turned to Vesna, who said, "From time immemorial, there have been conflicts between various factions in the Never-Never. Mimicking the conflicts in our human lands, there has been a struggle for supremacy. Control. Dominance. Mainly between two factions. Queen Mab of the Winter Kingdom has battled her sister, Queen Maeve of the Summer Kingdom, for a millennium. It has been a low-level conflict for centuries, but recently, it has heated up. Both here on Earth and in the Never-Never. They are at swords' point and are busy collecting allies. That is why she contacted you with her minion in the unauthorized portal that you recently found."

Finally, someone who knew something! I exclaimed, "I thought as much. Did any of you know of this portal?" Grannie Meg spoke up, "Aye, so we did, darling. We know of several that we can tell you about. We keep an eye on such to see that nothing comes over from the other side that might be dangerous. Or at least dangerous enough that we have to take action."

Tiwa spoke next. "Each of us has contacts with the fay. Some are on one side, and some are on the other. The one thing we can all agree on is that we must not take an active part in the conflict. Because if we do, we might unleash the power of the fay on our peoples to such a degree that has not been seen since the Age of Gods and Heroes before the walls of ancient Troy."

The Cuban Warlock took up the narrative. "Once we knew you were contacted, we had to bring you into our little 'familia.' You must not go to the other side to join in the fight. If you do, you will cause irreparable damage both to that world and this one. We ask you to join us as we work to keep this realm safe from the conflicts of the other side. I put the question to you. Will you join us? Or suffer the consequences?"

I was stunned to think that my Grannie would be a party to this. I didn't take kindly to ultimatums or threats. "Consequences? What do you mean, consequences? Are you threatening me?" Vesna jumped in to make a conciliatory gesture. "Alejandro is just excited, Speranza. He did not mean it that way. Did you, Alejandro?" The suave Cuban Warlock shot his cuffs and sat back in his chair. "I apologize. In my zeal to get you to join us, I misspoke. I am not making threats. I am only beseeching you to join our fellowship and help us make this war pass us by. Please forgive me."

Grannie Meg seconded the emotion. "He is a hot head, dearie, but he means well. It is your duty and your destiny. Most of all, we need you. Your youth and strength might make the difference. The hunt is on already with the Queen of Darkness. You surely must be a predator, or you become the prey. Join this pack and help us. It is what I have trained you to do. It was what Nonna has trained you to do. Ask her if you must. She would never join us, but I know she supports our aims. You don't have to answer now in full, but you must think long and hard about both the opportunity and the duty you owe to you and yours. I know you like to keep yourself to yourself, but it is time to come and join the fight."

That was the longest speech I had ever heard Grannie Meg make in all the years I had known her. It was obvious that she was passionate about this. I couldn't reject it out of hand, no matter how much I wanted a peaceful existence.

"I understand, Grannie, and I will hear you out. But you must tell me more about this. I need to know a lot more before I make a final decision. At least I will sit with you for now. Let's talk."

I have to find out what is *really* going on before I make up my mind.

Chapter Twenty – Table Talk

"I still don't fully understand why we should be involved in this conflict in the first place. I've always thought our purpose was to protect this realm from incursions from the other side. Isn't it our goal to keep the knowledge of Magic away from ordinary mortals? It always turns into a disaster when they find out about Magic, and we must stop that from happening at any cost. I don't think we want to see Witch trials on the Internet." I looked at each of the others, in turn, to see who would reply. It was Alejandro who took up the torch.

"This is very true, but not all of the story. Throughout history, humans have taken part in conflicts with the fay. It is the basis of many stories and myths in many traditions. In this case, the two rivals are almost equally matched, and they are looking for an advantage. Your participation would be an advantage that they would do almost anything to acquire. You might ask why that is so. I will ask your abuela to explain it to you."

Grannie Meg stopped for a minute to sip from her cup of tea that had somehow magically appeared. Beverages had appeared in front of each of us, and I didn't notice how it happened. I had thought to myself that I could use an espresso, and one just appeared in front of me. Drinks had materialized for each of us. It was, dare I say, Magic. The room had read our thoughts and answered our wants and needs. I took the espresso in front of me and took a small sip.

Fortified by her precious tea, Grannie Meg took up the tale, "Well, you see, darling, you are uniquely powerful because of blood. Our bloodlines, to be exact. When your mother married your father, they joined together two powerful bloodlines. That of Italia and my homeland of Eire. It is very unusual for this to happen, and the heir of such a coupling will create an offspring of unusual power. It has happened before in human history. Merlin the Wizard was one such. Circe was another. They were powerful beings whom the fay enlisted in their disputes. Queen Mab wants you to be the next one to be exploited. It never ends well for those with that power. Merlin was imprisoned in a tree. We do not want that for you. That is why your other grandmother and I have been tutoring you in the craft. To give you the tools to survive when this day would come. I only hope it has been enough." She reached out and grabbed my hand. The love that she had for me shone from her eyes. Her physical touch was very disconcerting. She's not the touchy-feely type. I knew I had to work hard to be worthy of her love and concern. Was I up to the task?

Runa spoke up, "We don't know precisely why Mab is looking for you to join in the battles with her sister. You must have some specific power or ability that even you are not aware of. It could be something that would only become manifest if you take up her offer. We wanted you to join us so that we might help guide you. The offer to gain more power is often tempting." Runa took a breath and continued in her normal, deliberate manner, "Many in the past have chosen the easy way. I don't think that you will, but we are here to help. If you will let us."

Nikolai scoffed in his normal brusque manner, "It is up to you, my dear. In the end, only you can decide to stay true to yourself. All the training and help will mean nothing if you do not want to be free of the influence of the Winter Queen." He seemed almost livid in his misogynistic attitude, "It is best if you refuse any contact with her. I know this to be true. Don't listen to these old women. That is the only way for you to be safe. Trust me. I know. Contact with the Gods only results in heartbreak. You can be sure of that."

Vesna spoke in her normal soft manner. "Queen Mab is not quite a God, Nikolai." She continued in an almost derisive tone in contrast to Nikolai's sexist bombast. "She is a very powerful being and one of the most dangerous entities in the Never-Never. It ill behooves us to grant her more power. Getting Speranza as a willing vassal exponentially increases her might. I know that is not something you would want to do, Speranza. You have free will. Queen Mab cannot enforce her demands outside of the Never-Never. Her powers are great, but not unlimited. We have protected this mortal veil from her for many years. I think it might help if we tell you about the history of our Council so you might understand us a little better."

"That would be great, Vesna," I said. "I would like to know more. When did it start? Are you all original members? Who else has been a part of it?"

Runa took the floor in her normal deliberative cadence, "It started many centuries ago. Right before the Civil War, here in America. Many different groups emigrated at that time. Although the Irish dominated as they were already here in great numbers, there were enclaves of several other ethnicities. My Scandinavian ancestors were here in Bay Ridge. Mainly seafarers and sailors who bought property and built homes. With it came the practitioners whom they went to for various services. Divination. Protection. Spells of one sort or another. It brought them into conflict with other traditions. When riots began between different groups, these practitioners joined the fray. In 1844, there were terrible riots instigated by some English and Welsh practitioners who influenced their people to attack the Irish because they feared their power. A riot ensued that was only put down by the authorities when Cardinal

John Hughes of the Catholic Church threatened to burn the city down if they did not stop the attacks. What he meant was that he was going to burn the Witches, even if he had to burn down the rest of the city to do so. The Church has long been the enemy of our kind, and those English Witches recognized that, so they backed down. A low-level conflict continued until the time of your Civil War. When the Draft riots began, it was the Irish against the rest of the city, and it threatened to destroy the city itself. That worried the Irish practitioners of Magic because they no longer had control over their people. They could not ride the whirlwind, so they reached out to others of the craft to see what could be done. Several of them had banded together to stand against the power of the Irish, which was almost overwhelming at that time. They were shocked when the Irish reached out to them for help, but they agreed. The combined group took action. They killed Cardinal Hughes and several of the leaders of the Irish revolt against the draft. Curbing the power of the Church and the Mob so the craft could survive. They were able to do that and leave the Irish practitioners' hands clean."

My eyes glazed over. I am not a history buff like Sean. I needed him here to be my Wikipedia so I could just get the Cliff Notes and not the whole backstory. Too much information. Squirrel!

"Aye, that was very important, my dear," Grannie Meg piped in. "The Irish had a long history of informers and traitors, and they didn't want the masses to turn against them. The service that Runa's forebearers provided led to trust. Trust enough to form this council. As new groups came in, they were granted a seat at the table. Each succeeding generation would send its leaders to join and maintain the peace in the magical community. Through wars and pestilence, the alliance has held. As it should. Now it is your turn to join and help us maintain the peace."

"Maintaining the peace is just part of what we do, Speranza," Alejandro said. "We also adjudicate any disputes amongst the various factions who practice Magic. For instance, I am aware that one of my compatriots did a spell on your turf and that you are upset. Just know that she did not tell me about it, and she will be disciplined. It is vitally important that we respect each other's prerogatives and not tread on each other's toes. You can be sure that will not happen again."

"That's fine as far as it goes," I said as a feeling of relief flooded my consciousness. I would not have a dispute right off the bat with the obviously powerful Cuban Warlock. "But what does this have to do with the problem of the Queen? Shouldn't we develop a plan or something? I imagine she will keep trying to contact me, and I am still in the dark as to why. I understand that you say I have some nebulous power that I am not aware of, so what should I do?" I was starting to get perturbed. I was not getting a definitive answer with a clear choice of action. My ADD was kicking in big time. I hated history, and it sounded like they were reading a dictionary. It took me back to Catholic school when the nun made the class read out loud. It was so confusing, especially with all the different accents. Enough already with this mishegoss.

"Queen Mab's desire to bring you to the other side could have several different purposes," Vesna said as she sipped her cup of tea. "She could simply want to utilize your powers as a Witch with a great deal of ability. Strong even for the Never-Never, let alone in this realm. She might want to co-opt you simply to keep you from the other side. There are many possibilities."

"It has happened before in our history," Runa said. Great! Another history lesson. I wanted to run out into traffic just to make it stop. Runa played with some sugar cubes. She had lined them up in front of her plate. It was as though the cubes were runes, and she was casting a divination. "In the history of several of our traditions, this is a common tale. Perhaps the most famous was the case of Merlin, who is the one practitioner most often depicted in popular culture. Of course, as usual, they had it wrong."

I was confused. Again. "How did they have it wrong? I thought Merlin was the Wizard who helped King Arthur and guided him after he drew the Magic Sword from the stone, Excalibur." "Yes, that is the myth, dear," replied Grannie Meg. "The fact is that Excalibur was not the Sword in the stone. That was Caliburn, which was the one Arthur drew out of the stone to prove that he was the true King of England. It was later destroyed, and

Arthur was given Excalibur by the Lady of the Lake. She had been its steward and only presented it to Arthur as he was the chosen one. He returned it to her before he died, proving his worth. While all the time, Merlin lusted for it. He wanted to take the Sword for himself. It was only through the offices of Morgan le Fay that he was stopped. She imprisoned him in a tree for all eternity, so this Sword of power was kept out of his hands. Magical artifacts can be very dangerous in the hands of the fay. Especially if they want to use the power to dominate and control others."

Alejandro took up the tale, "The use and indeed the misuse of magical artifacts are part of the history of Magic since time immemorial. Gods and demons have often tried to obtain such power and used human agents to do so. The Golden Fleece was one such, as was the torque known as Draupnir, which gave its wielder unimaginable wealth." I started to lean over as though I was going to collapse. I can't take it anymore! No more history, please! I had a recurring mantra in my brain: no more history, no more history, no more history. But Alejandro continued his pedantic rant, "The Gods sent out humans to seek out these items because, for one reason or another, they could not do so directly. That was, in fact, why Arthur had to pull the Sword from the stone. Magical beings don't have the ability to do that, so they enlist human agents."

"What are you saying, Alejandro?" I asked. "Queen Mab wants me to find something for her? To bring it to her? Why would I do that? I don't owe her any loyalty. I am not her vassal here or in the Never-Never. I've never passed over to the other side and have no knowledge of it. Only what I have gleaned from people such as you or the few fay that I have come into contact with over the years. If she is so all-powerful, she must realize that I would not turn anything so deadly over to someone like her." I was truly bewildered at how we had come to this point in our discussion. Didn't they know me? At least Grannie Meg should have given them some indication as to my character.

Strangely, it was Tiwa who answered my questions in a lilting Caribbean accent, "Oh, Child, it might not be that at all, but that is our best guess. She will not order you to do it or try to compel you by threatening you or your husband, or even your grandmothers. No, she will try to persuade you. Trick you. She will make it seem to be the right thing to do. She will take advantage of your compassion. Your empathy. Your kindness. Which is both your greatest strength and your greatest weakness. You must not let her mistake your kindness for weakness. She will try to get you to her Court and get you on her side by showing some atrocity that the other side has committed. While hiding her culpability in equally as foul deeds committed by her minions. She will make up be down and black be white and will work to confuse and bedazzle you. You must be aware of her wiles and be sure that you stay strong."

Nickolai chimed in with his harsh Russian accent, "Or this could all be borscht. It might have nothing to do with her interest in you. She might just want you as a soldier in her army. I think that is most likely, though I don't see why. All of this is just guesses. I was against bringing you in, but the others voted for it, so here you are. It would be best if you stayed away from Mab and not deal with her in any way."

Grannie Meg disagreed. "That won't wash, Nikolai. You know that Queen Mab is trying to contact Speranza and get her to visit her Court. She will not stop until she gets what she wants. Right now, it is gentle persuasion. But it could turn to threats or violence. It might be wise to find out what she wants and then come back here to let us figure out a strategy. I don't think ignoring her will work. It has never worked before."

"Am I hearing you right, Grannie?" I was shocked. I felt the anxiety rise in my chest. "Do you *really* think that I should go to the Never-Never and put myself in the clutches of Queen Mab? I admit I am truly curious, but it seems very dangerous. Why would I subject myself to this, and why would you want it for me, Grannie?"

Grannie Meg shook her greying head sorrowfully and replied, "I don't want it for you, darling girl, but I don't think there is a way in God's Green Earth that you can avoid it. You have to face up to it. You're strong enough to do it! Everything that your other grannie and I have taught you will be enough to see you through." I remembered my life. Now it was obvious that it had led to this moment. Grannie Meg continued in a tone of regret and sorrow, “It is better to face up to the challenge instead of waiting to see what the Winter Queen will do. It will be much worse if you don’t.”

“You must know she will come for you!” Nikolai banged his hand on the table. He began to pontificate in his usual arrogant and dismissive manner. “I change mind. You must face her, or she will destroy you. Find a way! Talk to her without committing yourself. Queen Mab will be patient with you. She has been remarkably patient so far. She has not commanded you to attend her. That is very unlike her, so you must have something she wants. Use that to protect yourself and our realm.”

“For once in his life, our Russian friend has it right,” said Vesna in her heavy Croatian accent. She did speak softly, but it was as if Dracula’s sister was setting me straight. “You can dissemble when you meet her. Tell her just enough of the truth to seem plausible. Find out what she wants and pretend to agree. Of course, you should not enter into any magical pacts or accept the status of a vassal. I feel confident that she will allow you to return to think about her proposals and decide how best to implement them. If her desires revolve around matters in this realm, then you will be obligated to return. If you come back to us, we can help you formulate a response. One that protects you and all of us.”

“I fear that is the only response you can make, darling girl,” Grannie Meg murmured in her soft Irish brogue. “You will have to take that leap. I just pray that it will turn out the way we envision. I just don't see any alternative."

I have to say I was *really* flabbergasted. My own beloved Grandmother wanted me to travel to the Never-Never to confront a powerful and dangerous Queen. All of these other very experienced practitioners agreed. I felt abandoned. It was as though I'd been thrown to the wolves. I threw up my hands in a gesture of surrender. "Alright, already! I have to think about this. I will let you know what I decide." I took Grannie's arm and led her toward the door as I whispered in an undertone, "I want to leave now, Grannie. Let's go home. I feel like I am going to throw up!"

I need to speak to my husband. I won't tell him the details, but I could not hide such a momentous decision from him. He deserves to know what is going on.

Most of all, I had to speak to Nonna. She will help me decide the right thing to do.

Chapter Twenty-One – The Red Caps Are Coming!

We were silent on the ride back home after the meeting. You could hear a pin drop. There was so much to download. I had reached maximum capacity. I didn't want to freak out, so I put on my poker face because I knew Grannie Meg wouldn't be sympathetic. She was very much a "stop the nonsense and act like an adult" kind of person. Right now, I don't feel like adulting. I just need a hug. I usually went to Nonna for emotional support. I went to Grannie Meg for the unvarnished truth. Boy, did I get it in spades.

Grannie Meg dropped me off in front of my house, and I said, "Thank you, Grannie. You certainly gave me a lot to think about." "Aye, Speranza, there is, but don't you fret too much. I know you are going to consult your other Grannie. That stands to reason. If she needs any information or wants me to make anything clear to her, just ask, and I will be available. Have a grand night, and say hello to that handsome husband of yours." "Ok, Grannie, thank you."

That was major! Grannie Meg never wanted to interact with Nonna. You could count the number of times they had met in person on one hand! For her to offer to meet with Nonna just underlined how important this situation was and how much she wanted me to listen to her warning. She was willing to come to Nonna to convince her to let me do what the Council asked. Obviously, she must think that Nonna was going to try to convince me to do nothing. It was a major concession for her to be willing to plead her case to someone who had been her rival for many decades. A rival not just in Magic, but in their influence over me. I'm beginning to feel like the monkey in the middle.

I went into the house and immediately had a smile on my face. Here was my hug. Sean was in the kitchen with seventies disco music blasting in the background. I could hear him singing off-key as he bustled around in his apron, dancing to "Staying Alive." This is home. This is what truly matters. It was up to me to make sure that all of my loved ones stayed alive!

Sean was making zucchini fritters. He had finished shredding the zucchini and had already salted it and drained most of the water out. He had included some shredded mozzarella and a couple of eggs. He was in the process of adding the breadcrumbs to firm them up as patties to fry in olive oil. Sean never used cheap vegetable oil. It was olive oil all the way. This dish was one of my favorites. I loved zucchini. I loved them even more the next day. I didn't know what I was going to do about Queen Mab, but at least I know what I am having for lunch tomorrow.

Sean looked up from mixing the breadcrumbs, "Hey Babe! How ya' doing?" I put my bag down and went over and hugged him from behind. He was my rock. He grounded me. I felt safe when he was close to me. "I'm okay, just a lot going on. How was your day?" Sean laid his hands on mine that I had wrapped around him, and we rocked to the music in unison. "It was fine. Just paperwork, mostly. That's why I was able to come home early and make one of your favorite dishes. How does that sound, baby?" "That sounds great. When will it be ready?" "Just give me fifteen minutes and it'll be done, and a little salad to close the deal." Sean chuckled as he always did when he was about to make a wise-guy crack, "You know the zucchini is not enough to satisfy you." "Me? What about you? A whole pizza doesn't satisfy you! Maybe you need a little pizza with your salad, big boy!" I giggled and gave him a kiss on the back of his neck.

We sat down to eat, and I had to decide what exactly from today's madness I was going to tell him. I couldn't tell him everything because he would lose it. He was smart, so I had to selectively edit things so he would know what was going on without unduly worrying him.

"I went to a meeting in Bay Ridge with some of Grannie Meg's cronies. It was very informative." "That sounds interesting. Were they nice?" "I don't know if I would exactly call them nice. Some of them were pleasant enough, I guess, and some of them seemed more like an acquired taste." "Are you planning to join their group on the regular?" "I think I have to because they are going to be a rich source of information. They are all practitioners from various parts of Brooklyn, and it's better that I'm in contact with them than not." "Sounds right, I guess," Sean said as he speared another zucchini pancake. "Just don't do it if you don't enjoy it. Life is too short to do something you don't enjoy. How was Meg?" "Strange, actually. You know, I spend a lot less time with her compared to Nonna, so I am not as used to her quirky little ways. I'm learning, though, and that's always good."

We continued eating and chatting about everyday stuff for another hour. Then I helped Sean clean up and put the dishes in the dishwasher. He went off to bed since he had to be in Court in the Bronx very early in the morning. I decided I couldn't wait. My nerves are getting the best of me. I have to go talk to Nonna right now.

When I got to Nonna's house, I opened the door and walked down the hallway to the kitchen. As usual, Nonna was at the table working on a project. Instead of knitting, she was cataloging and translating her recipes. She had a square wooden box with index cards. I had a flashback to the days when I would visit Nonna with my mother. I'm holding Mommy's hand, and Nonna would look up and give us both the biggest smile. Nonna delighted in having us sit and work with her and her recipes. She would chat with my mother in Italian, and they argued about what to include and what to leave out. Those loud, boisterous voices and loving arguments were among my fondest memories. They were the soundtrack of my childhood.

The box contained handwritten recipes that Nonna was leaving to me. The only problem being they were all written in Italian, so she had to translate them. It was particularly important because the cards did not just contain recipes for her Italian food. They also had recipes for various healing potions, nostrums, and the occasional mild spells that related to household matters. She put down the card she was writing on and smiled at me.

"Speranza, Mia Bella! How are you? I didn't know you wanted to come by tonight. Sit and let me get you something." "No, Nonna, let me do it. I will brew up some tea. It's too late for coffee." I put the kettle on, which was very ironic since I usually had tea with my Grannie Meg and espresso with Nonna. I prepared two cups of fennel tea and sat across from Nonna, who had continued transcribing recipes.

"So, why are you here, Mia Bella?" "I want to talk about Grannie Meg and her friends. I imagine you know about the group that meets in Bay Ridge?" Nonna looked down at her hands, which were clasped around her teacup, and avoided eye contact. "Yes. I know of them."

She seemed very non-committal. As though she had something to hide. That was not like my Nonna. I got right to the point. "Why aren't you part of the group, Nonna? You're certainly a strong enough Witch. I would think that you would want the Italian community to be represented." Nonna shook her head gently as if in sorrow and regret. I don't know if she regrets not being in the group or if she regrets not talking to me about it. Is she hiding something? "Yes, I was invited several times to join. But I never did because I think they are wrong in what they do. They try to manipulate events based on their whims. I have always stood for independence."

Nonna sighed and looked up at the ceiling as if to search for divine guidance. "For decades, these people scorned the Italians until they wanted our power joined to theirs. They try to put on a sly face and fool me into joining their group. I will not be their monkey as they try to be the organ grinder. My own grandmother warned of them. She cautioned me about the Irish, like your Grannie Meg. I have come to tolerate her, but I will not join in with her and her other friends. Some of them are truly bad. Like that Cuban Warlock. And the Russian. Yes, the Russian is an exceptionally vile man. I would beg you to be wary of them, Speranza. They will betray you in the end. No good will come of working with them."

I … was … devastated. This reached me to my core. "I thought you and Grannie Meg had overcome your differences and were in a good place. Was I wrong about that?" Nonna smiled grimly and said, "We only came to an agreement because of your mother getting married. It was a long and tedious negotiation, and one of the main points I insisted on was that I was not going to assist in the attempt to dominate the craft by her little group. I've kept to it 'til this day, and I don't see the need to change."

"Circumstances might force you to change, Nonna. You know that there is a great upset in the Never-Never? Queen Mab has reached out to contact me. Do you have any idea why that happened?" I was hoping against hope that Nonna could clear this up. "No, I have no idea. It can't be good. I would advise staying away from her," she said in an almost dismissive tone. "Nothing good can come of it. You have managed to live this long without traveling to the other side, and now is not the time to start." I don't get it! Nonna had always been my rock, but now she is blowing me off as if all of this is just a "fairy tale." I tried to get her to take this seriously. "I don't know if I have that option anymore to just blow this off as though it is not important. This Queen is very insistent. How am I going to hold her off if she demands my presence? The others seem to think I should at least hear her out. They gave me some ideas about why she wanted to see me. What do you think? Do you have any guesses?"

Nonna shook her head. "She might want a soldier. Cannon fodder. That is why you should not get involved with the Winter Queen. She will destroy you." I sat and thought about what Nonna had to say. She wasn't being very helpful. Just fearful. Which was unusual for her. She was always very reticent about using her powers and getting me involved.

Suddenly, there was a tremendous noise coming from the cellar. I stood up and said to Nonna, "Did you hear that? It sounds like it's from the cellar. Could it be Mello?" "Go and look," Nonna said, "But stay at the top of the stairs." I went to the cellar door. Opened it and went down two steps. Mello was lying in a disheveled mess on the floor. His red tunic was ripped, and his staff seemed to be broken. Wait a minute. It looked like he was bleeding.

"Nonna!" I screamed, "Come quick! Mello is bleeding!" I ran down the steps, and Nonna slowly followed me in a more deliberate manner as she had to use her cane for support. She gripped the cellar railing so hard that it squeaked as it held her up as she hurried as best as she could. We went over to Mello. He was huddled on the floor in a fetal position. He had been severely beaten. I got down on the floor and cradled his head. Nonna handed me the thick white linen handkerchief that she always carried in her pocket. I applied pressure to the wound.

A shimmering haze materialized on the wall of the cellar. It must be the opening of a portal. A figure hurtled through, hit the floor, and bounced twice before skidding to a halt. It was Mello's acolyte, Luca. He had been eviscerated! His body was a mass of cuts and blood and gore. He had been murdered! The portal pulsed again.

Another being had crossed over. Not one that I had ever seen before.

A short and brutal-looking faerie stood over the bloody corpse of Mello's student. He had a hunched and gnarled frame with long, bony fingers that ended in razor-sharp claws. The fearsome figure looked about in an aggressive manner as if he couldn't wait to kill. His long tunic was stained with blood, and his odd little twisted body was topped by a redcap. Wait! That's who he was! A "Red Cap!" One of the most dangerous and evil faeries to be found anywhere in the realm of the fay. He turned his evil gaze to us and snarled.

"I found your familiars, Witch, and I've returned them to you," he spat in a guttural voice that caused you to feel it in your chest. "Let me finish with the fat one, and I will have completed my task." He took a step toward us, and I hovered protectively over Mello. Nonna stepped in front of us and said, "Halt, Varrik! I know you from old! The Queen's executioner holds no sway here! You will not hurt anyone in my home! Be gone!"

The evil imp laughed in her face, "You don't command me, Witch! The Queen has called for their blood. Stand aside, or I will do the same to you!" Nonna pointed her cane at him and chanted, "I have given you authority to trample on snakes and scorpions and to overcome all the power of the enemy; nothing will harm you." Nonna had cast a quick spell to counter the evil intent of the bloody-handed Red Cap.

As Nonna said the words of that simple bible verse from the Book of Luke, the Red Cap began to shake and struggle. He was gradually but inexorably pulled back into the vortex as if a tractor beam had been engaged. He cursed and raged, but he was still sucked into the void as quickly and efficiently as I have ever seen before.

"What just happened, Nonna?" I asked as I tried to staunch Mello's bleeding. I think I had it under control, even though everything else seemed chaotic. "Not now, Speranza. I will tell you later. Let's get Mello upstairs and tend to him. Pick him up and carry him, Mia Bella." I looked at Luca's tiny, mangled corpse. "What about Luca?" I asked. "We can't just leave him here like this?" Nonna was insistent, "We cannot do anything for him. He is gone. Just go upstairs."

Nonna took a small blue tarp from off the wall and laid it reverently over the murdered faerie. "Just go," Nonna commanded in an imperious voice as she waved her hand at me as if I were an annoying fly. Nonna turned back to Luca's body and made a hand gesture as she mumbled a spell under her breath. There was some movement under the tarp as though Luca's body was changing and returning to its original form. She must have cast a spell to reconstitute his corpse. I wonder why she did that. Is she trying to hide something? This doesn't make any sense.

I picked up Mello. He was as light as a feather. I hurried up the stairs.

I hope we can save him.

Chapter Twenty-Two – Do You Believe in Santa?

We rushed upstairs and took Mello into the living room to lay him on the sofa. Or at least I rushed upstairs as Nonna had to walk as fast as she could with her cane. I grabbed a clean towel and wet it, and tried to wipe away some of the blood to see where he was hurt. It seemed that he had several deep lacerations and bruises, but none of them were all that life-threatening. I took the first aid kit from under the sink and started treating some of the cuts with alcohol. Nonna came up and pushed me aside.

Nonna looked at Mello's wounds and raised her hands over his prostrate body. She took a deep breath and started an incantation in Italian, "*Con luce d'armonia, guarisci ferite e dolore, Nel fuoco di vita, torna sano il cuore.*"

It was a healing spell that Nonna had often used on people who were ill. Especially in our family. Roughly translated, it means: "With the light of harmony, heal wounds and pain; in the fire of life, bring back a healthy heart." It took me back to my childhood when I would go to Nonna to heal all my hurts. I couldn’t go to my mother because nurturing wasn’t her thing. She didn't have healing powers; she just slapped on a Band-Aid and told me to get over myself. Mercurochrome was her go-to, not hugs. Mom was more intellectual than spiritual. Nonna was the heart and soul of our family. Some Italian grandmas gave you pastina, but my Nonna weaved a spell. I hadn’t thought about it in years! It was so funny; it just popped into my head like a favorite movie clip. Even with all of this chaos, this memory gave me a warm feeling as I remembered how much I miss my mom. I never got closure, and sometimes disasters like this remind me of what I am missing. I’ll put it aside, but as always, it pops up at the most inconvenient time.

It was a simple but powerful spell, as the healing was generated from Nonna’s power and not just from the words of the spell. Magic often worked that way. The more powerful the practitioner, the more powerful the spell. I hope that someday I might be as powerful as my Nonna.

Mello sighed as his wounds began to magically heal. The blood disappeared, and the wounds were shut without a line or scar to indicate that they had ever existed. He murmured under his breath to himself as he was still unconscious. Nonna gently stroked his brow and called to him in a soothing, gentle voice, "Mello, Mello, come back to us." Mello's eyes opened, and he looked around frantically. "Where am I? What happened?" I leaned over him and said, "You came through the portal in the basement. You were wounded. It seems that you were in a fight. What happened?" Mello closed his eyes and sighed deeply as a single tear coursed down his cheek. He opened his eyes and pleaded with Nonna, "Luca?" She shook her head in sadness and said, "He's gone, Mello. I am so sorry." "Can you not use your powers, Señora? There must be something someone of your strength can do?" Mello raised his arms in supplication as though he could will the response he wanted. Frankly, it was owed to him by his faithful service to my grandmother. "No, my old friend, he is beyond my help. They made sure of that before they tossed him back to us like so much offal. He is well and truly gone. Hopefully to a better place because he was a good and faithful servant to you and deserves to have his rest."

"What happened, Mello?" I asked in an anguished tone. This brutal murder had chilled me to the core. I need to know why he was attacked! Was it because of a conflict in the Never-Never? Was it because I was avoiding the Queen of Winter? Or was it simply some personal grudge? The fay often indulged in personal fights that could get extremely violent. Just not to the extent that would see acolytes flayed and eviscerated.

Mello had his eyes closed as though he still felt his wounds, despite the fact that they had all been magically healed by Nonna's spell. Mello's voice was weak as he murmured, "We were walking along a pathway toward my village when we were viciously attacked. By a vile Red Cap named Varrik. I have had dealings with him before." Mello took a deep breath and continued, "It's not the first time we have met in anger. It was the first time he was bold enough to attack me. He ran at us with a snarl and a curse, without a care in the world. It seems he was of the opinion that there would be no consequences for attacking us." Mello's breathing began to increase to the point that he was almost hyperventilating. "He threw me to the floor, and before he could savage me, Luca jumped on his back and tried to choke him."

Mello stopped speaking for a moment. I took a cup of water and tried to make him drink. He was so upset that I was afraid he would hurt himself in the retelling of the tale. Nonna gently placed a cool cloth across his brow and motioned with her eyes to encourage him. Mello steeled himself to continue, "The vile beast threw him down and ripped and tore poor Luca to shreds. I can still hear his screams." Mello reached out and grasped Nonna's hand. He swallowed hard and began to softly weep. He said, "When he had finished murdering my friend, he took his filthy red cap and mopped up the blood and gore as though he were Mab's maid." Mello looked at Nonna beseechingly and said, "The Queen must have given him license since he has long been her toady and tool. When he turned his back to me, I quickly opened a portal to come here. Only to have him toss poor Luca's body in after me. As you know, he jumped in to finish his attack."

I looked at him skeptically. "Why would Queen Mab send her minion to attack you, Mello? He sounds like an evil beast! Maybe he just attacked you out of pure viciousness. How do we know that Queen Mab sanctioned the hit?" I said as I helped him sit up and lean back against the sofa cushion. Mello looked at Nonna when he answered, "We know why he did it. He is entirely a creature of his Queen and would not have done this without her permission." Nonna nodded in agreement, "He is right, Mia Bella. She had him do this thing as a message. To you and to me. We need to address it, or she will continue to attack those we hold dear. Notice that for all of his viciousness, he did not kill Mello." That was something to think about. I asked, "But what about Luca? He did kill him!" Nonna scoffed, "He is nothing to them. A lesser being who is of no account. She wouldn't think twice about destroying him. We must talk seriously about what we will do."

I thought to myself that the only answer was for me to confront the Queen. Everything seemed to point to that outcome. I have been getting mixed messages from everyone. Nonna says do nothing! Grannie Meg and the Council say go to the Never-Never and find out what she proposes! I know that Sean would tell me to stop doing Magic altogether and let them fight amongst themselves. The Queen seems to have her own agenda. She's trying to force a meeting and has gradually escalated her efforts. From simply having the Silvani ask me to, to now attacking and killing our friends. Who knows how far she would go to force me to dance attendance on her court?

"Nonna, I think it is clear that I will have to go and speak with Queen Mab myself. I can't allow this to continue and put everyone at risk. Grannie Meg and her friends seem to think it is the right thing to do. I can at least hear the Queen out and not commit to anything." Nonna seemed to get very upset after I said this. "No, Speranza, no. You cannot be serious. She will force you into her grasp. You are not strong enough nor experienced enough to avoid it. Don't be so arrogant as to think that your powers will allow you to resist the Queen of Winter. I did that once, and I cannot let you repeat my mistake."

"What do you mean, Nonna? How did you come into her power?" Nonna stood up, "Mello, you must rest now. Let us take care of him, and then we will talk." She put a pillow beneath his head and covered him with the knitted afghan she had draped over the back of the sofa. She gently patted him on the head and then took my hand and led me into the kitchen. We sat at the table and looked at each other.

It was the moment of truth.

"You must understand, Speranza. I have a long and difficult history with Queen Mab. As I have told you, I spent many hours in the Never-Never in my youth. I learned a great deal, and Queen Mab was one of my tutors. Perhaps the most important one. That knowledge came at a price. I became her vassal. You see, the Queen does nothing that does not benefit her. In the folly of my youth, I thought she was good and kind, if somewhat imperious. But she is not. She will teach you many things, but eventually, the bill will become due."

"What does that mean, Nonna? What did you have to do?" Nonna looked very troubled. "I was forced to fight for her. In the last war in the Never-Never. But not only in the Never-Never if you can understand. I was forced to fight the vassals of her opponent here in the earthly realm. The predecessors of this so-called Council that your other Grandmother took you to meet. Some were creatures of Maeve, the Queen of Summer. Or at least most of them were at that time. The battle was long and hard. Some died. I am not proud of what I did. Ever since then, I have stayed away from conflict. Never visited the other realm despite many messages from the Queen. My Queen, I am still her vassal, after all. She can command me if I come into her realm. You cannot expose yourself to her. She is very seductive. She will grant you many powers. You will learn a great deal. Become very powerful. Almost unrecognizable. It is what you will have to become to gain that power that will ultimately destroy you. Or at least the person you are now and the person you want to be. Please, I beg of you, do not think of going there."

Nonna seemed genuinely frightened for me. I did not see an alternative to at least meeting with the Queen. I respected Nonna's opinion, but all I've heard were vague explanations. I had to get more concrete facts if I was going to make an informed decision. "Nonna, I love you, and I believe everything you're telling me. But please … tell me what happened. Exactly. In detail. I need to know what I am facing if I do come into contact with the other side. What did you do that is so terrible?"

Nonna took my hand and looked at me with great affection and love. She softly said, "I killed people, Speranza. Murdered them, in fact. Other practitioners decided to fight on the opposite side of the conflict. The fight between Winter and Summer has endured for a millennium. Neither side will yield to the other. They will snipe at each other until the smoldering embers of enmity are fanned into a full-scale war. Which seems to have happened." I looked at her in disbelief. "I find it hard to believe that you murdered someone, Nonna. I can't believe that you would do such a thing. Maybe someone might be killed in a fight, but to out-and-out murder? That's not you. That's not *my* Nonna." I loved her with all my heart, yet a tiny bit of doubt had started to leak into my soul.

Nonna was very troubled and upset. I guess confessing to her granddaughter was not something that she ever wanted to do in this life. "That might be so, Speranza, but it is true nonetheless. The Queen looks for any advantage that she can glean from any source of power. She wants it all. That includes the powers to be found in this realm as well. Many gods and demons have come to our Earthly realm over the ages. Their power and influence can surge or wane. This power is based on the number and fervor of their followers. A god might have been worshiped by multitudes and might now be forgotten. Diminished and forlorn but still retaining a mere glimmer of their power. A flickering flame adrift in the Universe."

I thought for a moment and said, "Do they come to Earth to try to gain new followers to get their power back?" Nonna shook her head. "Some do try, yes, but often fail unless they have some help. Often, they are helped by tools or artifacts created by their believers. A sword or a staff. Maybe even a magic cloak. When their worship declines and their followers disband, the power lies dormant. It is still available to those who can find a way to utilize it." My eyes had glazed over again, but this time, I pinched myself to stay awake. I do think that I've got the gist of it. Power was contingent on having believers. I asked, "So, you have to believe? You mean like believing in Santa?" We both giggled to break the tension. She said, "You see, Speranza, Magic can be the key to unleashing whatever power remains in those tools. That might be what the Queen seeks. That might be why she wants you. To be her instrument to obtain these tools. Or even to be the tool yourself. I was her instrument once. To my everlasting shame."

"All of this is about things?" I asked in an unusually querulous tone. That is not like me at all. I almost sounded like Birdie for a minute there. Mental note! I have to keep my *tête-à-têtes* with her to a minimum from now on.

"So, you're saying that there are things that the Queen wants that are only to be found in this earthly realm? Weapons that she can use in her war with Queen Maeve?" Nonna looked off into the distance as if she could find an answer there. "Yes, it was one such weapon that I took from the dead hand of Carlos. The grandfather of the current Warlock, Alejandro. He had an artifact in his possession, and the Queen desired it over anything else in this world. I took it from him. He died to protect it. I did not realize what Queen Mab would do with it. She used it to humiliate and humble her sister. Queen Mab used it to win her battle and then proceeded to kill thousands of the Summer Court. It was pure meanness. Evil. So many, so many." Nonna started to rock forward and back as though she was keening for the dead. She was starting to scare me.

Nonna whispered as she shivered, "I could not stand it, Speranza. I left the Queen's realm, never to return. The knowledge and power she offers is not worth the price. Now it appears that she wants you to be the one who gets something for her. Don't listen to the counsel of fools who want to entice you to heed her call. They may have an ulterior motive. Especially that Cuban Warlock. He did not forget his grandfather's fate. I know he will want revenge. You know that Spanish saying? Revenge is a dish best served cold. He does not have your best interests at heart. Do not trust any of them. Stay away from Queen Mab. I beg you."

"I don't think I can, Nonna. I just can't walk away and pretend that I am not involved. I have to find a solution. We can't let this go on and let the Queen escalate. Who will be next? Oona? Sean? I refuse to let anyone else die because I was too afraid to face my destiny." I stood up and started packing up my stuff. "Are you going to be ok with Mello? Do you need me to stay with you?" Nonna stood up in turn and hugged me. "No, we are fine, Mia Bella. Go with my blessing. Just think about what I have told you. Please do not do anything in haste. I beg you."

I walked to the door and turned to her. "I hear you, Nonna, and I will give a lot of thought to what you have said. I will let you know what I decide." I walked out the door and turned toward home.

I had to make some tough choices. I want to talk it over with Sean. The only problem is … he doesn't believe in Santa.

Chapter Twenty-Three – Off to See the Queen!

When I got back home, my head was spinning! I needed to speak with Sean right away. So many things have happened in the past couple of days. I feel overwhelmed! I caught myself and sadly realized that I couldn't discuss anything. The Council! Luca! Nonna! Geez Louise, Nonna. All the murders! Oh, and there's the little matter of me going to the Never-Never to see The Queen! Without a Scarecrow or a Tin Man to help me! How could I possibly tell Sean any of this?

What would he say? This was the one subject that separated us to the core. My anxiety was off the charts because I knew Sean would become irate and forbid me from going. You can see my dilemma. Sean would try his best to convince me and even beg me! Which would break my heart. Despite the potential cost. "Save the World, Lose the Shopkeeper!" Sean would never go for that. The effect of Magical disruptions to the earthly realm would not weigh in with his practical view of the world! I hate it when I know he is right. Remember, it is better to ask for forgiveness instead of permission.

I had to find a way out of this predicament, and the only way I could see forward was to confront the Queen in her element. In the Never-Never. Despite the risk, it seemed the only path forward. I am sure that I can go and stay noncommittal. Even if she makes demands, I could defer my final decision until I return to the mortal realm. Since the Queen wanted my willing support, she would not harm me, as long as there was a possibility that I would ally with her. I will sleep on it and decide what to do in the morning. I went to bed without discussing it with Sean and hoped that I would wake up with a clear head to decide the best course of action.

The next day dawned before I was ready. I felt exhausted. I was riddled with anxiety dreams all night long. Dreams of Sean finding out what I was up to and who was involved. I followed the smell of coffee to the kitchen like a bloodhound. Sean was waiting with a cup for me, just the way I liked it. "Hey Babe, have some espresso, or maybe I should make it a double? You tossed and turned all night. What's going on with you? If I didn't know better, I would think that you have a guilty conscience." That's the problem. He does know me, and I will be hard-pressed to hold anything from him. I would have to dissemble. "I haven't done anything wrong. Yet. I may have to strangle Birdie. The grandmothers were no help. I wasted my time, even though it was great to see them." Sean was amused and said, "That would be justifiable homicide. Any shyster would beat that wrap. I am glad you got to hang out with The Grannies."

I felt so guilty that I just gulped down more of my coffee. Sean snickered, "Take it easy, champ. Take Human bites or sips!" Sean was a card. I made a face and said, "Great call back, old man. That was from a commercial from forty years ago!" I bumped him with my shoulder and almost spilled the rest of my coffee. I covered up by saying, "How about a joke from this decade, buddy?" Sean took the coffee pot and refilled my cup as he kissed me. He wasn't fooled. It is very hard for me to fool him. "If you want dinner tonight, you better laugh at all my jokes in this House of Comedy or at least tell me what is bothering you." Sean left his cup in the sink. He gave me a final kiss goodbye and headed off to work.

I can't believe that I got away without lying to his face when Sean knew something was up. I really couldn't ask him to weigh in because I already knew what he was going to say. I had to find someone with a new perspective or a different angle on all of this. Not Sean, not Nonna, not Grannie Meg. Then I had to make up my mind quickly, or it would be too late.

I went and opened the store. I did what I always do when I have to make a big decision. I sat with a big sheet of thick paper and my colorful markers. I listed the pros and cons of the situation and the possible outcomes. I had only put down one thing in each column when Oona popped out of her little faerie house and hopped up onto my counter.

"Oona, I am so glad to see you! How are you? How are the Sidhe? Are you involved in the troubles that seem to have been starting in the Magical realm?" I was so happy to see that she was unharmed. If they were harming our allies in the Never-Never, then Oona would be a prime target.

Oona sat on an ornate box on the counter that held tarot cards. Her gossamer wings fluttered as she settled down and looked up at me with her luminous blue eyes. Eyes that looked troubled. Almost haunted. Or was I reading something into them that was not there?

"I came to warn you, Speranza. The war between the houses appears to be breaking out into actual violence. This conflict has been going on for as long as there has been a Never-Never, but now it appears to be bursting into flame. You need to take steps to protect yourself and the earthly realm." Finally. Someone is going to tell me the truth. I replied, "It seems that I am already involved. As is my Nonna. Her friend Mello was attacked and thrown back to us as a warning. His student was brutally murdered. I am afraid for you! If they are attacking our Magical friends, you are one of the people most likely to be attacked." Oona's eyes fluttered faster than her faerie wings. I wonder if she is about to lie to me. After all, it was her brother Aiden who had scooped up the wounded Aoife from Grannie Meg's house the other night, and she hadn't mentioned it. Is she ignoring that completely? Does she want to cover up the Sidhe's involvement in this war? Is it her loyalty to the Queen? Or her fear of the Queen? I have to be careful what I say.

Oona said, "No, that is not very likely. I am a good and faithful servant of Queen Mab, who, after all, is the Queen of the Sidhe, my tribe and clan. She would never stand for anyone hurting me. Who attacked your Nonna's friend? Do you have any idea of who is responsible?" I still think she is hiding something. Maybe I'm not going to get the truth after all. The Sidhe can never be straight with you. They always come at you from an angle. Let's play the angle.

I thought about how to describe what had happened in the most accurate and detailed manner. "He was a Red Cap. You know, those vile beasts who are used as attack dogs by powerful beings who want to cloak their involvement. Murder, Inc. for the Fairy World. Violence is second nature to them. I have to assume that it was Queen Mab since he is known to be one of her people. He claimed the Queen demanded he do it. But to be fair, he didn't name which Queen."

Oona shivered, and her little wings quivered as though a cold wind had blown through the store. "You might be right, Speranza, but I have no certain knowledge of what happened. Who can fathom the actions of the exalted ones? We can just keep to our place and hope we escape their notice. Which is what I advise you to do. Stay away, and you will stay safe. Don't worry about me and your other friends. You cannot protect us if the Queen decides to take against us as she did with your grandmother's friend. There is nothing you can do. I came here today to warn you to stay away. You have no concept of what might happen if you venture into the other realm."

The doorknob to the store rattled as someone was trying to obtain entry. I had locked the door when I came in because it was before store hours. Oona squeaked and ran and jumped into the door of her faerie house and slammed it shut. I got up and walked to the front of the store to see who it was. Oh. It was Ginny. She was standing outside with two large coffees and a grin on her face. Usually, I went to her shop to chat, but today she had come to me. I wonder why?

"Hey, you," she said as she came in after I opened the door. "Nunzio is covering for me at the store. He owes me because he has been slacking off lately, so I am going to make him work. Keep him focused, if you know what I mean." Nunzio is her brother who has a "part" interest in the family coffee shop and is a perpetual problem. He's typical of the neighborhood knock-around guy who dabbled in casual criminal activity in some Brooklyn neighborhoods in the eighties. He is a wannabe, half-a-gangster. He wouldn't do violence, but he would boost a load of steaks that he would sell from his trunk or maybe pick up a car that he would bring to a chop shop for some walking-around money. Nunzie had more or less been on the straight and narrow for the last decade, ever since their brother Charley had been killed. Charley was the one who was mobbed up, as he was a known associate of the Columbos. Their family had long been associated with the boys, and it was only in Ginny's parents' time that they more or less tried to go legit. It just didn't take.

Ginny has been trying to keep Nunzio away from "The Life." Which was tough because some of the boys were always hanging around the café and might seduce Nunzio back to his old ways. She had to keep him occupied. Still, she wasn't his mother, so she had to give him a little rope. Letting him run the café in the morning was a good first step.

"I was going to come by in a few minutes, Ginny," I said as we went to sit by the counter and sip our coffees. "You beat me to it." "No worries, Anna. Well, maybe some worries because the last time I saw you, it seemed that you were worried about something. That's not like you. You are everybody's therapist. Their go-to for help. You're never worried. You are where we go to stop worrying. What's up, buttercup?" I sighed and said, "I just have a lot on my mind. Plus, I am tired of being everybody's unpaid therapist. When did I get that job?" Ginny scoffed at that complaint. "You've had that job ever since we were in the first grade, kiddo. You always took on everyone's problems. I bet it's a bitch when you have a problem and need reassurance. Can't you talk to

Nonna about it? She is usually your go-to with things that bother you."

Ginny could cut to the quick like nobody else because she had been my best friend since the first grade. Even when we were kids, she would always call me out when I was acting foolishly and give me that wake-up call that all of us need from time to time.

"I can't talk to Nonna about the problem this time, Ginny. Mainly because this time, she's the problem. She has been hiding things from me. Important things. Things I need to know. Believe it or not, Grannie Meg has been more helpful." Ginny was incredulous. She almost spit up some of her coffee before saying, "What? That's crazy. I know you were never close to Grannie Meg. I thought you were a guinea through and through. None of that Danny Boy bullshit for you. You keep that omerta, baby. Only talk about it with the family. Your Italian family. Like you did your whole life. Come on, spill, sister. It's magic stuff, right? Sometimes, I even believe it's real, you know." I huffed at that and said, "It's real, Ginny. I have told you again and again. What do I have to do to prove it to you? Turn someone into a frog?"

Ginny giggled, "I've had enough frogs in my life. Every guy I dated for the past twenty years was a frog. And you know what? No matter how hard I kissed them, they never turned into a prince. Forget the freaking frogs, babe. Tell me what is bothering you. Maybe I can help." Although Ginny was my oldest friend, there was nothing she could do to help me make this choice. But there was one thing she could do.

"You know, there is one thing you can do for me, Ginny. Have you been talking to that Alice girl? You know the hipster who moved into Sackett Street." "Yeah, yeah, she's been coming into the café on the regular. I think she likes to think she is in with the 'in-crowd' now because some of the old-timers treat her nicely. This is only happening because I told them to do it. You do remember that you told me to cultivate her. Why?" I had to give her a good reason to do what I needed her to do. "I want you to call her up and get her to hang out with you today. Do you think you can do that?" Ginny shrugged and said, "Sure, no problem. Are you going to tell me why?" This manipulating people is getting to be too much for me. "Not really. Just know that it's really important. Text me when she is by you, and then I can go do what I've got to do. Capisce?"

We finished our coffee as we chatted about inconsequential family matters. She left to go to the store and call Alice. I waited around for about an hour until I got a text from Ginny to tell me that Alice was in the café.

The coast was clear.

I closed down the store and put a sign in the window. I didn't like to do that too often, but needs must. It seems to have become a habit these days.

I walked down Sackett Street to the front of Alice's condo and looked around to see if any of the usual chiacchierones were out there watching me. But no one seemed to be paying attention.

Normally, you have to get permission to cross over someone's threshold, but that wasn't the case here. Since I had put heavy wards over the door, this was my threshold. A simple spell and a wave of my hand, the locks magically opened, and I was inside.

I went up to the spot I had previously opened, and did an incantation to reverse my spell to open the doorway. I sidled down the corridor to where the door was protecting the portal to the Never-Never. I examined the wards and markings and saw that no one had tampered with them from either side. Once again, I raised my arms and placed my palms on the wards. A few words of the reversal spell, and the wards fell away. I put my hand on the doorknob and opened the door. The room that had formerly been there was gone!

In its place was a garden. Or, more correctly, a meadow. I stepped onto the grass and looked around. The sun was bright, and beautiful flowers were undulating in the gentle breeze. It seemed so peaceful. Then, the wind seemed to pick up and blow more fiercely. I heard some sounds. Sounds that seemed like a song floating on the breeze. In a swirl of wind, some bright and cheery figures could be seen dancing, playing, and singing as though they were at a party. They were the Filletto who were speeding about, making designs in the dust and dirt as they played what looked like a game of tag. One of them broke away from the group and flew in front of me with her gossamer wings beating a mile a minute. In a sweet, melodic voice, the air faerie sang, "Walk toward the wood, Witch … What you seek is waiting for you there." With a whoosh, they all flew in formation toward a wooded area that was about a hundred yards away. I looked around to try to remember where I was. Sean would be proud. He was a Boy Scout and tried to teach me woodcraft, so I want to leave a trail to follow. I don't have breadcrumbs like Hansel or Gretel, so I will just have to remember my way back. I started walking toward the woods.

When I was ten yards away, a hooded figure stepped out. Clad all in vibrant red furs, it was the Silvani that I had met before at Alice's house. She looked at me without expression and then shook her head in mock disdain. She spoke to me in a harsh voice, "It appears that you have come to your senses, child. Come, the Queen wishes to speak to you. We must not tarry. She has waited long enough for your foolish earthly whims. Follow me."

She turned and walked deeper into the woods. A path seemed to magically appear through the dense vegetation. I hurried to catch up to her. I was off to see the Wizard.

Or at least the faerie Queen of Darkness. Lucky me.

Chapter Twenty-Four – The Grass is Always Greener in the Green Room

I followed the Silvani Witch as we walked silently at a steady pace. A path magically appeared as we went deeper into the forest. The trees, shrubs, and vegetation simply disappeared as a pink gravel roadway sprang up. It was made of pink pieces of gravel that looked like candy. The kind of nougat candy your Nonna would give you. The candy with layers of sugar, pistachios, roasted almonds, and cherries. The treat I would get instead of cotton candy at the Feast of St. Rosalie when I was a kid. This candy was square blocks of deliciousness wrapped individually in cellophane. Nonna wanted to give me the good stuff, not the junk sold by the carneys at the feast. This pathway reminded me of my Nonna. Is that why it looked this way? Do my memories serve to influence my perception? Am I creating this reality from my mind? The path stretched forward invitingly.

Despite its shiny appearance, it was surprisingly not slippery or sticky. Can I walk on this? I wasn't walking on sunshine; I was walking on candy. It did seem very secure and inviting. The pathway molded itself around my feet. It offered the feeling of a comfy pair of slippers that wrapped around each foot. With each step I took, I felt a sense of safety and security wash over me. It was as if the path itself was guiding and protecting me on my journey. I continued to follow the silent Silvani, who plodded forward with grim determination. I let the gentle guidance of my candy road lead me toward whatever adventures awaited me in the Never-Never.

The forest seems alive with the symphony of nature at its most beautiful. Melodious birdsongs fill the air, and the gentle rustle of leaves whispers the secrets of the fay. Fragrant blossoms had fallen all around us, their sweet perfume mingling with the earthy scent of moss and damp soil. Shafts of golden light filter through the dense foliage, casting enchanting patterns of sigils and star signs on the forest floor. I could fleetingly glimpse figures passing through the outer reaches of my perception. Some of them seemed very familiar. Anyone I know? Fairies, like Oona or Aiden? Look! A tall woman with brown hair who, from the back, could pass as my mother, flitted at the edge of my peripheral vision. She would not let me see her. Am I imagining this? I see strange creatures, eyes brimming with otherworldly intelligence. They stare back at me with an unhealthy curiosity. Perhaps even malice. I could not tell for sure, so I had to keep moving and hope for the best.

After treading along the path for what seemed like twenty minutes, but could have been hours, we approached a structure that appeared part castle and part Vegas Casino. It's funny; the Never-Never did seem like Vegas to me. I never knew how much time had passed, and the air seemed like drug-induced euphoria and confusion in equal measure. I was distracted by it all. I need to concentrate on my goal to meet the Queen of Winter and find out what she wants.

Two ogres were standing in front of the door like bouncers at a strip club in Vegas. Amazingly ugly, they seemed seven feet tall and were unbelievably muscular and forbidding. Wait a minute! What are they wearing? Members Only Jackets? Tight polyester trousers and platform shoes? Am I having an eighties flashback? Or is it as I thought, my memories are shaping my experience?

The two ogres were holding huge axes, which they crossed in front of the door to deny us entry. One of them croaked a challenge from his huge misshapen lips, "Who goes there?" The Silvani Witch battered the axes away and hissed in a venomous tone, "Enough, fool! I am on the Queen's business, and you dare not delay us if you value your worthless skin." One of them stood in front of the door, and the other leaned his axe against the wall. He magically produced a clipboard and growled, "Name?" He started to go down the page using his massive, hairy finger to point to each line. It felt like we were trying to get into the Limelight on opening night. The Silvani Witch was not happy with this delay. "You know my name, fool! With the Witch, the Brooklyn Witch, the Queen has summoned!" I spoke up meekly to the ogre, "That's Speranza O'Rourke. O, apostrophe R—" The Silvani Witch interrupted in a furious tone and said, "Just put her down as my plus one. Now, let us pass." The ogre made a notation on his clipboard, and they opened the doors for us to pass through.

We entered a passageway that was tiled with black and white checkered squares. The walls were covered with decorations that seemed both garish and Magical. I tried to study them as the Silvani hurried me along, so I couldn't see what all of them were. Was that a vintage poster of "The Breakfast Club?" Is that Ally Sheedy shaking the dandruff from her head onto her desk? Instead of ancient tapestries, there are movie posters from the eighties. They are "totally in my head, *totally*."

At the end of the corridor, there was an old-fashioned phone booth with a folding door. It looked familiar. The Silvani pushed me in and closed the door. The pay phone on the wall rang. The Silvani said, "Answer it, Witch!" I picked up the receiver and put it to my ear. A nasal voice whispered, "Welcome, Speranza. Welcome to the Never-Never." "The Never-Never? This seems more like 'Back to the Future,' if it were set in the eighties." I could hear a laugh as the disembodied voice said, "The Never-Never is what you make of it; you made it into a John Hughes movie."

All of a sudden, the phone booth started to move. Down. Fast. As though it were an elevator plummeting to the basement. It slowed and eventually stopped. I tentatively pushed the door open and encountered a gnome. He was dressed in jeans and a plaid button-down shirt. Strangely enough, he was wearing a headset and carrying a clipboard with a page titled "Call Sheet." "Name?" he asked brusquely as he checked his sheet. "Speranza O'Rourke," I said timidly. "Ah, The Brooklyn Witch! Ok. Got it. Follow me." He grabbed my arm and pulled me in front of a door marked "The Midnight Show." In a slot on the door was a piece of paper marked, "The Brooklyn Witch. Speranza O'Rourke." He opened it and pushed me inside. "Wait a minute! What's going on?" I pleaded as I stumbled into the room. "This is the Green Room, dearie. You wait here until I call you to come on the show. Everything you might desire is here. Help yourself," the gnome muttered as he pulled the door closed. I put my foot in the door to block it and said, "Wait, who are you?" "Norm," he said as he forced the door closed. Norm the Gnome? What the hex-a-roni is going on here?" This is getting weird.

I stared at the door for a moment in bewilderment. What time is it anyway? Again, with the Vegas no-clock thing. I turned to look at the rest of the room and almost fell over. Norm the Gnome was right! There was an infinite closet placed before my eyes. Everything I ever wanted was in this room. Or at least every material thing. I sat down on the super comfy tufted ottoman to take it all in. I felt tired and anxious. Almost overwhelmed. I need to relax. If only I had some champagne. Immediately, a bucket materialized with a bottle of Dom Perignon on an exquisite table with a flute already poured for me. Holy Macaroni! If I just wish for it, will it come true? I took a few sips and refilled the glass. It calmed me down. Let's think about this for a moment.

But first, a couple more glasses of champagne.

It's like the "desert island" question. If you were stranded on a desert island and could only bring one record, what would you bring? What should I wish for? Maybe I should upgrade my wardrobe to go see the Queen of Winter. This was going to be tough. Too many choices were always my downfall.

I started to wish myself through the wardrobe.

I wished for new dresses, accessories, and many different "looks." I became a whirling dervish as I went from outfit to outfit in an increasingly frenzied way. Did you know that when you wish for a new look, the old one you were wearing ends up on the floor? I sure didn't! I am now surrounded by piles of all my discarded choices, no closer to an outfit, "Fit for a Queen." Plus, I am a little tipsy. Maybe a little more than tipsy. I think I need to eat, pronto. How does this "wishing" thing work anyway? I need carbs to sober up. I need bread to soak up all the champagne. I giggled to myself. I rubbed my hands together as though I was going to touch the Genie's Lamp. "I wish I had a nice, crispy piece of Italian bread with tomatoes, mozzarella, and lots of salt and olive oil. Like Nonna used to give me when we went to the beach when I was a kid."

Suddenly, the sandwich appeared in my hands. Geez Louise! You'd better watch what you wish for. I should have asked for a filet mignon with bearnaise sauce. Now that appeared right on the table in front of me! There was even a side of scalloped potatoes just like the dinner Sean and I loved when we went to Chez Jay in Santa Monica. So that is how it works. You ask for food or even just think about it, and it appears. I am in so … much … trouble! But first, I am going to have some of this filet. I need to sober up.

Soon, there was nothing left but crumbs. And a sleepy Witch. I wish I could take a nap. BOOM! Lights out. Wish granted. I awoke in a sinfully comfortable feather bed under what felt like five-thousand-count sheets of the softest cotton. There was a banging on the door, and I heard Norm the Gnome yelling, "First warning. You should be ready to go. They will be calling for you soon!" Oh no! What am I going to do? I stood there looking at myself in the mirror, wearing the most luxurious silk pajamas that I had ever worn and that I didn't want to take off. Can I wear this to see The Queen? Probably not. I will just stuff them in my bag like Birdie would do with the dinner rolls when the Columbiettes went to Brunch. Ugh, I need a bigger bag.

I rubbed my hands together excitedly and recited my wish in a firm voice, "I need a stylist, STAT!" There was a gentle knock on the door. A melodious voice asked humbly, "Speranza, it's Silvie! May I enter?" I opened the door, and Silvie the Sylphine Fairy flowed seamlessly into the room. She was slim, stylish, and ethereally beautiful. Her mere presence screamed fashion icon. Silvie was dressed in flowing silks, a diaphanous cloud of beauty that was not of the earth. She must have been a sylph who appeared in answer to my plea.

"Hello, Silvie. Obviously, I am in dire need of your help," I pleaded as I indicated by pointing to my pajamas. "What must I do to be properly dressed to have an audience with the Queen?" The elegant sylph gently nodded her head and said, "Don't fret, Speranza. I can help you. I think we will try to go with casual elegance with an overlaying sense of restrained power and strength. Perhaps a silk dress under a moto jacket in homage to your obsession with the eighties?" She got me! I could definitely work with her! "That sounds great, Silvie. But on second thought, I think it is too on the nose, if you know what I mean. Can we come up with something more in line with what people normally wear when they have an audience with the Queen?" I attempted what a curtsy should look like. Oh boy, that's going to need some work.

"It is all about your perception of the Never-Never, dear," Silvie said as she took out a tape measure and did a few quick calculations. "It is best to understand where your mind goes when you imagine what your perfect world would be. I wouldn't put you in a hoop skirt or a Victorian corseted dress, or even a miniskirt. You must be true to your school. As the saying goes." I have to agree. Still, we have to come up with something. "Fair enough, but eighties fashion included everything from Joan Collins to Joan Jett. We have to narrow it down a little," Speranza continued in a little girl's voice. "I always like the way Princess Di dressed. Can we do something along those lines?" Silvie burst out a beautiful smile and answered, "I loved the way she dressed, too. Let's work with that."

A stunning aubergine crushed velvet strapless gown just appeared on my body. It fit perfectly, and the rich color enhanced my natural skin tone and the color of my hair. A strappy sandal magically appeared on my feet, along with a pedicure that I didn't even know I needed but matched the exact color of the gown. We have to patent these shoes. It was like walking on marshmallows.

Silvie looked me up and down with a critical eye. "Something is missing, ahh!" She handed me a pair of opera gloves to complete the ensemble. I felt great, but I still needed to figure out the jewelry. Something simple, not to take away from the glamorous gown. I rubbed my hands once more, and my gloves created a friction that was both pleasing and effective. I wished for a simple layered twisted pearl choker and matching earrings. Classic. Elegant. They appeared on my body as soon as I thought of them. Did I have to rub my hands together, or was that just theatre and not necessary at all? I would test it out with my long hair. I thought about a larger-than-life, teased, voluminous, half-up, half-down, curly-style that would be hair-sprayed within an inch of its life and defy gravity. I saw it in the mirror instantly. Silvie oohed and aahed in appreciation. My look was complete. Oh, except for a bag. A quilted Chanel clutch materialized in my hand. Brava! That proves it! I only have to think about it to make it so.

There was only one more big problem. I was starving! I always get hungry when Magic is involved. Don't think about food. Don't think about food. I know. Think about lipstick or the rest of my makeup. Or even baseball. Anything to not think about food.

I don't want to show up to the Queen with a chicken cutlet in my velvet glove.

Chapter Twenty-Five – Let Them Eat Cake

Norm the Gnome knocked feverishly on the door, "It's time to go, dearie!" Oh boy! Here we go! I haven't forgotten that I was starving, but we are playing for keeps now. No food thoughts. DO … NOT … THINK … OF … FOOD! I started singing a childhood song in my head as a distraction: "The Spades go, tulips together, twilight forever, bring back my love to me." Great. Tragedy averted. I am not thinking about food. That should keep my wishes under control. I give myself a last look in the mirror and an internal pep talk. I vogued back and forth to see my outfit from different angles. Perfect!

I turned to look at Silvie, but she was gone. I guess once she did her job, she went off to whatever she was doing before I wished her into the room. The door slammed open, and an excitable gnome burst inside the room. He was dressed as before, but with headphones that were now over his pointed ears. Strangely enough, now he had a "Flock of Seagulls" hairdo. "Let's go, dearie. You are up next." I turned to him, and he grabbed my arm and started to propel me out of the room. "Ok, Norm. I am coming. You don't have to be so handsy! Give a lady a second, I have heels on." The excitable gnome immediately let go and said, "We don't want to be late. The Queen doesn't like it when you are late. This way, please, dearie." He turned and walked down a short hallway to a large double door. It opened automatically, and we walked into a darkened room. It appeared to be backstage at some sort of show with several gnomes with the same "Flock of Seagulls" haircuts bustling around. Fiddling with cameras, lights, and other equipment, they all seemed on the edge of panic. So was I. What is this? It was very busy. But very quiet at the same time. It was as if someone had lowered the volume to zero. I turned to Norm the Gnome and asked, "What is this place?" He said in a condescending tone," Why, it is backstage at the 'Midnight Show.' You are up next." I almost shivered with fear. "What show?" Another gnome leaned over to me and laughed in my face. She looked like a girl. A female gnome! I never knew there was such a thing. She chuckled, "Don't listen to my stupid boyfriend. You will be fine, honey. It's a piece of cake!"

I looked down, and a big piece of birthday cake with multi-colored sprinkles, including a lit candle, had appeared in my elegantly gloved hand. Oh no! She made me think of cake, and it's not even my birthday! "Geez Louise, now what am I going to do?" I wailed. The girlish gnome said, "Oooo! I love cake!" She grabbed the cake out of my hand and inhaled it, candle and all. Impressive. The smirking gnome with the icing all over her face said, "Now wish for a pizza!" I ran the names of the 1998 Yankees through my mind. Bernie Williams. Andy Pettitte. Derek Jeter. I had to name all of the Yankee lineup so I wouldn't think of food. Thank God Sean loves baseball and dragged me to so many games.

All of these crazy gnomes with the "Flock of Seagulls" haircuts and boyfriend jeans were running around getting ready for the show. I had to prepare for my entrance. A cherubic-faced gnome said to me that I should dance my way onto the stage. My new friend, the cake gnome, said, "Don't listen to Izzy, he's a jokester. Just walk out and be natural. The Queen knows all and cannot be fooled."

Then an elf got into my face, or at least I assumed she was an elf. Tall, slim, and elegant, she had pointed ears and very blond hair. It was not a dye job. "Speranza O'Rourke, The Brooklyn Witch? That's you, I presume. You are the Queen's next guest. I am your segment producer. I will run you through what is going to happen next. You are going to be announced and will walk through the curtain. You will walk up to the stage and sit in the chair next to the throne. Do not attempt to touch, hug, or otherwise come in contact with the Queen. She will say hello and start asking questions. The rest is up to you." I winced at the thought of being so close to the Queen and said, "What does she want of me? I'm still in the dark." The beautiful elven woman said, "I don't have any idea. You'll find out soon enough. That's your cue. GO! Go to the curtain."

Music started to play. It was "Lucky Star" by Madonna. I wish it were "I Will Survive," because all I want out of this is to survive and to find out why the Queen summoned me to the Never-Never. The two gnomes pushed me to the curtain, and it slowly opened. I stepped out into a darkened room, and all of a sudden, a spotlight illuminated me. Blinded, I started to walk forward, and a Monticello, who could have been Mello's twin, took me by the hand. He could have been his twin except for the fact that he was dressed like Michael Jackson, one glove and all! He whispered, "Don't fret, Speranza, Mello told me to take care of you. Walk this way." He turned to face me and moonwalked backward across the stage. Am I supposed to do that? It was still very dark as I simply walked forward. Then the lights went up, and I got to see what was in front of me.

There was an elevated stage with a huge Throne and several club chairs lined up on one side. They were all occupied by various types of Magical beings dressed to the nines. Or, more accurately, the eighties. On the impressive Throne sat a very beautiful woman. She was majestic and alluring, with a voluptuous figure. She had jet-black hair in a messy, curly style with a lace headband. She had startling blue eyes that seemed to burn right through you. Strangely enough, she was dressed like Madonna circa 1984, in her iconic outfit from the "Like a Virgin" video. Only she was in black, not white. A skirt made of layers of black tulle with shapes of moon and star cutouts adorning it. A tight black bustier with layers of black pearls and chains in her decolletage. Madonna's trademark, "Boy Toy" belt, was replaced by one with the word "Queen" embossed on it. Multiple matching black pearl bracelets graced her long, black lace fingerless gloves. Huge star earrings accessorized the look, and a pair of black pumps finished it off. Geez Louise, I am in the middle of an MTV video!

I advanced to the front of the stage and looked up at the Queen. She smiled at me. I couldn't tell if it was a warm smile or a cold one. But at least it was a smile. "Come, Speranza. Sit next to me." She turned toward the crowd, "Everyone, let's give 'The Brooklyn Witch' a warm welcome!" As I turned and sat down, I saw the crowd begin to clap and howl as though they were the rabid audience of the "Tonight Show" with Johnny Carson in his salad days. A huge Ogre windmilled his arms to encourage the crowd's response. It was a motley crew. Dozens of different types of faeries, nymphs, sylphs, and even monsters were cheering for me. Somehow, I thought many of them wanted to tear me limb from limb. But for now, I was under the Queen's protection.

"Welcome to the Never-Never, Speranza," the Queen said after the ovation had died down. "I am happy that you are finally here." Now, we can get to the crux of the matter. I said, "Thank you for having me. I know you wanted to speak with me. So—" The Queen cut me off. "We are at WAR, Speranza! I have been attacked, and all of my allies must join in the fight! Am I right?" She gestured to the crowd, and they all began to howl even more rabidly than before. They began stomping their feet or whatever served them as feet and banging various weapons on the floor. They were almost out of control until the Queen snapped her fingers, and then you could hear a pin drop. A Red Cap in the front row dropped a dagger, which made a loud clang. He bowed shamefacedly, picked it up, and put it back in his belt. A Red Cap! So, they are part of the Queen's gang! She must have ordered the attack on Mello. What am I getting myself into here?

"Your grandmother, Justina, would normally be here to represent the mortal realm, but I understand she is indisposed," the Queen said in what was superficially a very reasonable tone. Queen Mab leaned forward and asked mockingly, "Is she not feeling well? You must realize that she could reside here with us, living painlessly and thriving without a care in the world. The pain of the mortal realm does not exist here in my domain. Am I right?" The Queen gestured to the audience, and once again, they went wild. The Ogre on the sidelines encouraged this response as if he were a cheerleader. The Queen snapped her fingers again, and the crowd came to a complete stop. Dead silence.

The Queen adjusted herself and seemed to become even more regal and commanding as she said, "Now is the time for you to decide, Speranza. Are you with us, or are you against us? You can't go against the family. You and your grandmother have always been members of our family. If she cannot come to our aid in this time of need, you must stand here in her place. It is your duty. Your destiny. Your fate. Welcome to the bosom of your family." The crowd let out another vociferous shout of agreement. This time, the Queen didn't even have to prompt them. It looks like I have been adopted into the Queen of Winter's family. It's not the Columbo's, but I bet it is just as dangerous if I tried to get out of it. I could be a good soldier, or I could be dead. Another fine mess I got myself into.

What can I do to weasel my way out of here without making any commitments that would come back to haunt me? I know! Maybe if I compliment the Queen and play on her obvious vanity, she might cut me some slack and let me go without signing my life away. First, I will compliment her ensemble. I turned toward the audience and shouted as I stretched out my arms in enthusiasm, "Doesn't the Queen look absolutely gorgeous! Am I right?" Crickets. Dead silence. Not a response to be heard. Awkward. I shriveled in place at the lack of response.

Seriously? She looks exactly like that Madonna video, but so much better in black. I turned to the Queen and said, "You look a million times better than Madonna ever did, and you totally pulled off the black!" I clapped my hands feverishly to prompt the audience to join in. Nothing. Geez, Louise, this is so uncomfortable. I almost wish that a trap door would open up and take me away. The Queen was not amused and said in a tone of weary contempt, "Speranza … Speranza … Speranza. I do not need a lickspittle. I need a warrior! Your grandmother never stooped so low. Have some dignity."

She shook her head back and forth in dismissal of my attempt to curry favor with her. The Queen said, "I would have thought that Justina would have taught you better." There it is! An opportunity to wiggle my way out of this. "She taught me well, My Queen. I need to consult with her to best serve you. She can guide me to be the best possible vassal as she has been to you for so many years. As much as this is a place of wonder, and I love being here, I must go back and arrange my affairs. I do have a husband and a life to place in order so that I might better serve you." The Queen did not like that. At all. She grimaced and stood up and stomped her foot in what almost seemed frustration. I think the only thing that saved me from her wrath was her wish to have my willing compliance. She could compel me, but that would lessen my powers. "Fine, Speranza. You may go back to the earthly realm. You can consult your grandmother. Finalize your affairs. Briefly. But you must return in a fortnight. Or you will indeed incur my wrath!" The crowd turned on me and began to boo and hiss. Some of them shook weapons in the air, and I felt like I might be attacked. I don't know what to do. I stood up and made a tentative move to shake the Queen's hand to say thank you and goodbye. That made the crowd's reaction even worse. I immediately recoiled as I remembered that I was not to touch the Queen's person in any way, shape, or form. Then, someone stepped forward to save me.

The chubby, cheerful Monaciello, who was the Michael Jackson doppelganger, ran up and took my hand. "Come, child. You must go. You know what you must do … Beat it … Just beat it. You have to show them you're not scared, you're playing with your life, this ain't no truth or dare!" Is he quoting a Michael Jackson song? If he was going to do that, he should have quoted "Thriller" based on the looks of this crowd. This can't get any weirder. But it's still good advice.

He grabbed my hand firmly and pulled me along toward the door as the audience continued to menace us as if they were about to attack. We were magically transported back to the road, and we hurried along through the enchanted woods. When we reached the end of the wood, the Silvani crone appeared.

She looked me up and down and said contemptuously, "You wore that all day? You look horrible! Does nothing for you! Did you wear that to see the Queen? Fool! Tell me you were not so foolish as to think that these are the proper garments to honor the Queen of Winter! Never mind, follow me." She turned her back and mumbled to herself as she strode forward down the path. I stumbled for words. What do you say to that? Hold on, I don't owe this crone an explanation.

"You weren't there," I said petulantly. "Just show me the way back to the earthly realm as the Queen has commanded!" Two can play this game.

The Silvani didn't reply. She didn't say another word as we left the wood and went through the meadow back to the portal. The Michael Jackson impersonator bid me farewell in a high-pitched kind voice, "Come back to us soon, Speranza. Talk to your grandmother and return to your rightful place. We will be waiting for you. O—, O—, O—Hee-hee." He absolutely was channeling Michael. I waved goodbye and stepped forward.

I stepped through the portal to the earthly realm and ended up back on Sackett Street.

Now, I just have to explain why I am dressed for a Madonna video. Sean is gonna love this.

Chapter Twenty-Six – The War of the Grannies

After I left Alice's house, I started the trek back home. One thing was for sure. The Magic was gone! The heels that felt like I was walking on clouds are now killing me. I would love to take them off, but I would never walk barefoot on the streets of Brooklyn. It looked like the "walk of shame," even though it was the middle of the afternoon. Sean would love this outfit, but I need to get home before he does and change.

As I turned the corner and stumbled the last few feet to my door, I passed my neighbor's luxurious crop of basil in the front garden. I heard a hiss. I looked around to see who was hissing at me. Something was moving in the garden. It was as if something was pacing back and forth, like an expectant father waiting for his errant daughter to come home. Was it a cat? No! It was Hob who stuck his head out from under a huge basil plant. Holy Moly! What was Hob doing outside? In sunlight, no less. It must be urgent because he would never risk being seen by a mortal who did not have Magic.

"Speranza, Speranza! Bend down like you are fixing your shoe so you can hear me," Hob urged in an insistent voice that demanded I obey. I knelt and started to rub my aching tootsies. He stage-whispered, "Your husband is home early today, lassie. You need to be able to explain your attire if you want to conceal your activities in the Never-Never." I was startled. How did he know where I was? "How did you find out about that, Hob?" The Brownie snorted and said, "That's my favorite show. Next to the Real Housewives, of course! Now, heed my words if you please." After he gave his final warning, he disappeared into the garden. Great. Now I have to do some fast talking to get out of this one.

I walked into the kitchen, and Sean was standing at the island, eating a sloppy ham and cheese sandwich. I hoped the pepper ham and roasted peppers would distract him. But no such luck. His eyes looked like they were going to pop out of his head. He choked a little as he loudly asked me through a mouthful of sandwich, "Where are you coming from, Babe? I didn't know it was prom. My tux is in the cleaners." "What? This old dress?" I wasn't lying. It was old enough to fit into the eighties. "I was just perfecting my costume for an eighties party next month. We all did a trial run. You know how crazy I get when we go to a costume party!" Sean started to laugh, "You mean the way you went 'overboard' when you dressed up like Dead Natalie Wood with the life preserver and the seaweed in your hair? You know your motto about that. Anything worth doing is worth overdoing. You are the Queen of Costumes. I guess that is why you did the full hair and makeup, right?" He gestured with his sandwich up and down my whole ensemble. He continued to munch on his sandwich as we bantered. I might have deflected his questions. Wait. Queen? Crap that reminds me I only have two weeks.

"Where is my costume? Am I going as Robert Wagner again? You know, with the captain's hat and the blue blazer? You know that no one could figure out who I was supposed to be. They kept calling me Captain and asking me where Tennille was, or worse, they called me Mr. Howell. Maybe we can come up with a better costume this time? I am sure we can pick an eighties guy that I would like." I laughed in turn and said, "You can just wear your regular clothes. You dress like it's the eighties anyway, so just break out the Member's Only Jacket." I only thought of that because of the bouncers. But that's not fair. Sean is not an ogre. "Do you want to be Crocket or Tubbs? You know, Miami Vice? Or you can shave your head and suck on a lollypop, and be Kojak? Your choice." Sean deadpanned, "Who loves you, baby? That's the seventies, not the eighties. Why do I have to be a cop anyway? I can wear a T-shirt, a fake mullet, and a leather jacket and be Bon Jovi. How about that?" I chuckled at his dad humor. "Later, potater. I need to go out for a little while, so I have to change," I said to end the conversation. Sean said, "Yeah, I have to go back to work, too. I just came home for lunch. I will see you tonight." He kissed me and got some mayo on my cheek as he walked out the door, still working on his sandwich. That's my Sean.

I quickly changed and put my hair in a ponytail. I hurried over to Nonna's and let myself in. No one was home. "Hello? Nonna? It's me. We need to talk." Mello poked his head into the room. "La Señora is not here, Speranza. She went out for a walk." "What? She doesn't do that." Not as far as I know. But what do I know these days? Nonna has become a big mystery to me.

"Where does she walk, Mello?" Mello came into the room and replied, "She almost always goes to the same place. Valentino Park on the Waterfront. In Red Hook. When she gets melancholy, she likes to go and stare at the Statue of Liberty and remember how her people came to America. It gives her hope." How do I not know this? Mello had a bottle of wine that he swigged as he continued, "I think that she got your friend Ginny's brother, the criminal, to give her a ride. At least that is what I overheard when she was on the phone." So that's how she got down there! It was way too far for her to walk. I was flabbergasted. I didn't even know that she knew who Nunzio was, let alone that she could call him for favors. I need to catch up. "Thank you, Mello. I need to go find her." I wanted to ask him about his relative in the Never-Never, but that will have to wait. The clock is ticking. That is all I can think about for the next two weeks.

I called an Uber, and it took me to the entrance of the park. I got out of the car and looked down the long pier and saw two figures arguing as they sat on a bench in front of Lady Liberty. To my surprise, it was Nonna and Grannie Meg who seemed to be in a big fight. This must be about my trip to the Never-Never. As soon as I set foot on the pier, they immediately stopped talking. They must have sensed that I was there. I walked up to the bench and wiggled in between them. "How's tricks," I spat out as my tone got combative, "Cause Trix are not just for kids, they are for Grannies who don't want to tell me the truth!" I was angry at them for not giving me a heads-up as to how the Never-Never worked. "My anxiety was on 'ludicrous speed' in the Never-Never. Why didn't one of you warn me that my brain would dictate how it would look? I was lost in the eighties when I was there! At least I could have been prepared." Nonna looked at me like I was crazy, "Mia Bella, what are you talking about? I am confused. The Queen was there, no? She looked like Sophia Loren. Very pretty, no? Did you meet her, Chamberlain?" Nonna stopped for a moment and chortled, "Mello's cousin who looks like Elvis? That's the Never-Never!" Nonna turned to Grannie Meg as if to get her agreement, but she just shook her head no. "Never been. Irish need not apply," Grannie Meg said in a tone of virtuous snottiness. If that's a thing. "Who cares what it looks like?" Grannie Meg asked plaintively, "What happened while you were there, darling girl? We have differing reports from our familiars and other sources. Can you give us the real story?"

What is the real story? Do I even know anymore? "The bottom line is that Queen Mab has demanded that I become her willing vassal. Much as we had already discussed. She has amassed an army of faeries, goblins, and monsters and wants me to join. I don't want to! But I feel that I will not be able to fool her. What am I going to do? I only have a fortnight."

Nonna was clearly upset and implored me, "You don't have to go back. I am sorry that you feel that I misled you. I did not. Everyone has a different tale to tell of their time there. It is never the same. I hope that you realize the Queen is not someone to trifle with and that you should remain here in the mortal realm. Please learn from my mistakes. Do not give yourself over to her. You would live to regret it. As I have for these many years." Grannie Meg interjected in a furious tone, "Live to regret it? She might not live at all you great booby! The Queen's demands must be met, or she will send her minions to enforce them. Or to destroy those who deny her. You are a coward, Justina. You surrendered to her and became her minion. Speranza is strong enough to avoid that. That's the Irish in her. We don't bow to tyrants. She has to play the long game. She has to do something to placate the Queen of Winter, or she will suffer. As will all of us."

Nonna let out a deep sigh as if she couldn't believe that I refused to listen to her. "You don't understand, Margaret. The Queen operates in the same manner as the 'honored society.' What you call the *Mafia.*" Nonna turned to look out over the water. "They have a saying. 'Once in, never out.' When you come to the Queen's notice, you must acquiesce to her demands or perish." Nonna turned to look back at me. "You must be willing to do anything. Kill your best friend. Destroy your family. Betray your blood. Anything she demands. You do not want this." She grabbed my hand with surprising strength and pleaded with glistening eyes, "Please listen to me, I beg you. Learn from your Nonna's mistakes. You must stay out of her control. You can never go back to the Court. Don't listen to Margaret. She did not resist the Queen because of her integrity, as she claims. She just escaped the Queen's notice, that is all." Nonna glanced at Grannie Meg and sniffed in superiority, "Margaret is not all that important in this world. Don't let her all-too-human arrogance become your arrogance. You cannot fool the Queen of Winter. You must become her vassal if she demands it. Or Die. Unless you never go back. I am so sorry, Mia Bella, that I brought this trouble to your door." Nonna started to weep silently.

Grannie Meg was livid. She was practically hopping up and down in her seat. She grabbed my arm and forcibly turned me toward her, "Tosh and balderdash! We all have free will! That is why the Queen could not compel you to be her slave. Which is what your Nonna is, so don't let her fool you. I noticed that she returned to the mortal vale to escape Queen Mab's control. You can do the same if you go back." Grannie Meg stared directly into my eyes, "I am not the only one who feels this way. The rest of the Council agrees. The Council that your Nonna has so arrogantly refused to meet with for decades." Grannie Meg stood up and declared, "Justina, I now formally demand that you present yourself to the Council or suffer the consequences." Grannie Meg waved her hand in the air, and an elaborate gold-encrusted scroll appeared. She held it up in front of us and let it fall open. It had a gold leaf stamp with a demand that Nonna appear in front of the Council. What was this? A "Witchy Subpoena?" Shit just got real! Grannie Meg said with an angry lilt in her normally soft Irish brogue, "I have shielded you for too many years because of Speranza. Now it is time to pay the piper."

The two witches stared daggers at each other. The only sounds to be heard were the cries of seagulls as they swooped and fought along the shoreline of the pier. I needed to get them to agree to avoid an all-out war. The Cold War that had existed for so long seems to have come to an end.

I stood up to interpose myself between them. "Nonna, it's not such a bad thing to speak to other practitioners who have knowledge about the Queen." I want to bridge the gap before they start to fight for real. "Seeking other sources of information is the furthest thing you can get from being arrogant. We have to acknowledge that we don't know everything, Nonna. You taught me that. You are the sum of your experiences. Other people had different experiences that will help me make an informed decision. So, how about it? Let's at least talk to them, Nonna. Please."

Nonna bent her head down as though she had a great weight on her. Nonna murmured, "Fine, Mia Bella. We will go to that silly talking shop. But you should know that your other grandmother is not the only old woman who sits on the Council. I think they have nothing to add, but I will go with you so I can set you straight when they offer the wrong advice." She stood up and started to walk out of the park. Grannie Meg scurried to get in front of her as I trailed behind. We walked out to Van Brunt Street, and lo and behold, Grannie Meg's car was parked there. We all got in with Nonna in the backseat and proceeded to Bay Ridge.

"Don't touch the window," Grannie Meg growled in an irascible tone. "I have to have it fixed, so leave it alone. Don'tcha see the blue tape? That means no touchy!" Nonna huffed, "Do not worry, Irisher, I will not touch your filthy car. At least not until you clean it properly." Which was a dig since the car was spotless. I didn't understand why there was blue painter's tape everywhere since Grannie Meg used Magic to maintain the car. Maybe it was a series of wards to protect the people in the car. You never know with Grannie Meg. I had to tamp down the spark of disagreement so it didn't burst into flames.

"Ladies, you know I love you both and that you both love me. So, I beg you to stop this bickering and let's go in peace to discuss our problems. We have enough to worry about without fighting amongst ourselves." I hoped that would work. They quieted down, and we were silent for the rest of the trip.

I don't know if it was Magic, but it seemed that we were in front of the door to the Council's Chamber in a matter of moments. Grannie Meg opened the door and ushered us in. The other members were all in their seats. Another extra seat was placed away from the table where all could see. It was set on a platform as though she were in the dock in some Magical courtroom. That must be for Nonna, as she did not have a seat at the table. Grannie Meg and I sat in our seats, and the meeting began. I gave a full accounting of what went on and waited for their reactions.

The verdict was split. Grannie Meg, Alejandro, Vesna, and Nikolai all supported going back to the Never-Never, while the others agreed with Nonna that I should stay away. Nonna halfheartedly joined in the debate, but it was clear that she had very little respect for the Council or most of its members. In particular, it was clear she despised Nikolai and Alejandro. Not just for their opinions, but their character. It was an unforgiving side of Nonna that I had never seen before.

The meeting broke up before we came to a decision. Everything was still up in the air. Nonna got into a discussion with Vesna, who seemed warm and very friendly. Grannie Meg was speaking with Tiwa as Alejandro sidled up to me and spoke in a very low tone. I said, "What? I can't hear you!" I am not good with accents in the first place, and I'm half deaf to boot. You need to understand that the eighties ruined my hearing from standing in front of large blasting speakers in "The Brooklyn Zoo." The new wave club, not the animal prison.

"Speak up for those in the back of the class," I said jokingly. Alejandro rolled his eyes for a brief moment and then said, "I need to tell you that your friend Lorraine Russo has set up another ritual. This time, at her mother's house in Carroll Gardens, with the same Santeria Witch who serves under my purview. I think we should attend. To put a stop to it before something untoward occurs." That little beyotch. She is becoming a real stone in my shoe, as my Nonna might say. "Yes, let's put an end to this once and for all. I will meet you in front of the Russo's house tonight. When is this ritual supposed to take place?" Alejandro gave me a sarcastic smile and said, "Midnight. I am sure that will be very convenient for you. Ha."

Great! Now I have to make up an excuse for Sean. Maybe I will just say I have to stay with Nonna and will be home very late. He will buy that because it has happened before. Luckily, the Yankees are on the Coast, so he can listen to the game in his man cave. I will leave him a note.

I am just digging the hole even deeper. Double your trouble, two Grannies in one.

Chapter Twenty-Seven – To Tell the Truth

We drove home in Grannie Meg's car in total silence. There were no arguments. No discussions. No meeting of the minds. Simply an icy silence that did not bode well. I want to have everyone reconciled because I will need all of them to survive. The clock is ticking.

We finally arrived at Nonna's house; I walked her in since she was very tired and not steady on her feet. Grannie Meg pulled away without another word. A real "Irish goodbye!" I guess she felt that made her position clear. This was the way she usually treated me. As an adult who could make her own decisions. As long as I did what she wanted me to do, everything was fine. On the other hand, Nonna had a tendency to treat me like the little girl she remembers sitting at her kitchen table listening to her tales of Magic.

I sat her down in her favorite chair and said, "That was a lot, Nonna. Let's sleep on it, and we can regroup tomorrow. I will come and see you then. Ok?" Nonna was slumped over and said, "Si, Mia Bella. Tomorrow. I just need to rest now." I touched her shoulder, walked out, and went the few blocks over to my house. I need to leave Sean a note and find somewhere to hang out until midnight. I guess I can go to Ginny's.

I quickly jumped in the shower to wash off the Never-Never that seemed to still be clinging to me. Especially all that hairspray from the eighties. I felt like I hadn't showered since the eighties. I blew out my hair straight and decided to do a little extra in the makeup department. I wanted to look the part of a serious "Witch" tonight. Of course, I am wearing black, but then again, I wanted to up my "Witchy look" for this confrontation. Also, show Alejandro I mean business! I am taking this very seriously. They are on my turf now, so I have to be the boss! I want to look as confident on the outside as I feel on the inside. Black layers. Black lace-up boots with a flat heel, so I am ready for anything. As I looked through my closet, I spied a black shawl with armholes to keep me "hands-free" to throw a spell. I bought it in a thrift shop in Salem on one of my first vacations with Sean. I always wondered if another Witch had owned it. It did make me feel connected to my heritage. I put it on, and I was almost ready. Now time to accessorize. I grabbed a few crystal bracelets, mostly for protection, and my favorite amethyst necklace. Now I'm ready to go. Witches, start your broomsticks!

I went to Ginny's house on Clinton Street, which was conveniently a few blocks away from Salvina Russo's brownstone. Ginny had already closed the café, so I was pretty sure she was home and not out on a date. That would've required a plan like it was the Invasion of Normandy. I rang the bell and knocked on the iron gate at the basement door. I heard Ginny shout, "Be right there!" A minute later, she opened the door and laughingly said, "Trick or Treat, Smell my Feet!" We both cracked up as we thought about the childhood rhyme that we always chanted on Halloween. "Your costume looks great. You just need your little dog, too!" I pushed past her as I barged into her house and replied, "That was Dorothy! Get it right, sister. Don't be dissin' the Wicked Witch. She's my people." Laughing at each other, we moved into the living room. I sat on the sofa, and the plastic slipcover immediately started squeaking most embarrassingly. "Geez, Ginny, what are you, ninety or what? You are taking the ginzo grandmother vibe way too seriously." Ginny sat down next to me and playfully gave me a shove. "Don't knock it, girlie. It worked for my grandmother and yours, too. A better question is, why are you all dolled up? What's up with all the make-up? If I didn't know better, I would say you were stepping out on Sean-o, but I know that would never happen. Spill."

I had come to the fork in the road. And I had to take it. Should I clue her in to what was going on? It could be very helpful to get the perspective of my oldest friend. Plus, she is a full human with no magical taint to influence her reactions. I think it was time to spill the cannoli beans.

"I have something important to tell you, Ginny," I said as I took her hand. "Oh, No! What's up? Did somebody die? Are you getting a divorce?" Ginny glumly asked in a sing-song voice slathered in doom and gloom. "What? No!" I waved her off with a get-out-of-here gesture. "Where did you get that idea, you dope? No, I want to talk to you about ... you know," I took a beat and said, "Magic!" Ginny was nonplussed and said, "Magic? What do you mean, Magic?" I have to finally tell her the truth. "You know how I have been doing Magic all these years. Like my Nonna before me. Well, I have to tell you … Magic is real. All of it." I waved my arms like an umpire calling the runner safe! Only nobody was safe.

"The faeries, the ghosts and goblins, and the spells. It's all real. The spells are real. And it has all caught up to me!" I dropped my face into my hands. Ginny had a bulldog look of disbelief and pushed me until I looked up at her. She said, "What a load of bologna. And cheap bologna, not even Mortadella! I know you did a bunch of spells and made love potions and all that, but I thought it was just a scam to make money." Ginny held out her arms and shrugged her shoulders, "Not that it's a bad thing, but still. I just thought you wanted to keep the superstitious old ladies, like Birdie and Salvina, under control. What are you trying to say here, Anna? That you can *really* turn my ex into a frog?" Ginny started to laugh at me through the side of her mouth.

"Statazit, Ginny! I'm pouring my heart out here, and you're joking about deli meat!" I have to jump in with both feet now. "Speaking of Salvina and her beyotch daughter, Lorraine, I'm on my way to Salvina's tonight. They're going to try to do a fugazi ritual with some Santeria Priestess." Ginny interjected, "You mean like the fiasco with the housecoat covered in chicken blood?" I chuckled. "I wish it were that simple. I think they're going to try something much worse this time. I need to shut it down. I am meeting someone who will put the priestess in her place. He's her boss, and I need the backup, anyway." Ginny squared her shoulders and said, "I'll come with you, Anna! I'll be your backup," and started throwing exaggerated air punches like the Cowardly Lion. "I will *pulverize* 'em. I will *murderize* 'em. Hold me back." You had to laugh. I can always count on Ginny. I truly wish I could take her with me. "That's ok, tiger. I just need a place to chill until midnight when the ritual is scheduled to begin. Let's have a bite. What kind of food do you have here anyway that you feed your poor kids? You must have some Hot Pockets or Pop-Tarts or something." Ginny pushed me good-naturedly and scoffed, "Pop-Tarts? Disgrazia! Don't bust my chops. I can put on some gnocchi. I have some leftover sauce in the fridge." I said, "Don't go to all that trouble. Do you have any cold cuts? Just make a sandwich." Ginny said,

"Sure! I have a nice loaf of Italian bread from Caputo's." She took out the prosciutto, fresh mozzarella, and tomatoes. When she was done, we had overstuffed sandwiches that I would have gotten if I had wished for one in the Never-Never! It was a true work of art.

We ate, chatted, and laughed our asses off. I sipped some espresso, as I didn't want any wine because I needed a clear head for what came next. At twenty to twelve, I said goodbye and walked toward Salvina's house. As I approached, I saw a figure standing in front of the tree at the corner. When I got closer, I could feel the power of the Magic that oozed out of the site of the ritual. I wonder if they had started early? Oh great. Now I am starving. Again. Do you think I have time to grab a slice? As I dreamed about pepperoni, Alejandro appeared in front of me in a flash, without me even seeing him move. And he didn't have a pizza.

"Speranza! You ready? They must have started. This puta is incompetent. She doesn't even know she was supposed to start at midnight. I don't think we have any time to lose. Let us force entry." He said that because of the heavy metal gate on the door and the ward on the threshold. Luckily, I was the one who put it there, so we could gain entry without any fuss or muss. I murmured a quick opening spell, and the door flew open, hit the brick wall, and made that clangy echo sound like it was the door to a prison cell. We walked in. As we stood in the vestibule, it was loud, and the inside rooms were lit with flashing lights of many colors, like a cop car outside your window in the middle of the night. We heard screams, and all the hairs on my body stood up. Suddenly, it was quiet. Deathly quiet.

We looked at each other and rushed into the living room. We're not in Brooklyn anymore.

We had entered Hell!

Chapter Twenty-Eight – It's Hard to be Hummel

Salvina Russo's living room looked completely different from the last time I was there. What I saw before me was a symphony of chaos and violence. There was blood everywhere. On the floor. On the walls. Even on the ceiling. I saw Salvina, Lorraine, and her husband. Or more accurately, what was left of them. They were dead. Their bodies were torn apart in the most appalling way possible. Salvina, who was one of Nonna's closest friends, had terrible wounds. Her daughter and son-in-law were torn limb from limb. What could have possibly caused all of this carnage?

I could not believe my eyes! How could this happen to people I've known all my life? Could this be the end of their story? What does this mean for me? I suddenly realized my life was going to be very different.

Not the life my grandmothers had planned for me. Will it be violence and horror for the rest of my days? Is this the true legacy of Magic? Is this what my life will look like as a vassal of the Queen? What if I don't want to play this game? More importantly, how can I explain this to Sean?

I'm sure he will be assigned to this case. Fury and rage will come to dominate my life. Sean can't find out that I had any previous knowledge of this ritual. He would believe that I could've stopped it or at least warned him. This reads as premeditated, and that I had lied to him about going to Nonna's house. How could I have possibly warned him about what had resulted from their arrogance? I stood in disbelief at this battlefield. Then, my trance was disturbed by something that entered my consciousness. I heard a sound and looked at the wall directly across from me. A portal shimmered with dark energy. It was the source of the flashing lights that we had seen earlier. I had forgotten all about Alejandro and turned to look for him.

He was bent over the broken figure of a woman. She must be the Santeria Priestess who was the author of this disaster. She was breathing her last, as Alejandro put his ear to her mouth to get her dying declaration. The gruesomely wounded woman took one last gasp and expired. He stood up. Then he kicked her lifeless body in fury.

"Why did you do that?" I asked in horror. That was needlessly cruel. Is this his true nature? Is this why Nonna dislikes him, so? Alejandro had an angry glare on his face as he spat out, "She is the one who caused all of this! She told me that she performed a summoning." Wait? What's so bad about a summoning? I gingerly asked," Do you know who she summoned? Why would that cause all of this carnage? I do summoning spells all the time." Alejandro was very grim and now spoke in a furious tone, "This was an illegal, unsanctioned, outlawed ritual. She must have summoned something too strong for her to control. Or worse, she demanded something that resulted in this massacre. We need to find out what happened here if we are going to protect the mortal realm. Or, at the very least, we need to close this portal." That made sense, and I agreed, "Fine. Let's do that. Wait! What's happening?"

The lights in the portal began to pulse and flash brighter and stronger as a massive silhouette was visible through the haze of the open portal. It was huge and terrifying. Then it stepped through.

It was a seven-foot-tall figure with the muscles of a bodybuilder. It looked like an elongated Arnold Schwarzenegger in his prime, with a muscular physique that promised immense power and strength. The only thing he wore was a simple loincloth that barely covered him. He flexed conceitedly as he enjoyed the cool air on his sweating skin. Oh, and by the way, he had the head of a Bull. A gigantic snorting feral bull. I know that creature. It's the Minotaur!

The Minotaur is a monster straight from the myths of Ancient Greece. Well, I guess it wasn't a myth! He was a terrifying creature from Crete who guarded the Labyrinth and was killed by Theseus, the Athenian Hero. Obviously, he wasn't mythical or dead because he was here in the flesh. A lot of angry flesh that looked around to see who else he could kill. I thank my lucky stars that I occasionally pay attention to Sean when he talks about books he's reading when we're going to sleep. It never fails to put me out, but every once in a while, I remember something. I remember the story of the Minotaur because it scared the crap out of me. The description of this terrifying monster was enough to give you nightmares. Now, the monster in the mirror is closer than it appears!

I didn't realize how huge he was until he was right in front of me. Seven feet of rippling muscles and rage that, on closer inspection, was bathed in blood. His hooves were covered in gore. Hooves? And a tail? The Minotaur was so tall and imposing that his wide shoulders seemed to fill the entire portal. This creature was a perfect amalgam of Human and Bull. He was quite simply terrifying.

He must have been the one who perpetrated this massacre. But why? He seemed to be in a daze, but then his nostrils flared. He smelled something. He grunted with what seemed like a taste for destruction and gore as if the smell of death was something to revel in. The Minotaur turned toward me in a rage and wanted to attack. He smelled fresh meat and jumped forward from the wall and was right up in my face. He was as close as you could get without touching. I felt like I was in the movie "Alien," waiting for a third jaw to come out. He was about to do to me what he had done to Salvina. Then Alejandro intervened.

"Hold Asterion!" Alejandro shouted in a loud and commanding voice. "This is Speranza O'Rourke, the Brooklyn Witch, who is to be vassal to your Queen. You dare not harm her, for you will certainly incur your sovereign's wrath." The Minotaur snorted and spewed in my face with just about the worst case of bad breath that I've ever encountered. His chest was heaving as you could see he wanted to attack, but with a supreme effort of will, he stopped himself. I can't believe this. Not only can Alejandro talk to him, but he even knows his name! I didn't realize that the Minotaur was an intelligent being and not an animal. He seemed to be a "Raging Bull" if you know what I mean.

The smelly beast took one step back and slowly turned his massive bull head in Alejandro's direction. In a deep guttural voice, the monster said, "The Witch? I know of her." He speaks! What a surprise! A talking monster was not on my Bingo card. Alejandro replied in a commanding tone, "Yes, then you know her person is sacrosanct. She is the Queen's vassal, just like you. You may not harm her." The bull-man hissed like a tea kettle, "She has not sworn yet. She is still fair game until she takes her oath." Alejandro shook his head and said, "The Queen wants her. Do you want to forestall her wish? You would not fare well if you thwart her will." The Minotaur looked almost thoughtful for a moment and then took two steps back. He spoke in a deep bass voice, "You could be correct, Warlock. I will not go against the Queen. The Witch is under her protection. You are not." With that, he kicked out with one of his cloven hooves and sent Alejandro flying across the room, with claw marks almost immediately visible on his body. As the Minotaur moved in to attack, Alejandro had already recovered his composure. He stood tall and put his hands out to cast a spell. He mumbled words under his breath as he cast, to stop the Minotaur from hearing or perhaps to keep me from knowing his secrets.

The raging monster stopped in his tracks as a cosmic force hit him and forced him back. There wasn't any tangible reason for this; it was Magic. Pure, unadulterated, powerful Magic, worthy of a member of the Council. I had no idea what it was, and I don't possess any Magic like that. In fact, I didn't have any fighting Magic at all! And I needed some because I had to help him. What was I going to do? I've never been in a serious fight for my life! Should I pull his hair? Or better yet, his tail? I should've gone to those self-defense classes Sean taught, but I never thought I would need to fight a seven-foot-tall magical beast.

I looked around for something to use in the fight. I saw Salvina's silver tea set on the credenza, and lightning struck. I have it! I am going to "Beauty and the Beast" this dude. I put out my hand and said a word of power, "Ionsai!" Which is Gaelic for attack! It's my magical mantra to make an inanimate object fly out and bash something. I normally use it for mosquitoes because I'm deathly allergic to them. I'm very non-violent, but I make an exception for those disgusting creatures. Maybe it could work with a seven-foot-tall bull? The Teapot, the Spoon, and the Candlestick all flew and hit the Minotaur on the back of his big, fat head. He didn't even notice it. It's time to call in the reinforcements. I'm going to use "old lady magic" to help my friend. I need to use the tools at hand to make a difference.

Alejandro was still casting his spell to hold the monster at bay. The Minotaur was trying to walk forward to grab him. I couldn't hear what he was saying, but I was sure it was a complicated spell that required arcane knowledge that I did not possess. This holding spell was much different from the simple "Word of Power" that I used to transport objects to strike the monster. Spells require much more thought and elaborate rituals than the intrinsic strength of the "Word of Power." Whatever the spell was, it seemed to take a lot out of Alejandro, so I had to do something quick.

It was as if the Minotaur was walking in mud as he slowly but surely was getting closer to the sweating and straining Warlock. I turned to the curio cabinet and shouted my mantra at the top of my voice with all of my power behind it. The glass doors burst open and slammed against the sides to shatter. A platoon of Hummels jumped out like paratroopers and marched across the floor to attack the Minotaur. They stabbed at him with umbrellas, slammed him with spinning wheels, and tried to trip him up with wheelbarrows. The rosy-cheeked figurines struck with whatever was in their hands. It was the attack of the "Children of the Hummels," and the bull was not amused. He barely acknowledged the effect of their attack as he slammed his hooves down and smashed them if they got too close. That didn't stop those valiant children as the ceramic shards of the broken Hummels spun up and embedded themselves in the flesh of his furry legs.

I turned to the old-fashioned roll-top secretary desk that was behind me. A huge stack of cards sat there. Hundreds, used and unused. Birthday, Mother's Day, Christmas, and even Mass cards were in neat piles. I pointed at them and shouted, 'Ionsai," and swept my arms toward the beast. They flew across the room like a flight of angry wasps and started slashing him. It was "Death by a Thousand Cuts." Paper cuts, but cuts all the same. They were distracting him as he waved and tried to get them out of his face. I needed something better. Something to slow him down. I wish I had some help. Someone with good ideas. If only Ginny were here. Holy Moly! Ginny! That's the answer!

I turned to Salvina's sofa and waved my hands over the blood-stained furniture. The furniture itself wasn't blood-stained because like every good Italian of her generation, Salvina had them encased in industrial-strength plastic slip-covers. I waved my hands over them and issued an incantation. Not just a word of power. They ripped themselves off the furniture and wrapped around every inch of the Minotaur like cling wrap on last night's leftovers. I continued the spell to make it stronger as he struggled against its power. This was one of my best spells since I use it every day. Sean's cooking generates a lot of leftovers.

I looked around to see what else I could use. Salvina's knitting basket! I sent the knitting needles flying across the room to stick in the monster's face. I yelled at him, "Knit one, stab two!" That felt good. The unfinished afghan wrapped itself across his eyes to temporarily blind him as the rest of the yarn unraveled and spun around him to help the slipcovers hold.

I searched for anything else that would help. I looked at the bookshelves and set the outdated 1960-era Encyclopedia Britannica flying across the room and conking him on the head one by one. The refrigerator magnets flew onto him and served as another irritant as they stuck to him, covering his face so he couldn't see what was happening. I saw Salvina's pill dispensers on the sideboard that had each day marked. I cast a spell, and the lids opened, each in turn. SMTWTFS, an acronym for each day of the week, filled with pills and vitamins. I had them shoot across the room like bullets as each hit him in the face. It just seemed to get him even angrier.

While all of this was going on, Alejandro was still throwing a spell at him. He couldn't hold him much longer. He was losing his grip. We needed a solution to end this. I cast around for an answer. Hah! There it was on the recliner. Doilies!

There were lace-crocheted doilies everywhere! On the sofa. On the arms of all the chairs. Under the lamps, vases, and almost everything in the house, to protect the furniture. I can use them to protect us! I cast a more complicated spell that gathered all the doilies together to form a net. How do you get rid of a shark? You put it in a net and drag it behind your boat until it drowns. I learned that on Shark Week. This guy was as big and nasty as a great white. Let's do the same thing. Not to kill him, but to get rid of him before he kills Alejandro.

I set the net of doilies to the walls of the portal and extended it over the still-struggling Minotaur, who seemed to be ready to break free at any moment. I set my strongest compulsion spell to force the crocheted doilies to pull him back into the void. He started yelling and growling as he was slowly pulled back to the other side. He yelled something, but I didn't catch what he said. With a pop and a snap, he was pulled into the portal, and I immediately closed it with the strongest wards at my disposal.

I fell to the ground, exhausted. Alejandro was even more spent as he lay with his back against the sofa. "That was intense, my friend," he whispered weakly. "What was that last thing he shouted as he was drawn back into the void?" I said, "'Nobody puts baby in a corner?' Or at least that's what it sounded like to me." We looked at each other and started laughing helplessly. It was more a release from terror than a joke. It was good to be alive.

Now we will have to do something to clean up this mess. I am sure Sean will be called in to investigate these murders. This is his precinct, and he will be in charge. How am I going to explain this? All this mess. All this blood. All this horror.

Holy horror slasher movie, Batman!

Chapter Twenty-Nine – Take the Cannoli, Leave the Magic!

I feel like this was all a dream. No … a nightmare! Any minute, I will wake up in my bed, all cozy next to my husband, Sean. That would be a tall order because as I looked around, devastation. The broken furniture. Those poor Hummels. The dead bodies. The blood.

It wasn't just the destruction. It was the smell. An overpowering smell that I am sure a passerby would notice on the street. I hate this smell. I feel like I am going to throw up. My anxiety is off the charts. On a good day, I'm in fight or flight mode. Today, it was definitely switched to flight. Because the fight was over. I was still vibrating, and I couldn't move. What finally broke through the daze was the smell. I couldn't take it anymore, and I had to do something.

I turned to Alejandro, who was exhausted and breathing heavily as if he had run a marathon. "What are we going to do, Alejandro?" I wearily asked the formally natty Warlock, who looked like he had been through the ringer. "You know the cops are going to be all over this? My husband, for one! This is a triple homicide with special circumstances that will be all over the news. We have to cover this up! Fast!" Alejandro stayed slumped over with his chin on his chest as though he couldn't move. He raised his head and said, "Yes, Speranza. You are surely correct. Don't worry. This is not the first time I have had to cover up a magical massacre. It is one of the most common duties of the Council." I was surprised by his claim and asked, "I've never heard of any magical massacres?" He chuckled wearily and murmured, "Then we have done our job. Now it is time to do it again."

Alejandro grabbed the side of the sofa, lifted himself, and suggested, "You need to leave, Speranza. I will handle this. I have done it before. No one should know that you were here. Especially your husband. Go home to him and pretend that nothing is wrong." This didn't sound right. I asked, "Are you sure, Alejandro? I am in this too, and I won't let you handle it alone." "Don't worry, just go." I didn't like this because it seemed like he was rushing me, and I needed some answers. Some of them he can give me. Right now.

"What did the Priestess say to you before she died, Alejandro? Did she tell you why this happened? Do we have any idea what this was all about?" He looked at me with a deadpan expression as though he was deciding how much to tell me. "She didn't tell me anything of note.

Other than the fact that she was doing a summoning. We can make some deductions based on who responded to her summons," he said as he rubbed his arm that had been torn by the Minotaur's hooves. "The Minotaur is a guardian. Just as he was in the Myths of Ancient Greece. It must be because of this function that he responded to what Chaithra did." This was first-rate deductive reasoning. Is he the Spanish Sherlock Holmes? Or is he just trying to placate me?

I asked, "Who is he guarding that he went to such lengths to protect?" Alejandro simply said, "Not who. What. He guards the Queen of Winter's treasury. They must have tried to rob her. What you see is the result of their greed and foolishness." I almost lost my mind when I heard this explanation! It totally tracks. Lorraine was a greedy beyotch, and the money must have been running out as they've been spending like drunken sailors for years. Because of her greed, Nonna's best friend lies torn and broken in front of me. How will I ever be able to tell her what happened?

Alejandro was two steps ahead of me. He said kindly, "Don't worry about your grandmother, Justina. She has seen much worse in her day. She can be of immense comfort to you. As will your grandmother Margaret, who has some experience in these matters. I will cast a spell to return these bodies to some semblance of order. They will be complete if drained of blood. I cannot return the blood to them, but I can clean it up so it does not stain the walls. The smell will be gone as well.

We cannot return the room to its original state because it will take too much Magic. We will leave it as a mystery to the authorities. They will term it a robbery, as has happened many times before in our history." I had to laugh. Does he think Sean is going to accept that? "I don't think you understand how diligent my husband is as a detective. No blood? What is he going to think? That it was vampires that robbed them of their blood? What, there wasn't a blood bank available? That's just nonsense, Alejandro. We have to give them a better explanation than that!" Alejandro looked thoughtful for a moment and said, "You make a good point. I will put some Satanic symbols around the room and make it look like what it was. A ritual that went bad. The best way to sell a lie is to tell some truth. It will be a mystery for them to solve." I had to laugh at that conceit, "Maybe some hipster will do a podcast about it."

I was too exhausted to argue anymore. I just went home. Thankfully, Sean was not there as he was on a case, and I was able to shower and change into comfy pajamas. I hid my clothes because they needed a good wash. A magical wash to take off the smell and the bad energy. I hope my Brownie is a good Dry Cleaner. I examined my shawl for rips or tears, and it was surprisingly intact. It totally belonged to another Witch because it should have been in tatters after tonight's antics.

Believe it or not, I went right to sleep. Without eating. Which was amazing because I had been buried up to my neck in Magic, and I wasn't starving. I was just that tired. I dreamed of battles and teacups all night long. The next morning was rough. I had my coffee and checked my phone. Oh, no! Sean had texted me at the crack of dawn. He said he had bad news about Salvina Russo. He must be at the crime scene. The shit is going to hit the fan.

I have to talk to Ginny about all of this! She needs to know! Sean was my rock, but Ginny was my safe space ever since the first grade. It's time to spill the beans. The Magic Beans. I texted her and told her to come over ASAP! We can't talk at the café or my shop because the walls have ears. Too many ears. At least I know no one is listening here. Other than miscellaneous faeries who may be on the Queen's payroll. I have to watch what I say because I am going to tell Ginny all about it. Everything. I have to tell the story without disparaging the Queen or her motives. I can lay out my fears and get her no-nonsense take on it. One Brooklyn girl to another.

Ginny showed up with two large fresh coffees and a big bag of pastries. Her worried face told me that she already knew. Everyone knew. The neighborhood grapevine must have spread the news. At least to all of the old-timers. Not the exact details, but the fact that something bad had happened at Salvina Russo's house. The police were going in and out, and the morgue wagon was parked outside. The street was closed, and the CSI van was parked at the hydrant. Everyone is an expert these days because of all the TV shows, so there had to be many theories about what was going on. I can tell Ginny what *really* happened. It's not a story I want to relive. But I have to take her fully into my confidence.

Ginny put everything down and just hugged me. I felt safe for a moment. Then she pushed me, grabbed my shoulders, and shook me. She spit out a hundred questions, "What the hell, Anna? What happened? Are you ok? Are you hurt? How did this happen? What about Salvina and Lorraine, and the other people who were at this ritual you were talking about? Are they ok? Why is the morgue van parked outside their house?" I pushed her back and led her over to a chair at the kitchen island. "I have a lot to tell you, Ginny. You need to take a breath and calm down. I will answer all your questions. I know. This is crazy." I sat next to her and handed her a coffee. I took a big gulp of the other cup and prepared to confess.

I patted Ginny's hand and said, "I have bad news. The worst. Salvina, Lorraine, and her husband are all dead. Murdered." Ginny looked at me in shock and blurted, "By who? By you? I knew you always hated Lorraine, but you could never murder anyone, right? What happened?" I shrugged my shoulders and answered, "You are never going to believe me. It was the Minotaur." Ginny looked at me as if she hadn't heard what I said. "The Minotaur? Who the hell is the Minotaur? A loan shark?" Ginny had no idea what I was talking about. I had to spell it out for her in terms she would understand. "You know how they spend money like water, and that they were going to do a fugazi ritual? They did it to steal money from the wrong people. The

Minotaur was the enforcer who came in response to them trying to rip off his boss. He ripped them. To shreds. It was horrible. You wouldn't believe it, Ginny. The blood. I am still shaking."

Ginny looked at my ashen face and hugged me again. "I bet it was terrible. Who else was there? Did your friend come with you? What about this priestess you told me about?" I replied, "Alejandro did come with me. The priestess, Chaithra, didn't make it. When we got there, the Minotaur had already killed them and turned to attack us. We managed to beat him and send him back to the Never-Never through a portal that sent him to another dimension. It was Magic. Serious Magic that I had never done before. You know about my Magic from the spells and love potions. But *real* Magic … is a whole other thing. The Minotaur is a monster. A big, half-man/half-bull kind of monster. He came from the other side." Ginny was overwhelmed and started to tear up. "What from the other side? Like my cousin Ciro from Sicily? That Other side?" We laughed together like schoolgirls. "Not quite. More like from another planet. I have a lot of explaining to do, Lucy." Ginny handed me a cannoli and said, "Eat a pastry and get started, Ethel!"

So, I did. I told her everything as Ginny's eyes glazed over with several different facial expressions. Surprise. Disbelief. Amazement, and eventually Acceptance. She is a tough cookie and took it all in at face value. She knows I would never lie to her. Especially about something this important. I wanted to explain it to her in terms she would understand. I told her about the Council and the meetings I had gone to with Grannie Meg. Even the one with Nonna. I explained that she should think of the Council as the Five Families. Each of them has its territory and its soldiers. I told Ginny about how my family was involved and how I had taken over for Nonna. I laid it all out. Everything.

Ginny laughed, "So that makes you Michael and Nonna the Godfather? Or the Godmother? I am losing track here. This is a lot all at once, babe." I smiled back at her amusement. "You think you're overwhelmed? You need to walk in my pointy boots for a while. I didn't even tell you about the eighties party with the Queen of Winter. This is going to blow your mind." I went into detail about gnomes with "Flock of Seagulls" haircuts and ogres in "Members Only" jackets. I set the whole scene in great detail, but the longer I described it, the more comical it became. Ginny laughed even harder. "Now you are just making stuff up! Get outta here with that nonsense. "It's all true, Ginny, every bit of it," but then I suddenly sobered up, freaked out, and said, "Two Weeks! The Queen gave me an ultimatum. I have two weeks to make a decision." Ginny looked at me quizzically. "Two weeks? Like the Money Pit? I thought we were doing 'The Godfather.' Can we just stick to one movie?" We both took a sip of coffee and stopped for a moment. I had to make her understand that this was all too real.

"I've been speaking with Nonna and Grannie Meg, and they are advising me, but I still don't know what to do," I said in a downcast voice. "A decision about what?" Ginny said. I was going to tell her the truth. "She wants me to go to the Never-Never to be her vassal and fight on her side. As a Witch. Which is what I am. The Brooklyn Witch." Ginny looked at me like I was crazy. "Fight? When did you become a fighter? I always had to fight for you. Like the time that beyotch tried to steal your pocketbook off the dance floor? You ain't no fighter, babe!" "I know, but this time, I don't have a choice. She made me an offer I can't refuse." Ginny burst out in laughter at that, "Oh, back to The Godfather, are we? What's the worst that can happen? She leaves a Unicorn's head in your bed and glitter all over your fancy sheets?" We both started laughing hysterically.

I loved Ginny to death. She is helping me release some of the anxiety that was crushing me. That's why I had to tell her everything. But I think this is enough for now. We both need to get to work. "I have to get back to the café, babe," Ginny said as if she could read my mind. "Just one last question. If you are Michael in 'The Godfather,' does that make me Fredo?" I laughed, "Ha, ha. No. But I do have one thing to add."

"Take the cannoli and leave the Magic."

Chapter Thirty – The Games Afoot

I went to the store and spent the day doing normal things. Selling crystals here and there and trying not to think too much about what had happened. Especially the fact that Salvina was dead. I can't believe Salvina is gone. I had wanted to be the one to tell Nonna about it, but I guess I was too much of a coward. I took solace in doing mundane chores instead of facing the music. Nonna must know about it by now. Someone had to have told her. Probably Birdie. Since Birdie wasn't busting my chops, I would bet she is with Nonna and driving her crazy. I have to go help. It's the least I can do.

I closed up the shop after I put a sign in the window. "Closed Due to Family Emergency." That will tell the neighborhood people I am dealing with Salvina's family, which is now in crisis. Everyone else will simply accept that the store is closed.

I slowly walked to Nonna's house and carefully opened the door. I felt like I was sneaking in the way I did when I was in college. Tiptoeing in at the crack of dawn, trying not to wake Nonna. Now, I have a sinking feeling as a heavy energy envelops me. The sense of grief and depression was almost palpable and got stronger as I walked toward the kitchen. I could hear Birdie chirping away in a monologue that was dedicated to her sense of self-involvement. She had managed to make Salvina's death all about her. I need to rescue Nonna.

"Hello, Nonna. Birdie. I guess you heard what happened? What do you know?" Birdie jumped up and down in her chair as if she was trying to take flight, "See. SEE! I told you so. Salvina was in danger. I felt it, and you didn't believe me! Now she's dead." Birdie burst into tears and shuddered with emotion. Nonna reached out and took her hand. "Birdie, we need to be strong. For Salvina's sake. Her family needs us. The ones that are left. I hear that her daughter Lorraine is gone as well." Nonna turned and gave me an irritated look. "Isn't that right, Speranza? What is Sean saying about all of this?" That cut right to the heart of the matter. I said, "I don't know, Nonna, because I haven't seen Sean. I do know that he is assigned to the case, and he will be working nonstop for days. By the way, Lorraine and her husband were found there as well. At least, that is the rumor. I don't know anything official." "Don't you think you should speak to your husband, Speranza?" Nonna said in a peevish voice. "We need to know what is what."

Wait a minute! Why is Nonna calling me Speranza? She never calls me by my given name. It's always Mia Bella this, Mia Bella that? She must be so angry with me. I wonder if she thinks I had something to do with this. We need to talk, but I have to get rid of Birdie first.

"Birdie, don't you have to get ready for the wake? Isn't your niece and nephew coming to town for the wake? To stay with you, because they are too cheap for a hotel? You have to get the house ready for them. Right?" Birdie stopped short in a tone of righteous indignation and said, "You're right, Speranza. They are going to put it all on me. I have so much to do. I will be working like a dog until they get here. And they won't appreciate any of it. I have to go. I will see you later, Justina." Birdie grabbed her shopping bag and ran out of the house as fast as her wobbly legs could take her.

I sat down at the table and looked over at my Nonna. It was obvious that she was angry. "I can see that you are upset, but don't be mad at me. I had nothing to do with this." Nonna looked like she was going to spit. "Nothing to do with it. You had everything to do with it! This is what comes of dealing with the Queen of Winter. Terrible deeds. Horror. Death. I warned you, and you did not listen. Instead, you followed the lead of that drunken Witch Meg and her foolish friends who play-act like a puppet show."

I was taken aback that she would have this attitude. "First of all, I didn't take the lead from anyone. I am my own person, and nobody controls me. Not even you. This happened because Lorraine tried to steal from the Queen!" Nonna made a rude gesture and scoffed at that. She said, "What do you mean she tried to steal from the Queen? How does she even know about the Queen? What nonsense!" I had to set her straight without antagonizing her further. "She had the help of a Santeria Priestess and tried another unsanctioned ritual. To steal from the Queen's treasury. Alejandro and I went to stop her, but we were too late." Nonna got even angrier at that news. She almost yelled at me and said, "Alejandro? That fool? You put your trust in him! You silly girl." Nonna kept shaking her head in disbelief. "Has everything I taught you gone in one ear and out the other? Of course, you failed. He must have planned it that way. You can never trust that strunz." Oh boy, Nonna never curses. She really, really hates Alejandro.

"He didn't do anything wrong, Nonna. He saved my life! When the Minotaur was in my face—" Nonna immediately viscerally reacted to this news. She turned very pale and shook as she said, "The Minotaur? This is very bad. The Queen had many alternatives to stop a feeble attempt at theft. Instead, she sent one of her most powerful tools. To wreak carnage in the mortal realm. She would never do that unless she wanted to make a point. I fear she wants to make this point. To you! To show you what she is capable of. To bend you to her will." I didn't understand what she was getting at. "How does she know that Salvina has anything to do with me? Why would I care?" A drunken voice came from inside the cupboard. Mello stepped out from hiding and said, "Of course she knows everything about you, toots. She has the straight poop from the horse's mouth. Well, the poop doesn't come from its mouth but from my cousin who you met at the show. We talk all the time, and he knows all about Nonna and you and everything youse guys do." "So, you're a blabbermouth, Mello? Why are you informing on us to the Queen?" I couldn't believe that he would be so disloyal. Nonna answered for him, "He is a vassal of the Queen. As am I. He must tell her everything she might want to know. As I would if I entered the Never-Never. Mello is a creature of two worlds. That would be your fate if you gave your allegiance to the Queen." Mello nodded in agreement and said, "She made an example of Salvina and the others because she knew how you would react. She might step it up and make an example of your husband, the copper. You don't want that, do you, toots?"

I was starting to get pissed off. Now they're bringing Sean into this! Nonna is not helping. She is keeping things from me instead of giving me all the information I need to protect my family. "Why, Nonna? Why aren't you helping instead of keeping things from me? The clock is ticking, and I only have a little time until my two weeks are up. I have to make a final decision, and I need to know the truth!" Nonna shifted in her seat as if she were uncomfortable with my tone. "The truth. Whose truth? Yours? The Queen's? The Minotaur's? Many truths can all exist at the same time. What you must realize is that the Queen is dangerous. Deadly, as poor Salvina and her family have shown. Sean could indeed become another target if we do not take steps to protect him. You will not get anywhere depending on the likes of Meg or Alejandro! You must listen to me and only me!"

This is just not going to fly. I know Nonna loves me, but I am a big Witch, and I need to make my own decisions. She has to realize that it is my time. I am not her little acolyte anymore. I have to stand on my own two feet. "Nonna, I can't only listen to you since you're not telling me the truth. I need to know everything so I can protect us. You. Me. Sean. Ginny—" Mello piped up from under the table, "Don't worry about the Mafia girl. The Queen will never harm the changeling's grandbaby. She has too much invested in that family."

"Changeling's grandbaby? What are you talking about, you drunken imp?" I yelled as I grabbed his smock and pulled him out from under the table, "Spill it, Buster, or I will put a spell on all the wine in the house to turn it into vinegar! TALK!" Mello looked shamefacedly at Nonna, burped, and said, "Oops, I kinda spilled the beans there, sweetheart. We have to tell her about her friend." Nonna stared at Mello and picked up her cold cup of tea. As though she was trying to decide if she was ready to finally reveal the truth that she had kept from me for so long. She looked at me and wearily replied, "Your friend Ginny is a special case. Her grandmother was a changeling. The Queen's minions, the Silvani, took a different baby. To replace the stillborn that was to have been her grandmother. You know this because you visited the room from which it came. It was Capone's bastard child." I am furious! "WHAT? The baby from the story became Ginny's grandmother? How could you keep something this important from me? Ginny is my best friend. My sister. Family. You always say family comes first, and now you do this? What else have you not told me?"

Mello piped up in a mischievous tone as if to lighten the atmosphere and change the subject, "The Queen didn't tell you that you have more than two earthly weeks to decide what to do. Time is different in the Never-Never. Two weeks there is not two weeks here. Haven't you explained this to her, Justina?" Nonna was not amused. "Be quiet, monk. It is time for you to sleep it off before you get yourself in more trouble than you can handle. Begone!" Mello disappeared right out of my grasp. I don't know if he fled on his own or if Nonna had used a spell. It doesn't matter because the damage was done.

"This is another giant secret you've kept from me. I've been so upset! I feel like I'm going to throw up right now! Don't you know I haven't been sleeping, and my anxiety is running a thousand miles an hour? Don't you care about how this has affected me? I told you at the park that I had only two weeks. Why didn't you tell me then? It would have helped!" Nonna looked exasperated and said, "You didn't need two weeks, child. You don't need two minutes to know that you have to reject the Queen's summons and stay here where you belong. It is as obvious as the nose on your face. There is no doubt about this. You can only protect the people you love by staying out of her clutches! Not by becoming her minion. It is just not necessary. This is why I kept the time difference secret from you, because I knew in my heart that you would never agree to go. I never had a doubt. I know your heart, Mia Bella." I was irate. "Don't call me that, Nonna, when you are lying to my face! I won't lie to my family. That's why I told Ginny all about what was happening. She knows it all. Now I have to go back to her and reveal this giant secret. About her grandmother and Al Capone, of all people!" Nonna grabbed my hand and squeezed very hard, "Don't you dare tell her! She will not be able to handle the truth. Once she knows, the Silvani will contact her. They have been her protectors all these years. Of Ginny and her family. The Silvani watch and hear everything she does. They will bring anything you tell her to the Queen. You cannot confide in her." I tore my hand out of her grasp and said, "I don't care about the Silvani. They weren't very nice to me, but many of the fay seem not to care for me very much. Is that because of you, Nonna? Do you have more secrets you might need to share?"

Nonna sat back and showed all of her years. The emotions and feelings we had stirred up in this argument had exhausted her. I was all out of sympathy. I hate liars. I have to tell Ginny. Maybe even Sean. I need people whom I can count on. I could talk to Grannie Meg, too. I had to choose up my team like Ginny and I used to do in the schoolyard. No more fun and games.

"I have to go, Nonna. We both have a lot to think about. The next time we talk, I hope you will tell me the truth. All of the truth. Don't leave anything out to protect me. Those days are over. I will see you tomorrow after we both calm down. I need to go find my husband."

Sean would always quote Sherlock Holmes when he was investigating a tough case. He would say, "The games afoot, Watson!" Well, the game has started.

We are playing for keeps now.

Chapter Thirty-One – Rumor Has It

I left Nonna's house and walked back home. I thought about going to see Ginny at her café, but we couldn't speak freely. This new information about her grandmother was too much of a bomb to drop without some thought. I need to speak with Sean.

When I got home, I texted Sean and asked if he wanted to come for a late lunch. He replied that it sounded great and needed to shower anyway since he hadn't been home for twenty-four hours. So, I had to rustle up some lunch. I couldn't ask him to cook, so it was pizza all the way. I will call for his favorite pizza and some of those deep-fried calzones from the place on Columbia Street. That will make him happy, and maybe I can finesse what I have to tell him.

I want to tell him everything, but I don't think he can deal with it. The Queen. The Never-Never. The Minotaur? Can you imagine that conversation? Imagine telling him that a monster tried to kill me. That would be a deal breaker for him. I want to give him credit. He loves me with all of his heart and would never try to control me except when my life is in danger. Then he might try to put his foot down. He has seen too much as a cop to take a blasé attitude about this level of violence. I don't want to fight with him because I want my house to be a safe space.

Strangely enough, I am in the same spot that Nonna was when she withheld information from me. Funny how things come full circle. I always say I need to speak with Sean, but I never do. It's definitely a quandary, but it gives me some empathy for Nonna's choices. Still, I have to present enough of the truth to satisfy him and hold back as much as I can so he doesn't lose it.

Sean came in about half an hour later. "Hey Babe, I'm going to wash up. Be down in a few minutes," Sean said without really looking at me. That was weird. Not even a kiss hello? Something's up; I know it. I heard the shower running, and he came down a few minutes later in a new suit. He broke a record showering, but he isn't Superman, so he was still toweling his hair as he came into the kitchen.

"Speranza, we need to talk," Sean said in a very serious tone. Uh oh! When he calls me by my given name,

I know he's upset! "I have been working the case, and somehow, you are right in the middle of it." I tried to look all innocent and said, "Who, me? I have nothing to do with it. What do you mean?" Sean turned to me angrily and said, "You are in the middle of CCTV footage from Clinton Street, a block from Salvina's house." He said as he held his hands apart and then slapped them together. "Right at the time they died. Midnight! What the hell were you doing there? At midnight? With some guy who looks like the dude from Fantasy Island? Don't lie to me!" He clasped his hands together as if he were praying. He shook them at me in that classic Italian gesture. "Please, I beg of you. Tell me the whole truth, and don't leave anything out." This is a little over the top. I had to reply in kind, "Lie to you? Why would I lie to you? I always tell you the truth!" Sean folded his arms and stared at me like I was a perp. I'm not going to take that. Not now. Not from my husband.

"The guy's name is Alejandro. He is a magical practitioner just like me. He is part of a group that Grannie Meg introduced me to. Remember? I told you I met Grannie Meg's friends. He is one of them, and he is in charge of Sunset Park just like I am in charge of Carroll Gardens," I said in a snippy voice to put him off balance. I have to use at least part of the truth if I am going to explain this. Sean wasn't impressed. "Ok, that's fine, but why are you meeting at midnight? Down the street from three … dead … bodies? Riddle me that, Batman," Sean said as he had to throw in some of the TV trivia that he loved so much. I smiled. Thank God he's joking with me.

"Look, Speranza, I know you didn't do anything wrong. But I am not the only one you have to convince. I need to talk to this guy, and you both need to get your stories straight. Otherwise, you are both going to be put in a room while some cop sweats you for twenty-four hours straight to break you down, and it won't be me. So, when can I talk to him? The sooner, the better." I took out my phone and said, "I don't know, but I will text him right now and tell him to come here." Alejandro replied immediately as if he were waiting for me to contact him. "He says he will be right over." The bell rang. That was quick! Did he use Magic? I opened the door. It was the pizza. We both looked at each other and cracked up. Great minds think alike. Maybe we can get on the same page.

That calmed Sean right down. The Magic of Pizza and Calzones always works. We laughed and talked about nonsense like the old Adam West Batman show that we both watched as kids when we came home from grammar school. Sean was on his second calzone when the bell rang a second time. It was Alejandro. Maybe he did use Magic to get here so fast.

I introduced them, "Sean, this is my friend Alejandro. Alejandro, this is my husband, Sean. He has some questions for us about why we were on Clinton Street late last night." Alejandro looked at Sean and said, "Ah. The CCTV, I presume?" Sean smiled back at him thinly as if he was still suspicious and replied, "Yes. That and a bunch of Ring cameras that we were able to access.

Why were you both there at that hour?" Alejandro looked back at me and said, "You did not tell him, Speranza?" "No, I thought we could tell our story together." I turned to Sean and said, "We were on our way to stop an unsanctioned ritual. It was to be performed by one of Alejandro's students who was trespassing on my patch. We were going to stop it together, but we were too late." Sean was no dummy. He stared at me and said, "A ritual? Don't tell me it was at Salvina's house?" Alejandro suddenly waved his hands about, and Sean froze in place.

I yelled, "What did you do to my husband, Warlock? Set him free right now!" I turned my palms toward the Cuban and prepared to send a spell his way to stop him from attacking Sean. "Hold Speranza! I did not harm him. I just froze him for a moment so we can discuss what we are going to say. I did not realize how intimately he would be involved. I think we need a better cover story. Your husband will not accept random Satanists if he knows you are involved. We need to change our plans. Carbon Monoxide." I was totally confused and said, "What? Are you going all climate change on me? You sniffing Carbon Monoxide, or are you sniffing glue? Because that's the only way you would come up with something like that!" Alejandro smiled at me with an evil grin and laughingly said, "No, I picked the wrong week to stop sniffing glue." I was startled into a laugh, "Another 'Airplane' fan I see. Sean would have appreciated that joke. Now wake him up. Right NOW!"

Alejandro put out his hand as if to tell me to stop. "Slow down, Speranza. I didn't do anything that is irreparable or would harm your husband. Give me a minute to explain how we can make this work." I stomped my foot in fury and said, "You have ONE minute, and then I want my husband back," as I gestured with my index finger. I am livid that he would dare to touch Sean. I am not going to deal with an arrogant misogynist Warlock who thinks he can treat me as less than. I have to stand up for myself and Sean. I started to furiously clap one hand into the other and demanded, "Clocks ticking, so what's this big idea of yours?"

Alejandro tried to seem consolatory. "I think I have a solution. I can fix the boiler to show a carbon monoxide leak. People die from that all the time. Especially in an older brownstone where an elderly lady may not keep it up to standard. It is a plausible answer." I thought about it for a moment and then nodded in agreement. "Yeah. Maybe they were too cheap to install carbon monoxide detectors. That tracks. But what are we going to do about the bodies? They didn't ingest any gas, and they didn't have any blood. How do we fix that?" "With a spell. A mass hallucination spell," Alejandro said. "The Council has done this before. It is why we exist. We need three powerful witches. You. Me. Your Grandmother, Meg. The power of three. We can wipe everyone's mind, and they will accept this explanation."

"Fine. Let's do that. Now let Sean go, and we will call Meg." Alejandro looked quizzically at me and said, "I will do so. We agree." He waved his hand in an arcane motion, and Sean woke up. "Hey, nice to meet you, pal. I have to go back to work. See ya, babe." He kissed me goodbye and left without looking back. I angrily turned to the warlock and snarled, "What … did … you … do, Alejandro?" He said in an almost meek voice, "I wiped his memory. He will be confused until we do our spell. It is just for a few hours, but that is the best I can do." I was pissed. I know what happens when you wipe someone's mind. I know I sound like a hypocrite since I just did it to Alice, but I don't care. This is Sean. My husband. I don't want someone else to root around in his brain. He might alter it in a way that we can't predict. "I need to talk to Grannie Meg. I am not comfortable with this." The bell rang one more time. "Now what?" I opened the door. It was my grandmother.

"Don't leave me here in the vestibule, lassie. Let an old woman rest her weary bones," Grannie Meg said as she bustled into my house. She nodded at Alejandro and sat down. "How did you know that we needed you, Grannie?" I asked. Alejandro piped up, "I contacted her. I had a suspicion that we might need her help." He was not the only one with a bunch of suspicions. I am liking this less and less. It seems all too needlessly complicated.

I turned to Grannie Meg and said, "Do you know what's going on? This guy just wiped Sean's mind without telling me or asking for permission! Is that what you do at The Council? Because if it is, I don't want any part of it. You don't attack the mind of someone I love without consequences." Grannie Meg glanced at Alejandro, looked back at me almost with pity, and said, "Grow up, Speranza. Magic always has its price. Sometimes, those closest to us have to pay. Sean will be fine. I imagine we will have to wipe the minds of a great many people before this is all over. You are going to help. I repeat. Grow up. It is time to put away childish things." Now, I'm furious at Grannie Meg! I'm embarrassed that she was lecturing me in front of Alejandro. It's a betrayal. "I thought we should never go against the family? Or is that just an Italian thing? Why are you taking his side?" Alejandro spoke up, "There are no sides here. There is only the need to cover up this atrocity that came about because of Magic. The "Normals" must never know what happened. This is the task of our Council. I am sure you will agree, Margaret."

Grannie Meg leaned forward and said, "He's right, darling girl. We have to cover this up. The only question is, what is the best way to do it? I know you are worried about Sean. His job is to find out what happened, but we cannot risk that. You cannot risk that. We will have to use one of our standard ploys." Alejandro said, "The carbon monoxide tale. It is an old one, but reliable. We need to do a memory spell to wipe out the minds of those involved in the investigation." I can't believe that they think they can cover this up! I replied in a disapproving tone, "Everyone in the neighborhood knows about this. Are you going to wipe all of their minds? I don't see how we can do that." "Not quite, lassie," Grannie Meg replied. "We need not wipe everyone. The cops and the morgue people, to be sure. Everything else will be craic. Gossip. Rumors. We can live with that."

"We must do the spell now before the knowledge spreads of what truly happened," Alejandro said as he motioned in Grannie Meg's direction. "Where can we do this ritual?" "This is as good a place as any. We do not have to return to the scene for it to work. Let's move to the living room," Grannie Meg said as she laboriously got out of her chair and moved to the next room. Alejandro pushed the coffee table back to make room, and we gathered in a circle. We joined hands, and Grannie Meg intoned a spell. She called on the memories of all the police, CSI, and Medical Examiners to perceive that the cause of death was asphyxiation via carbon dioxide poisoning. Since it was early in the process, this would lead the medical examiner to alter her autopsy report. Anyone examining these deaths would be led to the same conclusion. Then, Alejandro cast a spell to provide the physical evidence of a faulty boiler. When he finished, we all stepped back and sorted out a chair. Even though I did not speak, the power of three called on all of our combined strength and power. It was exhausting, and now I am starving.

"So that's it? We're done? This all covered up, now? What about Sean? Am I the only one concerned about him? How does this spell affect *him*?" Grannie Meg answered, "He's fine, darling. He will be affected the same way as the rest. He will believe that it was an accident and will stop asking questions. Let it be a normal closure." Alejandro chimed in and said, "You should be relieved. You no longer have to explain yourself to this mortal." "Mortal? What are you talking about? That's no mortal, that's my husband, and he's more important to me than anyone in the Never-Never. Including the Queen!" I said as he began to infuriate me again. I'm beginning to see why Nonna hates him.

"I can see that you are upset, Speranza. I will leave you now, and we can continue with the full Council." With that last word, Alejandro simply left. Grannie Meg stood up and said, "I am disappointed that you are so childish. You need to work with the Council if you want to survive. Great powers are at war, and you need all the help you can get. I know that you want to protect Sean, but you must put your differences with Alejandro aside for the greater good. Otherwise, it will end in disaster." With a final, imperious sniff, Grannie Meg stalked out of my house.

I am finally alone. Except for my hunger pangs. I'm done with the pizza. I went to the pantry and looked for something sweet.

It's me and Lil' Debbie until Sean comes home.

Chapter Thirty-two – Alone Again, Naturally

This past week has been horrible. I've been fighting with Nonna, which I have never done before. When I say fighting, I mean that we are not speaking. Normally, I would talk to her every day. Today is Salvina's funeral, and it will be the first time I will be in Nonna's company since our fight. I need to put my differences with Nonna aside for today.

I drove with Sean to the funeral parlor, where people met up before traveling to Green-Wood Cemetery in Sunset Park, where Salvina and her daughter will be buried. A brief prayer was said inside before everyone got in their cars for the funeral procession. The funeral director, Vinny Martucci, gave every driver a plaque for their windshield that said "Funeral," along with directions to the plot in the cemetery. Vinny was a maniac when he did a funeral. I remember one time he got out of his limo and stood in front of oncoming traffic on the Belt Parkway. He waved his arms like he was landing an airplane to make traffic yield to keep the procession together. So, we had to keep up with the group to avoid an incident.

Sean had borrowed a big SUV to take us to the cemetery. We had Ginny, Birdie, and Nonna in the car with us. It was very quiet as I softly told Sean where to go based on the directions. Of course, Birdie could not keep quiet for the whole trip. She started her histrionics about how she had lost her best friend and was now all alone. She wanted to make it all about her, as usual. Finally, Nonna spoke, "Enough, Birdie. I am still here. You are not alone. Statazit!" Birdie was cowed for a moment but continued to mutter under her breath. I decided to take the initiative with Nonna to sort this out.

"Nonna, Birdie is feeling sad. I know you are, too. You three have been friends for many, many years, and I know this accident is devastating. We need to help each other get through this as best we can," I said as I faced forward so as not to look Nonna in the face. "Accident, humph." Nonna noisily cleared her throat in a tone that meant she did not believe me. "Birdie, it doesn't matter what happened. Salvina is gone, and we must carry on the best we can," Nonna said as she patted Birdie's lace-gloved hand to reassure her. Birdie was not so easy to comfort. She said, "I know, Justina, it is terrible. I can't believe she is gone. I don't understand why she didn't have one of those detectors. I have one on every floor. I thought it was a law?" Sean piped up from the driver's seat, "That's only for multi-family houses, Birdie. Salvina had a one-family, so she didn't have to put in anything. Not even smoke detectors." Ginny snorted in disbelief, "You know they're just too cheap. Not to speak ill of the dead, but they should have spent the money on that instead of cruises and mink coats." I had to rein in her sarcasm. "Be nice, Ginny. Now is not the time." I needed to change the subject.

"Did you change your hair, Ginny? What did you do differently today?" I asked as I glanced back at her through the rear-view mirror. I wonder if she has Al Capone's hair? No, that can't be, she would be bald. I chuckled to myself and had to cover it with a cough as if I suddenly had something stuck in my throat. "Maybe she washed it," Sean said with an evil grin. He always made jokes at funerals. "Very funny, coppa; at least I have a full head of hair," Ginny answered back. "You are getting a little thin up there, buster. I just changed the part of my hair to the other side, Anna. No big deal. Do you like it?" We bickered back and forth until we got to the entrance of the cemetery. I still did not address the fact that Nonna lied. That Sean's mind might be scrambled. That Ginny is a Mafia heiress. Squirrel! My mind was going a mile a minute, and I was getting more and more anxious. Let's go to a funeral now! Fun!

Green-Wood Cemetery is huge! It has been around since 1838, and you would think it would be full by now.

Salvina had a family plot where there was room for her and her daughter. I don't know what they did with the daughter's husband, and I didn't care. He was to blame for this whole fiasco with his meddling and bringing in a Santeria Priestess to rob the Queen. We followed the funeral cortege to the back of the cemetery near Section 20, off Lake Avenue, down Cedar Path near Sylvan Pond. The line of cars stopped, and we all got out and walked toward the gravesite. We walked uphill on wet cobblestones that could break your ankle if you were wearing heels. That's why I always wear flats at funerals, so I don't do a "Tumbelina" down the hill. I get so nervous at funerals that I once almost fell into a coffin. I need to be strong for Nonna, even though she's mad at me. There was a line of chairs set up for the family by the graves. They were surrounded by stand-up wreaths and big flower arrangements that Vinny had brought from the funeral home. There was already a crowd of mourners grouped around the gravesite. There was also a big surprise.

Grannie Meg, Alejandro, and the rest of the Council were standing in the back. I had no idea that they would be here. I thought Alejandro might come, but the others surprised me. I wonder why they are here. I helped Nonna and Birdie into their seats alongside Salvina's remaining family. Her two other daughters were seated with their husbands standing behind them. The Priest from Sacred Hearts started the final service to intern the bodies, and there was the sound of quiet tears from many in the crowd. When he was finished, the mourners took flowers and laid them on the coffins as they filed out of the ceremony. Vinny passed out invitations to the mourners with directions to the restaurant on Court Street. There is always food after a funeral. Italian food. Why am I so hungry? Is there Magic here?

I turned to Ginny and Sean and said, "Sean, do you think you and Ginny can take Nonna and Birdie to the restaurant? I need to speak with Grannie Meg and her friends. I will catch a ride back with her." I would rather go with Sean since I was starving, but I needed to hang back and speak with the Council Members. Why are they here? Did any of them even know Salvina?

Sean was incredulous that Grannie Meg was here. Sean said, "Fine. How did Grannie Meg know Salvina? Were they friends?" I answered quickly to avoid arousing his suspicions, "They had known each other for over fifty years. It's more of a respect thing." Sean looked at me quizzically and asked, "Who are those other people? That guy seems familiar to me somehow. Do I know him?" Great! This is evidence that Sean has lost his memory! What else will he forget? I want to punch that Alejandro in the face right now! "Those are Grannie Meg's friends. I don't know why they're here. They won't be coming back to the after-party." "Don't call it that, Anna," Ginny laughed. "That's right, babe, it is not going to be a party, that's for sure," Sean chuckled in turn. "I will see you there. Don't dawdle." With that, they helped Nonna and

Birdie into the car and drove away. I went to speak with the Council.

I walked up to the black-clad group of Witches and Warlocks. They were in civilian clothes and not their magical attire. I guess they must go "incognito" when they are out in the world. "Why are you all here? I expected Grannie Meg, but not the rest of you." Runa replied in her clipped cadence, "We came to see. To see if there were any further disruptions." "Oh, you are my Magical Security Detail?" I smirked at the ridiculousness of that claim. Grannie Meg snapped in a furious tone, "Wipe that smirk off of your face, lassie. This is not something to play at. This is a serious matter, and you need to drop your attitude." I saw Alejandro's fleeting smile as if he was entertained by my embarrassment. Grannie Meg is at it again. Belittling me as if I were a child. I need to nip this in the bud right now.

Vesna spoke up in her sonorous accent to stop my angry reply, "It is as they say … better safe than sorry. No?" I will take this up with Grannie Meg when we are alone. Just because she embarrassed me doesn't mean that I have to embarrass her. I can do that later. Privately. "We came here to make sure there were no further incursions by the vassals of the Queen," Grannie Meg said in a snippy tone as if she was angry at having to justify herself. "Thankfully, that did not happen, so we could go on our way." The others had been strangely quiet as if they didn't want to be involved in a familial dispute. As the others chatted, Vesna grabbed my elbow and said, "Can I speak to you privately for one moment?" She led me a few feet away from the group.

"I want to ask you something. Do you feel … the Magic?" Vesna asked. That's why I'm so hungry! I replied in a relieved tone, "Yes! I do! I thought it was just me. There is definitely Magic here. Could it be from restless spirits that might congregate in a cemetery?" Vesna looked at me as if I were crazy. "This is not a movie, Speranza. This is the real thing. There is an artifact of immense power here. I need to explain to you what it is and how it relates to you and your mission," Vesna said in what seemed to be a slightly condescending tone. Or it could just be her accent. I'm never sure. At least I can hear her as she modulated her tone to take into account my hearing difficulties. The eighties strike again.

"What artifacts are you talking about? Is this one of the ones we discussed when The Council met?" Vesna leaned into me and whispered in my ear so only I could hear, "All will be revealed. Tonight. Very late. A passerby cannot witness what we must do next." All the hairs on my neck stood up. In her Dracula daughter's voice, she made me think that she wanted to bite my neck. I can hear her say, "I vant … to suck … your blood." Stop it, Speranza! Get serious. "I guess I can do that. Sean will probably be busy tonight since he took time off for the funeral. How about we meet back here at midnight? That seems traditional for this Magical stuff." Vesna said, "It is good. We will meet then." As we turned back to the group, I noticed that Alejandro was staring at us with his head cocked at an angle. As if he were listening to our conversation. Chills again. I don't trust this, Warlock. Why is he still staring at us? He must have an inkling that I am furious at his abuse of my husband. I wanted to give him a piece of my mind, but this wasn't the time nor the place. His time will come.

Grannie Meg and I went to the car and turned to make our goodbyes. They had all disappeared in the blink of an eye. Was that Magic or just an Irish goodbye? We sat in an uncomfortable silence as we drove to the restaurant. I thought about telling Grannie Meg about the conversation with Vesna, but I decided to keep it under my hat. She didn't ask, and I am curious as to why. Her Irish pride is keeping her from speaking to me. I think I need to keep my cards close to the vest. No Grannie Meg. No Nonna. I need to do this on my own.

Alone again, naturally.

Chapter Thirty-Three – It's All Greek to Me

It was a dark and stormy night … no, wait a minute! This isn't the start of a cheesy novel. It's my real life. I'm standing outside the main entrance of Green-Wood Cemetery. At Midnight! Dressed all in black. Not to look cool. It's just so no one can see us sneaking around the tombstones. Or at least I think we are going to be sneaking around, because why else would we be meeting at midnight? Me and my big ideas.

Vesna was nowhere to be found. Then she's suddenly next to me. Magic! It never fails to startle me. "So, here we are, Vesna. What's next? I'll tell you one thing: I am not climbing this fence. I haven't done it since High School, and I'm not going to start now." Vesna said, "Do not fret. Follow me." We didn't attempt to use the entrance at the front gate. It was locked up tight, and there appeared to be a guard station. Vesna led me around the corner, and we walked to McDonald Avenue until we were somewhere in the middle of that side of the cemetery. It was a tree-lined portion of the street just past the bus stop that was bathed in shadows. A huge tree blocked anyone from the buildings on the other side of the street from seeing what we were doing. There was a hole in the iron fence. Or more accurately, a missing bar in the decorative wrought iron that we can squeeze through sideways. Lately, it seems I am always going sideways. I can't face any problems head-on. This is not a good omen.

As I squeezed through the tight space, Vesna pushed aside the prickly hedge that lined the fence. It snapped back and hit me in the face. Ouch! Vesna was a tiny slip of a thing and had easily passed inside. I had to wiggle my curves through a tight spot. I don't want to get stuck! Imagine that phone call. I could see having to get Sean to free me from the gates of a cemetery. Another fine mess I got myself into. Now Push! Push, push, through the bush! Why is my life always a Disco song?

I finally wiggled my way in and said, "Vesna, can you take it easy? You already hit me with a thorn bush. I want to get through this in one piece. Why didn't we use Magic to get inside?" Vesna replied, "Because Magic might alert certain forces that we are here. We don't want that." "Who are we hiding from?" I asked. "Everyone," she replied as we walked deeper into the cemetery. "Especially the guard booth. We need to stay out of his line of sight." We had slipped past the foliage that lined the cemetery and quickly ran into a copse of trees along Border Avenue. We walked behind the trees to avoid alerting the guard. We ran across the lawn, dodging tombstones until we reached a solitary mausoleum on Gladiodious Path. We hid in the shadows to catch our breath. We planned our next move like a S.W.A.T. team before we headed out down Chrysanthemum Path. It was important to tread carefully as we were walking on graves and could easily trip over a headstone. There was a grouping of Weeping Willows that gave us cover until we reached the circle of mausoleums. It was almost a nest. I don't know what you call a grouping of mausoleums. A herd? A school? I hope it's not a murder! Like with crows. We moved from one to another. I felt like the Pink Panther as we crept from one ornate structure to the next. I even walked on tippytoes, and I could almost hear that music in my head. I have to entertain myself somehow. Geez, Louise, I'm in a freakin' cemetery after all.

We moved slowly in the echoing darkness. Moonlight glinted off the polished marble headstones and threw off a faint, eerie light. I heard sounds in the background. At first, I thought it was my tinnitus, but that wasn't it. It wasn't music, but it sounded like a sad song. A song sung in grief and despair. Very appropriate background music for a cemetery. Cue the cemetery elevator music! It was almost as if tortured souls were moaning in unison. I was scared. Vesna looked at me and said, "Speranza, you are hurting me. You are squeezing my arm much too hard." I didn't even realize that I had a hold of her matchstick arm. I must be squeezing her arm like a blood pressure cuff! "Sorry. This is much too creepy for me. I'm trying to be brave, but all I can think of is lions, tigers, and bears. When are we going to see The Wizard?" Vesna let out a stifled laugh and said, "Let us hope we do not come upon any Wizards this night."

There are numerous mausoleums in Green-Wood Cemetery. They included everyone from old-timey Governor De Witt Clinton to Charlie Ebbets, who owned the old Brooklyn Dodger Stadium. This nest seemed to be an older section and was even scarier than those we had already passed. We came to a small section that contained many ornate mausoleums that were quite well-maintained. Eventually, we stopped in front of the final resting place of Charles Feltman, the creator of the hot dog! Hot dogs here! Several statues adorned this tomb, including a statue of Saint Michael the Archangel. Strangely enough, he was holding a sword, not a hot dog.

We took a few steps back to take in the view. Vesna looked up at the roof of the ornately decorated marble tomb. I looked at it in turn, as my eyes focused higher and higher. I tried to take in all of this immense edifice. I craned my neck back to the top of my shoulders. This mausoleum was huge. I hurt my neck trying to see what she was staring at so intently. She pointed to the statue of Saint Michael at the top of the cupola. He was holding a sword. Vesna spoke urgently in a tone of reverence, "It is here, Speranza. What the Queen is searching for!" She turned to look at me and said, "This may very well be why she summoned you to her side." I didn't understand. "She is looking for a tomb? Or a statue? What do you mean, Vesna?" Vesna looked very serious as she said, "She is searching for the 'Sword.' That Sword!" She shook her finger and pointed directly at the heroic statue of the Knight-Militant Saint Michael the Archangel. I looked at Vesna in horror and yelped, "If I wasn't going to climb a fence, I am surely not scaling this building." Vesna looked back at me with a sly smile and said, "Don't call me Shirley!" I was flabbergasted, "I must be rubbing off on you. Look at you pulling a line from 'Airplane.' I'm impressed!" Vesna smiled again and said, "That is how I learned English. Watching your American television."

"What's the big deal with the Sword, Vesna? It's part of a statue. I don't get it." I was truly confused. "We came all this way to stare at a statue? What gives?" "All is not as it seems," Vesna explained, "the Sword is hidden and cloaked behind a veil of Magic. I am the guardian of the Sword. It has been the task of my family for many generations. The Sword is a talisman of Magic. It cannot be wielded by just anyone who tries to use it. Only the truly worthy and pure of heart can access the Magic that it contains. It is an instrument of pure Magic. You are destined to be its Master." Vesna looked at me with a sense of anticipation, as if I were going to solve all of the problems of the world. "Me? You gotta be kidding me! Me! I don't know from swords. I hate sharp objects; they scare me!" She gave me another of her patented smiles and took my hand. She said, "This is your fate, my dear Brooklyn Witch. You have been chosen, and you must take up the burden of the 'Sword.'"

I broke away from her and put my hands on my thighs as I bent forward to take in a few deep breaths. This was all spinning out of control. Vesna brought me here under false pretenses. Is she like Alejandro, trying to manipulate me for her own purposes? I came here to find out about the Magic in this cemetery. It was simple curiosity. I certainly did not come here to become the guardian of an immensely powerful Magical artifact.

"Hold on a minute! I have a million questions, Vesna! First of all, how do we access the Sword without using Magic? You said we can't use Magic because we might alert the bad guys. Where did it come from? Why is your family involved? Why me? Tell me everything." My heart was racing, and I was becoming more and more anxious. Like I said, I … hate … knives! Let alone a Magical Sword! I don't like sharp objects at all. I won't go near a Hibachi Grill even though it's Ginny's favorite. Sean freaks me out when he does his fancy fast-chopping routine. I pull out the first-aid kit and wait for disaster to strike. If I have to swing this Sword, I'm going to need a lot of Band-Aids.

"I can give you a little history, Speranza. This is the Sword of Peleus. The Sword of Victory. Peleus was the father of Achilles, the immortal Greek Hero. The Greek Gods granted Peleus the Sword. It was magically ensorcelled to become the 'Sword of Victory.' Anyone with a pure heart who wields it in battle cannot be defeated. Many great heroes have held the Sword for a time. Agrippa, Belisarius, Roland, Cromwell, and Wellington have all been custodians of the Sword at one time or another. The last recipient was your General Grant, who used the 'Power of the Sword' to free the slaves. It was a noble purpose, and Grant could wield it in good conscience. But later, when he began the decimation of the native peoples, he lost his purity of purpose, and the Sword slipped from his grasp. My family brought it here to be concealed until a new worthy champion is revealed. You … are … that … Champion."

"Why your family, Vesna? You are Croatian, not Greek. I don't get it." Vesna looked away as if searching for words, "It was at the time of Belisarius … the great general of the Eastern Roman Empire. He was born in the Balkans. When he campaigned in Croatia, my ancestors served him. He revealed the secret of the Sword and swore them to be its Guardian. My family has served the Sword ever since." I am even more confused, "Wait a minute. I don't get it. If your family has been guarding this Sword since forever, why do you have such a thick accent? It's like you just got off the boat. If what you say is true, the Sword has been here for decades. What gives?" Vesna replied, "This task is one for my clan. When you are appointed the Guardian, you come here from the old country. I myself have been here for many years." "How long?" She looked directly into my eyes, "I have been here for one hundred and five years. You must realize. I am a Witch. Just like you." Holy AARP, Batman!

This brings up so much to rattle my brain. Will I live that long, too? What about Sean? Do I need to do a spell to make him live as long as me? Squirrel! One thing at a time. Now, back to our regularly scheduled cemetery visit.

"What are we doing here, Vesna? Thanks for telling me about the Sword and all, but so what?" I wanted to move this along. I am standing in the dark. I'm cold and I am starving. Magic! Vesna said, "I will show you." She raised her arms toward the statue and spoke in Croatian in a loud voice, "Podi—Sa—Mnom—Celik—Englesko—Hrvatski—Rjecnik!" The entire tomb started to shake and rattle. There was a flash of light that made me shield my eyes. A gleaming Sword had appeared in Vesna's hand. It seemed to fit her hand as if it were born to be there. The Sword was ornamented with jewels and inscribed with arcane writing. I did not recognize the language, but it gave off an unearthly energy. Shit just got real.

Vesna held the Sword in her outstretched hand. "Take it, Speranza. As Guardian of the Undying Sword of Victory, I hereby bequeath its powers to your stewardship." I was flummoxed at this ceremony. Did she mean that I was the new Guardian of the Sword? Or was I to be the Hero who wielded the Sword? Am I supposed to kneel or something? Is it like a knighting by the Queen? Should I at least curtsy? Suddenly, a loud voice commanded our attention. "Stop, Witch! The Sword is mine!" With that, Alejandro stepped out of the shadows. "I am Alejandro—Lopez—Garcia, prepare to die!"

Did he really quote the "Princess Bride?" Or did I just want him to say that? Because that would be cool. Unless he means it. That would be uncool.

I don't want to be in this movie.

Chapter Thirty-Four – Love is a Battlefield

Why is Alejandro here, and why is he demanding the Sword? How did he get here? Did he follow us? Did he use Magic to spy on our conversation? Why is he being so nasty? I thought he was my friend. We fought the Minotaur together for crying out loud. We had a bond, or at least I thought we did.

Vesna left the Sword in my hands and pushed me behind her. She spun around, raised her arms in a protective stance, and said, "Leave us, Warlock! There is nothing for you here. The Sword is NOT for you. It requires a pure heart. Something we know you do NOT possess!" Alejandro stared daggers at Vesna as if his mere look could kill. The elegant Warlock said, "Be silent, peasant. I need not deal with you. DIE!" He raised his arms in turn and threw a burst of magical energy at the Croatian Witch. It was a powerful spell, but Vesna was equal to the task. She put a protective shield in front of us to deflect this unwarranted attack. I held the Sword in a white-knuckled death grip. I don't know what to do. Do I use the Sword to attack Alejandro? I never took sword-fighting lessons. I only ever saw it on TV. I hope this doesn't end up like "Highlander." There has to be more than one!

Vesna and Alejandro were locked in a battle of wills. They threw Magical energy at each other. Offense and defense alternated as they struggled in silence. Or at least quietly as they muttered Magical incantations under their breath. I was at a loss. What do I do? Do I attack Alejandro? With the Sword? I didn't want to stab someone who had been my friend. But I certainly couldn't let him harm Vesna. I looked around for a less lethal weapon. Then I noticed the two statues in front of the Tomb. I know what to do! Hummels attack! I mean Statues attack! I can use the same spell that I used to fight the Minotaur to protect Vesna and not harm Alejandro. I didn't kill the Minotaur, and I don't want to kill Alejandro. I don't want to hurt anyone!

I sent out my spell to animate the statues on the tombs surrounding us. Several Angels woke up and descended on the battle scene. They did not attack anyone; they were Angels after all. They moved to interpose their stone forms between the two combatants, who were startled at their sudden appearance. Vesna took a step back and tried to catch her breath. Alejandro turned to look at me and said, "You cannot trick me with one of my own spells, foolish girl. Watch and learn!" Alejandro started to chant in Spanish in an undertone that I could not quite hear. It didn't matter that my eighties-damaged hearing had struck again because I don't speak Spanish. There was movement in the darkness, and I saw statues walking toward us like zombies in some cheap horror movie. Nope. I don't do zombies.

There were many different types of statuary represented in this motley crew. There were life-sized Civil War-era soldiers, dogs, cats, a Sphinx, and even a bear. I thought I saw Jesus, Mary, and Joseph! This wasn't going to work. We need to get out of here.

I grabbed Vesna, who had not fully recovered from her struggle with the mighty Cuban Warlock. I took her arm and started pulling her deeper into the Cemetery. It was huge, almost as big as Prospect Park. Maybe we can find somewhere to hide. Or at least put some distance between us. I turned to look back to see if my Angels had delayed the attack. They had not. The Angels who had our backs have been decimated. Their wings were torn off. Their heads were removed. The ravening horde led by Alejandro is following us. They were not moving in any fluid motion, as they herked and jerked along behind him. I need to find a way to protect us as we flee from them.

We moved as fast as we could, as Vesna was still disoriented and did not give me any guidance as to what we should do. Whenever we passed a statue that might serve to help us, I sent out a quick spell to animate them and have them join our ragged procession. Gargoyles, cherubs, eagles, owls, and even a huge kissy face joined our own motley crew. The problem was that Alejandro's army was catching up to us. It was growing in size as every statue that did not join us was joining him and chasing us with bad intent.

A stone gargoyle flew through the air with a shriek and landed in front of us. It immediately attacked a cherub from our gang and ripped off one of his arms. Three other cherubs attacked him in turn and beat him down with the bows and arrows that they held in their hands. They smacked him so vigorously that he fled back to Alejandro's gang. Two stone hounds jumped into our group and tried to savage one of the Angels, but a huge eagle beat its wings over them and forced them to retreat. It seemed that my statues were not as violent as Alejandro's. I didn't understand that because the Hummels that I had animated at Salvina's house were savages. They stabbed and used whatever they were holding to physically hurt the Minotaur. What was making these statues so wimpy?

"Come on, guys, hit them like you mean it," I said out loud. That was stupid, my spell is what controls them, not anything I say. Then Vesna murmured, "It is not in your nature to create such murderous monsters,

Speranza. You operate out of love. Not hate. It is Alejandro's nature to create murderous beings full of hate and violence. You can only reply with love. Love always conquers hate … eventually." I was incredulous at her advice and said, "We might not have time for that, Vesna. Alejandro seems very determined to do us harm. Now. Not eventually. You got anything that will help us now?" Vesna looked at me with a little smile and said, "Trust in your love, Speranza. It is your secret weapon. Your superpower. Don't stoop to his level. We need to hurry."

We had retreated to the "Field of Graves" bordering Battle Hill. Row upon row of tombstones that might serve our purposes. I conjured a spell to rip the stones out of the ground and send them flying toward Alejandro and his minions. They hit one or two of them in passing and served as a barrier piled up in front of them to block their passage. I aimed for their legs to knock them down and then piled more on top of them to stop their advance. I wanted to give us some breathing room. Especially so that Vesna could catch her breath.

"What should we do, Vesna?" I asked. She replied, "We must reach the top of Battle Hill. I can send out a message to call the other members of the Council. We are not alone in this battle. Come … let us walk as fast as we can." We started up the roadway toward the top of Battle Hill. I remembered from reading the guidebook that this was the highest natural point in Brooklyn. As we hurried, various statues came to life. A huge brown bear that was sitting on a gravestone looked up at me and started toward us. He must be one of Alejandro's. The bear snarled silently and rumbled in our direction. It looks like Yogi wants to give us some Boo Boo's. I need to bring out his inner Pooh. I waved my hand at the massive Kissy Face statue of a woman's head blowing a kiss. I sent it after the grim grizzly. The huge head rolled over to the bear and enveloped him in its embrace. "Pucker up, buttercup!" She began kissing him all over his body. Tickling him with her Medusa-like tendrils of hair. At first, the bear reacted violently. Slashing and snapping at the Kissy face. But gradually he started to giggle as if he was so ticklish that he stopped most of his violent actions. Yes! Love beats hate once again.

Vesna started to regain her strength. She pointed to a circular monument that was slightly off the path and shouted over the noises of the battle, "Let us lead our people this way!" She limped over to a huge circular monument that had tall columns at the front reminiscent of a Roman ruin. It was open to the sky and had enough space for all of us to quickly squeeze through. We immediately disappeared from view as we fled through a back door that Vesna then sealed with a ward. It was as if we had been teleported to another dimension, but we were just a few feet away. Alejandro's legion rushed to follow in our footsteps, not knowing it was a trap. When a large enough group had entered, Vesna cast a spell to start the massive monument spinning violently, which caused the statues inside to tumble into each other or try grabbing onto one of the columns. She lifted the whole monument several feet and let the floor drop out from under them. They ended in a vast pile of broken limbs and decapitated statues. "Holy Moly, Vesna! This is just like the Hell Hole in Coney Island." Vesna chuckled as she completed her spell, "Yes, I love the Coney Island."

Vesna's laugh soon turned to searing pain. Alejandro appeared with several of his minions. One of the cemetery's Civil War Heroes swung his bayonet robotically like in the March of the Wooden Soldiers. The stone soldier thrust his bayonet into Vesna's back as she screamed in anguish. She sent out magical energy to push the statue away as it stumbled backward, right into the Cuban Warlock. Alejandro immediately grabbed the rifle with the bayonet and thrust it into Vesna's gut with the impetus of his unearthly Magic behind it. It was too much for the diminutive Croatian, and she succumbed to the pain as blood gushed in torrents from her body. This wound seemed too severe for even her powerful Magic to counter.

I was stunned at how swiftly disaster had struck. Vesna lay broken and bleeding on the grass as Alejandro stood over her, gloating. Rage coursed through my body. The time for love was over. I took the Sword of Peleus in a two-handed grip and thrust it at the distracted Warlock with a primal scream. But it would not be that easy. The elusive Cuban Warlock dodged like a prize fighter and grabbed my arms as I stumbled over Vesna's body. We proceeded to wrestle as we both had a death grip on the deadly weapon. Alejandro was careful not to touch the Sword itself, as it would reject him as not being worthy of it. He could not wield it. He gripped my wrists and used all of his Magic as he tried to turn the Sword toward my body. He is immensely powerful because he has been a practicing Warlock for many years and has a vast reservoir of knowledge and power to call upon. I only had my untapped potential. It was very potent, and I held my own for a moment. Just as the edge of the Sword had torn my collar and sliced the skin of my neck, I felt two arms hug me from behind. They gripped my hands to lend strength to the struggle. It was enough to turn the tide. The Sword was reversed and pointed at Alejandro as he grimaced in disbelief and, eventually, in horror as he began to lose the struggle. With a final scream of anger, I broke out of his clutches and plunged the Sword into Alejandro's chest. His eyes rolled back, and he suddenly began to fade into dust. In a matter of seconds, he had been transfigured into a pile of ash. Ding Dong, the Warlock, is dead! I am horrified at what I have done.

Whatever was behind me let go of my hands. I slumped down to the ground to my knees as I was physically and emotionally spent. I turned to see who had helped me. I saw a shimmering image that looked remarkably like my dead mother. I looked through the haze at the apparition that was smiling and radiating a sense of love toward me. I threw my arms out to reach for her. "Mamma … is that you?" The figure shrouded in mist tentatively waved to me and disappeared. "Wait! Don't go! I have so many questions. Don't leave me again!" I wailed as she faded away.

Was that my mother? A ghost? A Spirit? Was it a magical manifestation of my desire to see my mother again? Was it a miracle born out of love? A mother's love? What did I just witness?

As I tried to catch my breath and calm my hysteria, I heard Vesna gurgle. "Oh my God … VESNA!" I immediately snapped out of it, and my sense of preservation kicked in. I must help her. I crawled over to her, but Vesna was clearly dying. I put pressure on her wounds to try to stem the bleeding, but it was hopeless. "Vesna, please hold on. Don't leave me. I will get help." Vesna whispered through labored breaths as she tried to say what she needed to tell me. Her Magic was enough to let her live long enough to speak to me. "I am finished, my love. My time is over. You are now the Guardian of the Sword. Continue as you have begun by defeating the Warlock. Keep it safe." I was weeping as she spoke and said, "Don't worry. I will put it back as it was and protect it as you have done. I will get my grandmothers to help me." Vesna said, "No! No!" She coughed as she tried to vehemently tell me what to do. "Not your grandmothers! Not the Council! No one can know!" Vesna looked up at me with her kind eyes that were starting to lose their light. "You must hide it in plain sight, as my family has done these past many years. You cannot put it back. This place is finished as a hiding place." "Vesna, I don't know if I can do this by myself. I need you! Don't leave me!" Vesna smiled her gentle smile and said, "I am not worried. You will protect the Sword. My burden is over, and now I can find peace." Vesna breathed her last. She had spent her last strength to tell me what to do. I had to honor her sacrifice.

I started to sob and rock back and forth as I held Vesna in my arms and stroked her hair. In the distance, I could hear someone approaching us. I sensed that there was no danger, but I had to take precautions. I used a spell to shrink the Sword down to the size of a small letter opener and hid it in my pocket. I looked up and realized that it was The Council with my Grannie Meg leading the band. It was good that I had hidden the Sword as Vesna had demanded. I leaned down in exhaustion. Let them deal with the cleanup and poor Vesna's body. My heart is broken.

Love conquers Hate. Heartache to Heartache. Love is a Battlefield.

EPILOGUE – EVERYTHING OLD IS NEW AGAIN

It has been two weeks since the blood bath at Green-Wood Cemetery. I still can't believe that Vesna is dead. I've never witnessed someone I knew die in front of me like that. And Alejandro! I'm not even sure it was me who murdered him. It was the hands of the entity that helped me push the Sword into his chest. It's all a blur. Who was that? What was that?

I know it's irrational, but I think it could've been my mother. Or her spirit. A piece of her soul that somehow came to the rescue in my hour of need. Did I manifest this? How can it be? She's been gone for so long. There's always something that reminds me of my mom, but lately, I've been catching fleeting glimpses of images that could only be her. I know it's impossible. I must be going crazy!

It's no wonder that I feel this way. So much has happened in the past few weeks. It's all so bizarre! Going to the Never-Never. Meeting the Queen, who is demanding that I become her vassal. Finding out about the Council and becoming involved in the machinations that led to the death of two of their members. Dead faeries. Dead babies. Al Capone! Fighting with Nonna. Fighting with Grannie Meg. Fighting a freaking Minotaur! Hiding the truth from my husband, and don't get me started on his mind wipe! The list of inexplicable occurrences is getting longer and longer with no end in sight.

I haven't heard from anyone in the past week, which is strange in and of itself. Nonna hasn't contacted me. Birdie's not busting my chops. Not a word from Grannie Meg or the Council. Even my faerie friends like Oona and Hob have been conspicuous in their absence. It seems as though the world is holding its breath.

I sat behind the counter as I toyed with the Sword of Peleus, secreted into the shape of a letter opener. I had transformed it into a replica of the one that Birdie always carried. Great idea, right? No one uses letter openers anymore. You can't open an email with a fancy letter opener. I eyed the photograph of my parents. I wonder what they would say about what has happened. They never had "the gift," but they always had to deal with the aftermath of what Nonna and I fashioned with our Magic. "Mamma. I wish you would come back to me—"

The bell above the door tinkled, and Birdie strolled into the store. I immediately dropped the Sword into my pen holder to conceal it. "Look who I brought with me, Speranza!" She stepped aside, and I saw my Nonna limping into the store as she leaned heavily on her cane. This was a momentous occasion. She had not come to the store in many years.

I jumped out from behind the counter to usher Nonna into a chair. "Nonna, why did you come here? I would have come to you. I know we need to talk, but—" I dipped my head toward Birdie to indicate that we could not talk freely. Nonna cut me off and said, "Yes. I know. We will talk, Mia Bella. So much has happened, we need to discuss." Birdie chimed in, "Yeah, I still can't get over the fact that Salvina is gone. It's enough to break me." Birdie snuffled as though she was about to burst into tears. I handed her a tissue and said, "I know, Birdie. It's terrible."

I had a sudden inspiration. The perfect place to hide the Sword is in Birdie's vinyl shopping bag! Talk about hiding it in plain sight! It's there for anyone to see, but luckily, no one ever pays attention to Birdie. Or wants to deal with her at all. Vesna would be so proud.

I put my arm around Birdie and stealthily replaced her letter opener with the Sword, which was an exact match. I had already placed spells on it. A protection spell. A concealment spell. A location spell, so I will know where it is at all times. I led Birdie to the other chair and helped her sit down.

Nonna spoke up, "I would like you to come for dinner tonight, Mia Bella. It has been too long since we have broken bread. Just you. We have things to talk about." "Ok, Nonna, that sounds great. How about around seven? Sean is busy tonight because he caught a big case, so it will just be the two of us. We can talk. I am looking forward to it."

We chatted for about a half hour about inconsequential matters. I called an Uber for Nonna because I didn't want her to struggle walking home. I spent the rest of the day running the store, trying to make sales even though I was very distracted. I reviewed the events in the cemetery as I prepared my case to make to Nonna. Should I mention my mother? Or was that just a fantasy? Would she believe me? Would she tell me the truth if she knew it? Was she keeping something from me for my own good? She's done it before! It's time for Nonna to fess up!

I closed up the shop and started to walk to Nonna's, but decided to stop at Ginny's first. When I got to the café, it was packed. Alice was sitting with a Ming Lao at a table on the sidewalk. They waved at me, and I waved back as I went inside to see Ginny.

"Hey Anna, what's up?" Ginny said as she poured another cup of coffee. Every seat in the house was taken. There were a bunch of neighborhood people, including a couple of hoods. Yes, some of the wannabe mafia guys who were friends of Nunzio.

"Hey, Nunzie, come and get the drinks for your pals," Ginny shouted as she put the final cup of espresso on the tray. Ginny had no time for Nunzio's hoodlum friends. She felt they were a bad influence on him and always got him in trouble. It is very ironic that Ginny hated the Mobsters when she was the great-granddaughter of Al Capone. She is quite literally a Mafia Princess!

I looked at Ginny as she ran around trying to get all the orders out. She didn't have any time for me. I called out as she whizzed by, "Ginny! I see you're busy. I will call you later." Ginny laughed as she gave a customer their change. "You got that right, kiddo. We need to have a 'sit-down' with some wine, and I need all the details! Don't you dare leave anything out! Capisce." "You got it! I'm heading to Nonna's now, maybe we can talk tomorrow? Ginny waved her arm in the air to acknowledge what I had said as she bustled into the kitchen.

I decided to go to Nonna's early since we had a lot to talk about. When I got to her house, I opened the door with my key and stopped. Something was off. I didn't smell anything. Usually, the homey aroma of Italian food would be wafting from the kitchen. I didn't hear any sounds of pots clanging or Mello gossiping. I felt like I was walking into a stranger's house.

I walked down the hall into the kitchen. All of the lights were out. Except for a single one in the hood over the stove that illuminated a small section of the kitchen.

Next to the stove on the counter, I saw Nonna's recipe box. It was as if a spotlight was on it, as the light seemed to coalesce as if she had used Magic to draw my notice. Tucked under the box, I saw an envelope addressed to me with Nonna's familiar handwriting.

I opened it and began to read:

Mia Bella,

As you can see, I am not here. I left to protect you. I know how troubled you are by the Queen's demands. Especially the demand that you decide within two weeks. I decided to go to the Queen in your place.

I have come to the end of my time in this earthly realm. I realize my body is breaking down, and I don't have much time left. I have gone to the Never-Never, where the rules are different. I will have many more years there, and Magic will restore my health.

Since I am already Queen Mab's vassal, I will attempt to get her to accept me instead of you in the coming conflict. I have fought for her before, and she knows my worth. If I am successful, you will never have to venture into this realm and serve the Queen of Winter.

I don't know if we will ever meet again. I beg you to avoid coming back to the Never-Never. I will make sure that the Queen will not try to force you to come to her. It is my final gift to you, my beloved granddaughter. You have so many happy years in front of you. You have the love of your Sean and your life together. You need not worry about me. My life has been fulfilled by taking care of you and teaching you what you needed to know to survive in this world of Magic and wonder.

You will be surprised to find that I took Birdie with me. She grounds me. I need to remember that I am only human, and nobody is more human than Birdie. She will whisper in my ear and keep my feet on the ground. She will have many more years here than she would have had back home, so she is content. Birdie insists I send you her love, even though she does not understand what is about to happen.

Goodbye, Mia Bella.

Remember, la familia is everything, and love conquers all.

Love, Nonna

What did I just read? My Nonna left me, too! First, Vesna dies, and now Nonna vanishes without saying goodbye. I have so many questions for her. What about my mother? Now, I can't ask her if my mother is still alive. I feel like I am going to be sick!

Wait a minute. She took Birdie with her? If Birdie went to the Never-Never, so did the Sword! I have to stop them. They don't know what they've done! Maybe they haven't gone through the portal yet. Which one would Nonna use? I'll never get to all of them in time. I can't ask for help from the Council because I can't reveal what has happened.

Exactly what the Queen wanted has come to pass. How can I safeguard the Sword or get it back if it stays in the Never-Never? Will the Queen sense its existence and try to take it away? Will my concealment spell be strong enough? Will my protection spell do the trick? The location spell only works in this realm! How will I ever find them in the Never-Never!

I have so many questions. Does Nonna know about the Sword and brought it as a peace offering to curry favor with the Queen? I hate to think that she would do that, but it is certainly possible. After all of the crimes she has admitted to in service of the Queen, I wouldn't put anything past her.

I promised Vesna that I would protect the Sword, and I have failed utterly. Vesna died protecting the Sword, and I was so careless that I lost it in the second week I had it. I tearfully shouted out to the Universe, "Vesna, I need you! Send me a sign! I have failed you! Give me a way to redeem myself!" There was no answer from the spirit world. I am on my own.

I started pacing back and forth as I became more and more emotional. I looked everywhere. In rooms, cupboards, closets, and even in Nonna's ancient valise. I hoped against hope that I would find the Sword. It was useless. There was no way I was going to find it since Birdie would never let that shopping bag out of her sight.

I have been silently crying the whole time. This seems like such a betrayal from the one person I've trusted all my life. I have to pull myself together. I went into the bathroom to splash some water on my face to calm my anxiety and ground myself. As I finished drying my face, I lowered the towel and looked at myself in the mirror. Who is that?

"Vesna? Is that you?" I had asked for a sign, and maybe this was it. But it couldn't be. This apparition had flaming red hair, and Vesna had jet-black hair. It spoke to me.

"No, it is not Vesna, my dear. We have not met. My name is Maeve, and I am the Queen of Summer. You may have met my sister, Mab. I like to call her the 'Evil Queen.' I thought I would contact you through this mirror." She softly giggled and said, "It is traditional, after all!" Queen Maeve smiled, and I immediately thought of Summer as a warm breeze blew past my face. I thought of sunlight in a meadow as wildflowers bloomed. She was the essence of Summer. For a moment, I felt safe.

"Let me tell you about your mother. She is waiting for you!"

GLOSSARY

Not from the neighborhood? This'll help you keep up.

Agita: *(Ah ·jee ·tah)* indigestion or a more general annoyance

Baccala: *(Baa·kuh·laa)* a fool or an idiot, or a smelly, tough, salted fish

Bailiwick: (*Bay·lee·wuhk)* is an old Irish way of saying territory

Beyotch: *(BEE ·otch)* a friendly use of the word bitch, or when someone gets over on you.

Capisce: *(Capeesh)* Do you understand?

Chiacchierone: *(Chiac ·chie ·ró ·ne)* someone who is very talkative, a gossip, or a blabbermouth

Chooch *(Chew ·ch)* **or Chooches:** describes a stupid or foolish person. Calling someone an idiot or a dummy

Craic: *(Krak)* is an Irish slang term for gossip

Cugine: (*Koo ·JEEN)* an Italian/American Slang term for cousin, or a good friend

Doilies: *(Doy·leez)* ornamental mats, often crocheted and lace-like decorations, placed under lamps, vases, or even on the arms and backs of chairs

Disgrazia: *(Dee ·sgrah ·tsee ·ah)* encapsulates a sense of something negative happening, whether it's a sudden event or a prolonged period of misfortune, also a loss of favor or standing, similar to being in someone's bad graces

Fugazi: *(Foo·ga·zee)* something that is fake, phony, or not genuine

Gagootz: *(Ca ·coot ·zah)* Italian for Zucchini

Guinea or Guineas: *(Gi·nee)* a disparaging term used to describe Italians.

Gavone: *(Gah ·VOHN)* describes someone who is a glutton, someone who eats a lot. It can also carry the connotation of being ill-mannered or lacking social grace.

Gavonie: a play on gavone when Speranza calls her Brownie a Gavonie

Hind: is an Irish term for a hut or small dwelling

Ionsai: *(Un ·see)* Gaelic for advance, approach, attack

Guido: *(Gwee·dow)* a man, especially an Italian American, regarded as vain, aggressively masculine, and socially unsophisticated.

Mishegoss: *(Mish ·eh ·GOSS)* a Yiddish term for a big mess

Mortadella: *(Mor·tuh·deh·luh)* a type of cured meat, specifically a large, finely ground sausage made from pork.

Moulinyans: (Moo *·lin ·YAHN*) Italian for eggplants

Nest: a home temperature controlling device

Pisan: *(PEE ·sahn)* someone of Italian descent who is a friend or compatriot

Ringolevio: *(Ring ·uh ·LEE ·vee ·oh)* a children's game that originated in the streets of New York City, where it is known to have been played at least as far back as the late 19th century. It is one of the many variations of tag

Sidhe: *(Shee)* the Faerie Folk of Irish Folklore

Skutch: *(Skuhch)* to pester or annoy

Strunz *(ST ROON Z)* or **Stugatz:** *(Stew ·gots)* a fool or an idiot

Stunad: *(Stoo ·nad)* is a stupid person

Sfogliatelle: *(Sfow·lee·uh·teh·lay)* is an Italian pastry

Swozzled: *(Swɒzəld)* Urban Dictionary is a derivative of swizzled, meaning intoxicated, tipsy, or mildly drunk

Queen Mab: *(Maeb)* Queen of Winter

Queen Maeve: *(May-v)* Queen of Summer

Ubriaco mio: *(oo ·bree ·AH ·koh MEE ·oh)* "Ubriaco mio" is Italian for "my drunk one."

Ubatz: *(OO ·bahts)* is Italian for out of your mind or crazy

Zeppoles: *(Zeh·puh·leez)* an Italian fried dessert served with confectioners' sugar

CAST OF CHARACTERS:

The Family (and Friends of Ours)

Speranza (Anna) O'Rourke: (Spai-raan-zaa) 58 years old. 5'6, long wavy brown hair, brown eyes that leave an impression, and a full-figured size 12-14. She is half-Italian and half-Irish. She is a witch, born into the bloodline of two grandmothers who were both witches. Married to Sean O'Rourke. They have one daughter, Melinda, 35, who does not possess Magic, and a 13-year-old granddaughter named Bettina (Betts) who is starting to come into her powers. Speranza is fiercely loyal to her family and friends. She will do anything to protect them. Mama bear energy.

Sean O'Rourke: Speranza's husband. 58 years old. He is half-Italian and half-Irish. He is an NYPD Detective who is 6'3" with a fair complexion, a full head of hair, and dimples on his cheeks. He has one blue eye and one hazel brown eye. He always wanted to be a cop, as his dad was, and most of his dad's family as well. He is aware of the existence of Magic but remains ignorant of the details. He loves his wife above and beyond everything and will go to any length to back her up in her crazy ventures. He secretly loves being kept on his toes with all her antics.

Fabrizia (Abby) Hennessey: Speranza's mother was a Tenured Professor of Archaeology at Fordham University. Died in a plane crash on the way to a dig in the Amazon. Would have been 78 years old if she had lived. She had an ambivalent relationship with Speranza, as she did not have Magic. She did not get along with her mother, Nonna, and rejected everything about her. She hated Magic and rejected her Italian heritage, refusing to speak Italian or even cook. She adopted the persona of a college intellectual with all that implies about her attitude and preferences. She was a fish out of water in the neighborhood with only one friend, her husband. The exact opposite of Nonna and Speranza.

Adam Hennessey: Speranza's father, who was an Adjunct Professor of Sociology at Fordham University. He was a kind man who supported his wife in her much more successful career. He was not involved in Magic. He was not aware of its existence and was estranged from his mother, Margaret, who is a powerful Irish Witch. He took up all the domestic slack in the household, including cooking, cleaning, and childcare. Speranza would always go to him first and was much closer to him than her mother. He also died in the plane crash on the way to a dig in the Amazon almost forty years ago.

Justina (Chris) Sorrentino: Speranza's Italian grandmother, who is affectionately known as **Nonna**. She is a powerful Witch at 95 years old, as witches are notoriously long-lived. She is an immigrant from Naples who was a famous beauty in her day (think Sofia Loren).

As an extremely powerful Witch, she became a vassal of the faerie Queen Mab of the Never-Never. She has vast powers that she does not utilize because she has done terrible things in the past in service of the Queen. She was afraid that she could do worse if she was not careful. She is the main influence on Speranza's character, serving as her tutor in the arts of Magic. Speranza is exceptionally close to her, and she either visits or speaks to her every day.

Margaret Liadán Hennessey: Speranza's Irish Grandmother. She was given one of the rarest and most unusual Irish girl names, Liadán, meaning "grey lady" because she was born with grey hair. Eventually, it changed to a dark brown in her early teens. At 96 years old, she was short and round with short grey hair and often wore a plain housecoat. She had blue-grey eyes that seemed colorless and nondescript, but her appearance hid her powers. She speaks in terms and allusions of an older generation and playfully dips into an Irish brogue in her theatrical presentation of her Irish heritage. Especially when she hits the bottle. She became estranged from her son, Adam, after he joined the army when he was underage. She actively dislikes Nonna and tries to drive a wedge between Nonna and Speranza. She instructs Speranza in the craft but with an emphasis on her Irish heritage. She introduced Speranza to her familiar Oona, one of the Sidhe.

Genevieve "Ginny" Gentile: Speranza's best friend and confidant. They went to grammar school, high school, and college together. She is 58 and divorced. She runs her family's coffee shop and is the third generation to run a business in that location. She knows about Magic, but not to the full extent of Speranza's powers. She had two brothers. One still works with her in the store, and the other was half a gangster and was killed by the police. Ginny has salt and pepper hair, more pepper than salt, green eyes, and a full figure with a petite frame. She has a no-nonsense way of speaking and does not suffer fools gladly. When excited, she lapses into Brooklynese. She is an old-school Italian in her attitude, but covers it up when dealing with new people.

Nunzio Gentile: Age 45, Ginny's brother, who has a Napoleonic complex because he is short and burly and a psycho. He is a wannabe gangster who has failed in his life of crime. He works at the café as his sister is trying to keep him on the straight and narrow, but occasionally, he slips.

Birdie Rubino: 95 years old, like her good friend Nonna. She lives in a Brownstone that she had inherited from her father. She was not only a spinster; she never went on a date in her life. All of her family were socially challenged and died alone. She ended up inheriting all of their money. She is very rich and very lonely. She is obsessed with her friends and overly involved with their lives.

Salvina Russo: 95 and widowed, she lives in a Brownstone that she had purchased with money she got from a lawsuit after her husband died. She is a neighborhood pisan and a lifelong friend of Nonna and

Birdie. She has three daughters whom she kept in money from the lawsuit. She was petite and round but always had a smile on her face. She puts up with Birdie because she knows that she is very lonely and overlooks when she goes too far. Her eldest daughter, Lorraine, tries to control her, but she puts her off by agreeing with whatever she says and then doing whatever she wants.

Lorriane Lopez: 58 years old. Salvina's eldest daughter and former classmate and rival of Speranza. She is married to a Cuban from Sunset Park named Peter, but everyone calls him Pepe to bust his chops. She has long been Speranza's nemesis and the only person that Speranza has had a physical fight with in Grammar School. She barely works for a dermatologist because she is lazy and inept. She scorns Speranza and Birdie and will do anything to separate them from her mother.

Alice Hoving: 23 years old, well dressed in designer clothes, but doesn't wear any bling. She is originally from Connecticut and just moved into the neighborhood. She bought a brownstone condo on Sackett Street near the highway, a new development between Henry and Hicks. She is good friends with Ming Lao. They went to school together at NYU. She introduced her to Carroll Gardens and encouraged her to move there. Ming told her about Magic and Speranza. She needs Speranza's help.

Ming Lao: 23 years old, a good friend of Alice Hoving. First-generation Chinese immigrant who went to NYU with Alice. She works in Fashion but is obsessed with Tarot and would come in for readings at least once a week. She based all her decisions on the Tarot. She buys every new deck that comes out. She is an avid collector. She often helped out at her father's Chinese restaurant in Sunset Park. He is involved in the Chinese Tong, which is a criminal gang similar to the Italian Mafia. She knows many of the current gangsters who frequent her father's restaurant, including some very violent hit men. She is petite and fashion-forward. She is always dressed to the hilt. Loves leather and seems almost elf-like when she is dressed up.

The Council: The secret governing body of Brooklyn's Magical beings. Composed of powerful Witches and Warlocks from several ethnic enclaves in the borough. Consists of Runa, Alejandro, Vesna, Nikolai, Tiwa, Meg, and Speranza, making 7.

Runa Johansan: A Nordic Viking Witch, heads up Bay Ridge. Descendant of Scandinavian parents. She is a master of Winter Magic and can freeze time for short periods and manipulate temperature. She is tall with silver hair and possesses a regal air with striking ice-blue eyes that seem to hold ancient wisdom. Her voice is calm and almost muted as though it were the atmosphere on a snow-covered street. Runa is very precise and deliberate in the cadence of her speech, almost as though she were autistic. Since English was her second language, she had to translate the words in her head first, and there was always a two-second time delay.

Runa's familiar: a Frost Faerie named **Icelara**, with wings that glisten with winter's frost. Her lightly blue-tinged skin and pointy ears were the basis of the legends of the elves that once inhabited the Nordic forests.

Alejandro Lopez-Garcia: A formidable Cuban Warlock, denizen of Sunset Park, and practitioner of Santeria. A distinguished-looking gentleman with a presence that commands attention. He has a charismatic aura and a hint of mischief in his eyes; he exudes an air of confidence and wisdom. He has a strong, sturdy build, as his physique mirrors the resilience and determination that define his character. His speech is very flowery and over the top. He is dramatic and almost operatic in his demeanor. Think of the biggest ham actor you have ever seen.

Alejandro's familiar: a Wind Sprite named **Zephyr,** who is a whirlwind of vibrant colors. His small form is adorned with shimmering hues of blues and greens reminiscent of the Caribbean seas, sparking waves as he fluttered his wings, a gentle breeze seemed to dance through the room, carrying whispers of enchantment and secrets only known to the wind.

Chaithra: Santeria Priestess from Sunset Park. Practices under the supervision of Alejandro, who is her superior in the craft.

Vesna Brankovic: a Croatian Witch from Greenpoint, Brooklyn. She has jet black hair and a ready, if sad, Mona

Lisa smile. She speaks in a soft, melodic Slavic accent as though she were a vampire that was falling asleep. She exuded an air of serenity that drew others to her. Her slow and deliberate tones were mesmerizing. Almost hypnotic as she drew you into her web. She is the Guardian of a vital secret that has the potential to change everything.

Vesna's Familiar: a Nixie Faerie named **Danica**, a creature adorned in hues of blue and white. A Nixie faerie is also known as a water nymph or sprite. They are graceful and alluring with long flowing hair that shimmers like water and skin that glistens with a soft iridescence. They are known for their enchanting voices and ability to lure unsuspecting travelers with captivating melodies.

Nikolai Kozlov: of Russian Origin. Represents Brighton Beach. His lineage is traced back to the mystical forests and vast steppes of his homeland. He seemed to possess a deep connection to nature and the spirits that resided within it. His appearance holds an uncanny resemblance to the terrible Tsars of the old regime. Towering and broad-shouldered, Nikolai's presence was both formidable and commanding. His russet hair, now streaked with strands of silver, flowed like a wild river. His eyes, a piercing shade of amber, mirrored the flickering flames of a bonfire as if Cossacks were gathering on the steppe before a raid into the hinterlands. His manner is very brusque and contemptuous. It came from a place of misogyny and arrogance.

Nikolai's Familiar: a Vila Faerie named **Radmila**, known for controlling the weather. She can weave illusions and mask Nikolia's presence. Loyal yet not submissive, but still wild and untamed. She appears in the form of a beautiful woman with long silver-blond hair, her eyes alternating from pale ice-blue to glowing gold. Although she rarely speaks, her voice carries a layered echo of many, like hearing a dozen distant women whispering in unison.

Tiwa: She represents Bedford Stuyvesant in Central Brooklyn. She is a tall, black woman with a lilting Caribbean accent almost singsong at times. Tiwa commands your attention with her regal presence. Her statuesque figure emanated strength and grace, draped in flowing garments that mirrored the colors of the stormy sky. Her skin, like polished obsidian, exuded an aura of mystery and power. Long, slender limbs moved with purpose, and her eyes, deep and captivating, held the wisdom of the ages. Crowning her head was a resplendent turban adorned with intricate feathers in hues of ebony, sapphire, and gold. Each feather whispered tales of the winds, carrying the essence of storms and the power of nature. Braids, intricately woven with tiny charms and beads, cascaded down her back. Tiwa is bright and boisterous with a regal manner, but very approachable all the same. Her voice bathed you like a warm Caribbean sun, so you feel safe speaking with her.

Tiwa's Familiar: a Mama Wata Faerie named **Fabienne**, a water spirit that is half-human and half-reptile. She is a shape-shifter and most often presents as a black woman whose lower extremities are those of a snake. She is a maternal figure with great power bound to Tiwa's family for generations and the waters of Jamaica Bay. She wields powerful water Magic in service of Tiwa's goals.

The Faeries and other Fay Folk of the Never-Never:
Faerie – (n.) A singular magical being of the Never-Never.
Faeries – (pl.) A group of individual faerie beings.
The Fay – (n., proper) The collective race or ancestral bloodline of magical beings from the Never-Never.

Oona: (OO-nah) a purple-tinged female Sidhe Faerie. Not a traditional "Disney Fairy," she dressed in a workaday smock and wooden clogs. Oona has wings and can fly around the room, but she would never do so in the light of day, where others could see her.

She first appeared to Speranza at the age of four. They didn't truly communicate until Speranza was thirteen and coming into her powers.

She is **Speranza's Familiar** and is her guide to the Never-Never. She is very shy and fearful, but musters up her courage when she needs to help Speranza. She loves spice drops, especially the purple ones. She has a Celtic Brogue and a high falsetto voice that turns into a squeak when she is emotional. She uses many terms of endearment and emotion when speaking to Speranza, as they have been inseparable for many years. She formerly acted like a big sister, but now that Speranza is realizing her potential, she is more like a little sister who now needs to be protected.

Aiden: a male Sidhe Faerie, who is Oona's brother and a leading warrior of the Sidhe Clan. He is contemptuous of women in general and his sister in particular. He has little patience for Oona's emotionalism as he is stoic in nature and focused on the upcoming battle.

Aoife: (ee-fa) a female Sidhe Faerie, she is **Grannie Meg's Familiar**. She is one of the first casualties of the war in the Never-Never.

Mello: a Monaciello Faerie, who is **Nonna's Familiar**. He is a small roly-poly figure dressed in what looks like a friar's robe. He often visited Nonna from the Never-Never for weeks at a time. A jolly little imp, he affected the voice and mannerisms of Edward G. Robinson of thirties gangster movie fame. He likes to pretend he is a tough guy, but he is actually a drunken sweetie who is much more interested in wine than in mayhem. When he is in distress, he reverts to a more formal way of speech, rather than his phony gangster style.

Luca: a Monaciello Faerie, is Mello's acolyte. He was murdered at the hands of a Red Cap Faerie at the beginning of the war.

Micha: a Monaciello Faerie, Mello's cousin, who dresses like Michael Jackson and serves as a confidante of the

Faerie Queen. He moonwalks Speranza across the stage during her visit to the Queen's Court. Stage name: Micha-Ciello.
Hob: a Brownie Faerie, a household faerie who lives in Speranza's home. He is only concerned with cleaning her house. Speaks with an old English accent. Old-fashioned words. Archaic words. Hob has lived in her home since it was built. A Brownie will clean your house if you leave an offering. Short and grubby in dirty homespun, the only mistake you can make is to offer them new clothes. Proud little beast.

Varrik: a Redcap Faerie, short and brutal-looking. He has a hunched and gnarled frame with long, bony fingers that end in razor-sharp claws. His voice has a guttural and viscerally angry tone, and his odd little twisted body was topped by a red cap. He uses his red cap to sop up blood to hide his crimes. He carries an ax and a long knife on his belt. The worst of the faeries.

Salvatrice: a Silvani Faerie, a wind Sprite from the woods of Sicily. She is short, only four feet tall. Dressed in a homespun frock, she has long grey hair and wears no makeup. She always wears red clothing. Her dark brown eyes blended seamlessly into the weathered skin of her face. Her toes are on the back of her feet. Famous for her love of children. Salvatrice is notable for her seriousness and grim façade. She only unbent when she was around children, specifically babies. She was the one who saved Al Capone's daughter, without permission from the Queen, and was severely punished.

Norm the Gnome: a male Gnome, short and thin. Full of nervous energy, he is part of the Queen's program staff. He normally sports a headset and clipboard and has a distinctive Flock of Seagulls haircut.

Sandra the Gnome: a female Gnome, Norm's girlfriend, who loves to eat and never gains any weight. Nickname: Sandro-zempic.

Silvie: a Sylphine Faerie, a fashion stylist who is humble and down-to-earth. She is slim, stylish, and ethereally beautiful. Her presence screamed fashion icon. Silvie is dressed in flowing silks, a diaphanous cloud of beauty that was not of the earth. To a Sylphine, fashion is not just about appearance, but about self-expression and empowerment, and she takes great pride in helping her clients look and feel their best.

Viola: a female Elf, who is tall, thin, and elegant. She has silver-blond hair and small, pointy ears. She is the Segment Producer of the Midnight Show.

Queen Mab: (Maeb) the Faerie Queen and Sovereign of the Winter Realm. She is of average height, but her voluptuous figure is both seductive and overwhelming. Her Regal presence commands your attention even amidst the frozen landscape of her domain. Her long, flowing hair cascades like midnight tendrils around her shoulders, gleaming with an otherworldly luster that shimmers like freshly fallen snow in the moonlight. Each strand is as dark as the deepest abyss, framing her delicate features with an air of mystery and enchantment.

Her face is a study in ethereal beauty, with high cheekbones and a sculpted jawline. Her skin is as pale as alabaster, flawless and untouched by the passage of time. Her eyes of ice-blue, which seem to hold the secrets of the winter.

Adorned in garments of shimmering silver and deep indigo, her attire is adorned with intricate frost patterns and delicate snowflakes. Around her neck, she wears a necklace of sparkling ice crystals, each crystal holding one of the 12-star signs.

Witch / Warlock:
Magical practitioners are bound to their bloodline, community, and Craft. Witches tend to use intuitive, ancestral power; Warlocks are often bound to deals, contracts, or corrupted Magic. Not all Warlocks are evil—but the good ones are rare.

The Patch:
A Witch's designated territory within Brooklyn's Magical map. Speranza inherits her grandmother Nonna's Patch, whether she wants it or not.

Never-Never:
The shifting, Magical dimension where the Fay and their Courts reside. It is not a place, but a perception. Anyone who enters sees what they fear or desire most. Time, form, and truth blur here.

ACKNOWLEDGEMENTS

I am deeply grateful to the people who helped bring The Brooklyn Witch to life.

To my husband, for being my late-night note-taker and daytime editor, my sounding board, and my heart. Your love and encyclopedic knowledge of history fueled so many pages of this book.

To my mother, who never stopped believing in my voice or my stories.

To my sister, the only person who has read every word of this book before publication. I love you so much. You can stop deleting my emails now, I've got it copyrighted!

To my lifelong friends from Brooklyn, you are part of every corner store, stoop, and shadow in these pages.

To my "Moon Gang," you believed in me back when this book was just a glimmer of an idea. It was always written in the stars, and you knew it would one day come to life.

And to the readers, may you find a touch of Magic between these pages, just when you need it most.

About the Author

Lisa Dolan is an artist, fashion designer, and Reality TV personality whose life and career have been defined by creativity. Born in Brooklyn to a fireman and a homemaker, Lisa has expressed herself through the arts from an early age, whether writing plays as a child or studying Graphic Arts in school. Her artistic path led her to become a fashion designer, launching a successful clothing line that caught national attention and culminated in starring in her own BBC/TLC reality series, Big Brooklyn Style.

Today, Lisa continues to evolve creatively as a novelist, with her debut novel, The Brooklyn Witch—the first in the series.

Connect with the Author

For more information, contact the author at:

www.thebrooklynwitch.com
www.leeleesvalise.com

Take the cannoli, leave the Magic—for now. The Brooklyn Witch returns in ***Spring 2026***.

The Brooklyn Witch II—Never Go Against the Family

www.ingramcontent.com/pod-product-compliance
Lightning Source LLC
Chambersburg PA
CBHW020946310726
48980CB00001B/70

9798999856227